Linda Newbery

SOME OTHER WAR

BARN OWL BOOKS

Some Other War was published by Armada in 1990
This edition was first published 2002 by Barn Owl Books,
157 Fortis Green Road, London N10 3LX

Text copyright © by Linda Newbery 1990, 2002
Cover artwork copyright © Lisa Kopper 2002
Linda Newbery has asserted her right
under the Copyright, Designs and Patents Act 1988
to be identified as author of this work

ISBN 1 903015 20 0
A CIP catalogue record for this book
is available from the British Library

Designed and typeset by Douglas Martin Associates
Printed and bound in Great Britain by
Cox & Wyman Ltd, Reading

Barn Owl Books are distributed by Frances Lincoln
4 Torriano Mews, Torriano Avenue London NW5 2RZ

*The photograph used in the front cover montage is reproduced with
permission of the Trustees of the Imperial War Museum, London*

TWINS JACK AND ALICE SMALLWOOD are approaching their eighteenth birthdays when war breaks out in 1914. Both work at the mansion of the wealthy Morland family, Jack as a groom and Alice as a chambermaid but the war catapults both of them into new and unimagined worlds. Jack goes into the trenches and Alice becomes a nurse.

While the newspapers report heroic victories, brother and sister see the grimmer reality. The narrative, alternating between the two characters, gives both a male and female perspective on the drastic events and tragic losses that characterise the First World War.

Some Other War is a moving and compassionate story of young people trying to maintain their integrity, courage and sense of purpose under the most testing of circumstances.

OTHER BOOKS

The Shell House · *Random House*
The Damage Done · *Scholastic*
Flightsend · *Scholastic*
No Way Back · *Orchard*
Break Time · *Orchard*
Windfall · *Orchard*

CONTENTS

Part One: 1914

GREENSTOCKS · 13

SUNDAY IN LITTLEHAYS · 23

GALLIARD · 29

AT WAR · 32

PARTINGS · 42

TRAINING CAMP · 52

Part Two: 1915

LORNA · 61

DEPARTURES · 69

NEW IMPRESSIONS · 77

TO THE FRONT · 88

NEAR LOOS · 93

AFTER CHURCH · 98

IN BROADLANDS GROUNDS · 107

TRENCH RAID · 112

Part Three: 1916

ON THE WARD · 123

LIEUTENANT MORLAND · 130

LAWRENCE · 136

THE SECOND WAVE · 142

RECKONING · 150

SOME OTHER WAR · 157

IN THE APPLE ORCHARD · 162

HOSPITAL VISIT · 169

THROUGH THE WIRE · 173

A LETTER FROM HARRIET · 183

Part Four: 1917

WINTRY SEA · 189

THE HOTEL IN THE PINES · 198

ARRAS · 205

OLD FORD ROAD · 209

WIRING · 219

GREENSTOCKS · 225

Northward, incessantly, the flickering gunnery rumbles,
Far off, like a dull rumour of some other war.
What are we doing here?

WILFRED OWEN · *Exposure*

Part One: 1914

Greenstocks

It was hot work, fencing. Jack Smallwood could feel the sun scorching the back of his neck, and the sweat trickling down inside his shirt. An old black-and-white mongrel, the farm dog, lay panting in the shade of the thick blackthorn, his share of the job done. The Ayrshire heifers, herded safely back to the proper side of the hedge, stood in a curious semi-circle, their big eyes watching Jack as he struggled to fit a new rail into the gap they had made. One of the bolder ones ventured closer, only to run back snorting as the end of Jack's rail swung round uncontrollably.

"Clear off, you silly blighter! Never seen a fence before?" Jack told it impatiently. It was already late afternoon, and he had plenty of work waiting for him; as soon as he'd finished here he would cycle down to the farm to see to the Shires, before returning to Greenstocks for evening stables. The heifer bucked sideways, stiff-legged, to join the others. Those on the fringe of the group were looking down into the valley now, their attention caught by something new. Jack, catching the sounds of voices and laughter, looked in the same direction.

Two horses, a bay and a chestnut, were cantering fast down the slope of what had been the hayfield. The bay was the new Greenstocks horse, Galliard, bought for young Mr Philip to hunt and to ride in the local point-to-points.

"Lucky so-and-so," Jack muttered, watching enviously through the gap. The bay was going easily, his long stride carrying him well ahead of the chestnut. He was a thoroughbred, a beauty, Jack thought; he looked as if he would be more at home in the parade ring at Newmarket or Epsom than in the stableyard of a country landowner.

13

Philip Morland turned in his saddle and laughed at the rider behind.

"Can't that old nag keep up?"

The second horseman was Geoffrey Montjoy, a friend of Philip's and would-be suitor for his sister Madeleine. The chestnut he rode was his father's steeplechaser, past its prime now; its neck and shoulders were damp with patchy sweat as it pounded after Galliard. Jack could imagine what Sedley, the head groom at Greenstocks, would say if he saw the two young men galloping about in this heat, with the ground hard as concrete from the prolonged dry weather.

Geoffrey's voice, with its distinctive rather whining note, rose in protest. "That's not fair. He's not fit. Wait till the hunting season . . ."

The two horses pulled up by the alders which fringed the stream at the lower edge of the hayfield. The riders' clear voices carried across the field to Jack, who watched unseen. "Tell you what," Geoffrey suggested with sudden enthusiasm, "I bet my nag can show yours the way over the hedge here. A guinea on it?"

Interested, Jack put down his tools. He was glad enough to stop for a moment. Fencing was uncomfortable work, with the sharp thorns stabbing his hands and the stupid heifers barging about, getting in the way. He was curious to see whether Philip would accept the challenge; curious, too, as to how well Galliard would perform. So far, Jack had only seen Philip riding him in and out of the stableyard.

Philip was eyeing the hedge dubiously. The point Geoffrey had indicated, at the bottom corner of the field, was high and dense. It would make a fairly imposing jump, Jack estimated; as an additional hazard, the ground on the landing side was a good two feet lower than the take-off, with a grassy ditch. Philip didn't seem particularly anxious to attempt it.

"Let's see yours jump it first, then," he replied finally.

"Nothing easier."

Geoffrey didn't wait for further discussion. He hauled his horse round and urged it into a short-striding, springy canter. The chestnut, veteran of many cross-country races, knew all about jumping hedges, and Jack could see it assessing the obstacle, its ears pricked. Geoffrey's heels drummed into its sides, and then the horse launched itself into a confident, economical leap over the forbidding obstacle, its hooves brushing through the highest twigs. Jack heard its grunt as it landed clear of the ditch, and saw Geoffrey's look of triumph as he wheeled round in a short circle to face Philip.

"Nothing to it," he shouted. "Coming over?"

Philip didn't reply for a moment. Then, his face set, he turned his horse away, spurred him into a canter and turned to face the jump. Galliard's ears flicked forward and back; seeing the hedge, he snatched at the reins and lengthened his stride, racing for the jump as if he meant to clear it and the next field all in one enormous bound. Jack saw the sudden look of panic cross Philip's face. He stiffened, throwing his weight back and pulling on the reins. Galliard, confused by the apparent change of mind on the part of his rider, planted his feet in front of the hedge and swerved to the right. Philip flew off over his shoulder and crashed heavily into the blackthorn.

Jack's irrepressible grin of amusement vanished quickly as he saw that Philip wasn't getting up, but lay winded in the hedge. One arm was still hooked through the reins, and Galliard, ears flat back with fright, tried to pull away. Geoffrey, from the lower ground on the other side of the hedge, couldn't see what had happened, and was in no position to offer help. After a moment's hesitation, Jack climbed through the gap and ran down the field, intending to calm the frightened horse or assist Philip, whichever seemed most urgent. As he approached, Philip struggled stiffly out of the hedge and disentangled his arm from the reins, turning towards the horse.

"You damn fool!"

He jerked at the reins as he spoke. The horse snorted and half-reared, plunging sideways and dragging Philip with him. Philip picked up the whip which he had dropped as he fell, and gave the horse a swift cut on the shoulder, the whip-mark creaming sweat. An exclamation rose to Jack's lips, quickly suppressed. Typical Philip bloody Morland, he thought, not really surprised. Philip always expected his horses to make up for his inadequacies as a rider.

"What's happened? Anything wrong?" Geoffrey's voice rose from the next field.

Philip turned to reply and stopped abruptly at the sight of Jack coming towards him.

"What are you doing here?"

Jack felt his face flushing with a mixture of anger, heat and embarrassment. "I was mending the hedge, sir, and I saw you fall." He could hardly keep the edge of insolence out of his voice.

Philip looked at him sharply. "Mending the hedge?" His tone suggested that he thought it more likely Jack had been idling in the fields, wasting his time. He glanced along the hedgerow, where the gap bridged with the new length of railing gave testimony to Jack's words.

"Yes, sir. I saw your fall, and I came to see if I could help you with the horse."

Philip spoke with the anger of hurt pride. "I didn't *fall*, as you put it. I was thrown when the animal stopped at the hedge – " He gave another jerk on the reins.

Jack bit back another retort, knowing full well that anything Philip might construe as insubordination could easily lose him his job. Philip was the master, he the servant. It was not for him to criticize Philip's horsemanship, sorely tempted though he was. He said nothing, watching Galliard's nervous fidgetings, longing to take the bridle himself, to get on the horse's back and ride him quietly away, soothing him and making him forget his fright.

The brief, uncomfortable silence was broken by the sound of trotting hooves as Geoffrey brought his chestnut through the gateway. "I say, what's going on here? Are you all right?"

"The brute stopped at the jump and threw me," Philip replied shortly. "I bought him as an experienced hunter – he'll have to go back if he can't cope with a fence like that."

Geoffrey's usually rather vacant face registered surprise at the anger in Philip's voice. His affable air vanished as he attempted to smooth things over. "Look, old man, don't get so worked up. Are you going to have another go?"

Philip, preparing to remount, turned his back on Jack before replying. "No, I don't think so. I twisted my wrist landing in that damned hedge – might have sprained it. I'll give the horse a better trial some other day."

Coward, Jack thought fiercely as the two young men rode away, Philip giving Galliard a flick with his whip to reassert his mastery. Jack felt a flash of sympathy for the horse, admiring its boldness and generosity of spirit – the way it had approached that fence! But the horse was subject to Philip's whims, just as he was himself.

He trudged back up to his gap, shooed away the heifers and began wedging a second rail into position, spearing his thumb on a thorn for his pains. The unfairness of the incident struck him anew – Philip had clearly been to blame, but it would be Galliard and Jack himself who would suffer. There had always been a latent hostility between Jack and Philip, which was, Jack knew, partly his own fault. He had more affinity and skill with horses than Philip would ever possess, and he didn't always succeed in concealing his contempt for Philip's bluster or the way he treated his animals, no matter how much he tried to adopt the blank-faced veneer required of a servant.

"I didn't fall off, I was thrown." Jack rehearsed the line a few times, mimicking Philip Morland perfectly. He'd amuse Jimmy Taplin with the story when he next saw him, he thought, embroidering a few details. Jack had gradually perfected his imitation of Philip, and this had almost brought about his downfall a few months ago. His mimicry caught with exactness Philip's public-school accent, his rather effete walk and the way he talked when trying to impress friends like Geoffrey. When Jimmy had called at Greenstocks to collect a dead foal for the Hunt kennels, Jack had been entertaining him with a lively impersonation of Philip when he suddenly became aware that his victim was standing by the harness-room, having come down to the yard with some order for Sedley. It had only been Sedley's going to old Mr Morland and speaking up for Jack that had saved him from being sacked for his impudence, and Philip had treated him with coolness ever since.

But Jack grinned now at the memory, selecting nails from the tool-bag and clenching them between his teeth as he reached for his hammer.

Alice Smallwood, shaking a duster out of the upstairs landing window, watched her twin brother with some envy as he cycled away between the hedgerows. In the winter it was different; she was glad then to be in the big warm house with its log fires, and sorry for Jack when he came home at night with numb fingers and ears reddened from the cold. But now she longed to be outside in the sunshine, breathing the smells of cut hay and roses and warm grass. She wondered whether Jack would be tempted to take his ferret out after rabbits when he had finished his work. It was late July, and the days were not far past their longest, but even so there was not much chance that she would be home before dark tonight, for the Morlands were having a dinner-party and she would be waiting on at table.

In spite of the late hours and the extra work, Alice liked social occasions, and for all her sense of confinement now she was looking forward to the evening with a small thrill of pleasure. She enjoyed preparing the dining-room, setting the polished walnut table with the best silver and candlesticks and damask napkins, arranging the flowers and lighting the many softly-shaded lamps. She liked seeing the ladies in their elegant gowns, especially Madeleine, who had an eye for the latest fashions.

The evening proved to be no disappointment. Madeleine had asked Alice to put out her newest dress, a dove-grey silk, and to dress her hair in the elaborate style she wore for special occasions. Alice enjoyed these preparations, too, handling the soft, expensive fabrics, so different from any garment she owned herself, and feeling that she and Madeleine were engaged in some feminine conspiracy. She looked on approvingly as Madeleine, dressed, perfumed and coiffed, selected jewellery from a tray. The new dress was rather daring, showing Madeleine's slender ankles, and her small feet in bar shoes of precisely the same colour as the silk of the dress.

"You look lovely, Miss."

Madeleine was used to being admired. "Thank you, Alice. You've done my hair beautifully." She held a pearl necklace against the neckline of the dress. "How does that look?"

"I think the garnets would look better," Alice said, considering. "Is it just the Groves coming tonight, Miss?"

"Mm. Perhaps you're right." Madeleine took a second necklace from her tray. "Yes, Mr and Mrs Grove — and their son, Robert. He's an officer in the Rifle Brigade, just come back from India."

The Groves were occasional guests at Greenstocks, but Alice had not seen their son before. She fastened the clasp on the garnet necklace, looking up to examine the resulting picture in the mirror. Madeleine, meeting her gaze, gave a quick, mischievous smile; Alice smiled back, understanding now the reason for the new dress and ornate hairstyle. She wished Madeleine a happy evening and went downstairs to the kitchen, where the hot steamy air contrasted unfavourably with the cool scent of roses and perfume in Madeleine's room. Mrs Sedley, the cook, was basting a joint, while Harriet, the second maid, was setting out coffee cups on a tray. They were discussing the dinner guests as they worked.

"Yes, the son's about Mr Philip's age," Mrs Sedley was saying.

"I know. Miss Madeleine's sweet on him," Harriet remarked.

"How do you know that?" Alice asked in surprise. She had just formed the same opinion herself, but Harriet's work kept her confined to the kitchen and scullery; she was not in a position to receive confidences from Miss Madeleine.

"Jack told me." Harriet threw Alice a smug glance. "He said that's why she goes riding so much lately. It's because this Mr Grove's home on leave."

"He won't be on leave much longer, I daresay," Mrs Sedley said darkly, "so she'd do better to set her sights elsewhere."

Alice had to contain her curiosity about Mr Grove until the guests were seated in the dining-room, and she went in to serve the soup. Mrs Morland, dressed in a high-necked lace blouse and cameo brooch, smiled at her briefly, but otherwise no-one glanced up as she entered. Young Mr Philip was there, elegant in his dinner-jacket, and opposite Madeleine sat the subject of the kitchen discussion, a slim, fair-haired young man in army uniform.

Alice served the bowls of soup, taking in fragments of conversation.

"What are your plans, Robert? How long are you expecting to be at home?" Mr Morland asked.

"I'm not certain," the young man replied in a rather drawling voice. "I only came back from India a few days ago – I shall probably get definite orders in a day or two."

"Everything's so vague," said Mrs Grove, a bony woman with a long neck rising out of a froth of lace. "But, if the situation in Europe gets any worse, he may be called back to barracks at any time."

"Yes, things have certainly begun to look serious since this

Sarajevo business, though no-one would have suspected it at the time," Mr Morland remarked. "It looks like putting the Irish question on the sidelines for the time being."

Carefully placing a bowl of soup in front of Philip, Alice noticed that he looked keenly interested in the conversation, evidently as impressed as Madeleine by the handsome young officer. However, at this point Alice was obliged to withdraw to the kitchen, having finished with the soup. That was one of the frustrating things about waiting at dinner; by the time she came in again the conversation would have moved on to a different topic.

"What's he like?" Harriet asked.

"Oh, quite nice-looking, I suppose."

"No-one can compare with Mr Philip, eh, Harriet?" Mrs Sedley remarked knowingly.

Harriet protested, but Alice knew that she did not really mind being teased. Harriet made no secret of her admiration for Philip. She was often scolded for gazing dreamily out of the window, neglecting her duties, as he strode down to the stables or set off on horseback across the park, and would defend him against any criticism, however slight, from the staff. It was a pity, Alice thought, that Jack in his turn was devoted to Harriet, and was often to be found waiting for her outside the kitchen when work was finished. Alice privately considered Harriet to be rather a silly girl, always giggling and gossiping. She admitted that Harriet was pretty, with a rosy complexion and softly-curling brown hair, but she wished that her brother would find someone more worthy of him. She hated to hear Harriet speak dismissively of Jack in the high-and-mighty way she copied from Madeleine in one of her haughty moods.

Alice returned to the dining-room to collect the dishes and take in the joint. The mood was altogether more light-hearted than it had been on her first entrance; Madeleine was entertaining the company with a description of the Fancy

Dress Ball she had attended at the Savoy, in London. She had had a special dress made, a Spanish dancer's, all frills and flounces, and Alice had seen the pictures in the papers of the guests in their wonderful costumes, like illustrations from a fairy-tale book. It all seemed far removed from the war rumours they had been discussing before, and Alice wondered if the trouble they had spoken of would blow over, as everything else seemed to. There was always trouble — trouble in Ireland, trouble in Europe – but it all seemed very remote. She had seen headlines in the paper mentioning the assassination of the Austrian Archduke in Sarajevo, and she knew that there had been some sort of ultimatum, but in the same paper there had been news of the latest ladies' fashions from Henley, so it didn't seem very serious.

A blast of hot air struck her face as she pushed open the kitchen door. "They're talking about the Midnight Ball," she reported.

Mrs Sedley plunged the used saucepans into a sink of scalding water. "Midnight Ball?" she repeated. "The only thing I want to do at midnight is fall into my bed, not go gallivanting about at all hours."

"Oh, it looked lovely, though," said Harriet. "I saw the pictures. I'd love to have gone. I'd have gone as a romantic medieval heroine, in a white dress with long flowing sleeves . . . " She danced a few steps with an imaginary partner, her eyes half-closed.

"Never mind that, Harriet, you can come and see to these pans." Mrs Sedley flung the soup-spoons into the sink with a clatter. "Otherwise you'll still be cleaning up here at midnight, never mind romantic dances and pretty dresses."

Sunday in Littlehays

Emily plumped up her mother's pillows and tucked the worn red blanket more firmly around the sides of the chair.

"Have you got everything you want?"

Mrs Smallwood smiled up at her elder daughter. "Yes, thank you, dear. You go along. Is Jack ready?"

As she spoke, a loud thumping of boots resounded from the narrow stairs and Jack appeared in the doorway, unfamiliarly smart in his best jacket and tie and with his hair neatly parted and damped down under his cap.

"Ready?" he asked his sister.

"Yes, and Alice has gone on with the children." Emily put on her brown felt hat and adjusted it in front of the small mirror. "Goodbye, then, Ma."

The small stone Norman church was dwarfed beneath the spreading branches of its yew tree, which was said to be as old as the church. The Morlands' Daimler was coming slowly along the village street, looking very shiny and new compared with the painted dog-carts which were the more normal mode of conveyance. Sedley was driving it, looking as if he would have felt more at home behind a pair of horses. He disliked motorcars as he did most things which smacked of modernity, but nevertheless did a good job on the Daimler, Jack noticed, admiring the sheen on the dark green bodywork. By the lych gate, Alice, in her best navy-blue coat and with her soft brown hair pinned up neatly under her felt hat, was talking to a tall dark-haired young man. Jack nudged Emily as he noticed the pair.

"See that? It's not the first time I've seen him single her out, either. I reckon he's sweet on her."

Emily tutted, amused. "You're just as bad as the village gossips. Edward's a nice young man and we've all known him for years. Why shouldn't he speak to Alice? It'd be rude of him *not* to, wouldn't it?"

"Well, he's called round a few times since he's been back from Cambridge, and I don't suppose it's just to see Ma and me," Jack pointed out.

Edward finished his conversation with Alice as the pair approached, raised his hat and asked after Mrs Smallwood, and went into the church with his father, who was the local doctor. Alice stepped forward to meet her brother and sister. She looked anxious, her hazel eyes wide with concern.

"Edward thinks there's almost certain to be a war," she told them. "He says Germany's declared war on Russia. He said he was in Chelmsford yesterday and everyone was talking about it."

Jack's expression showed excitement rather than dismay.

"So will we be in it, then?" he asked.

"Edward thinks so." Alice was alarmed to hear the note of enthusiasm in her brother's voice. She gave him a searching look and was relieved to see his attention swiftly refocused on Harriet, who was approaching with her parents. She was dressed in her showiest hat, really an old one transformed by a new piece of ribbon and a full-blown rose.

"Come on, let's go in," said Emily. "There's no point waiting for Tom. He must have got held up at the farm."

Inside the church, the Morland family sat in their front pew. Mrs Morland and Madeleine were more opulently dressed than the village women, and Madeleine commanded many admiring glances from the local youths. Philip sat beside her, neat and correct in his suit. Alice, watching him as he turned to speak to his mother, remembered Jack's account of the hedge-jumping incident, and was quite unmoved by Philip's undoubtedly handsome profile. Almost involuntarily, her glance fell on Edward Sidgwick, who was standing politely to allow an elderly lady to take her seat in the pew before him. Now there was a young man worth ten of Philip, Alice thought. He had a kind nature as well as good looks; she considered his dark hair and piercingly blue eyes infinitely more attractive than Philip's air of being far too pleased with himself.

Jack, settling down beside her on the wooden pew, his best boots creaking, whispered, "The rector looks serious."

Indeed, the rector's face did look grimly set as he climbed the steps to the lectern, and the low buzz of conversation which had been audible above the organ music dwindled and ceased as he scanned the faces of the congregation.

When the time came for the sermon, there was a longer pause than usual before he began speaking in a low, solemn voice. "I shall not be giving the sermon which I had intended for this morning. Instead I shall be speaking of the very grave news which has reached our village. You will be aware that the situation in Europe has been steadily worsening and that there have been rumours of war for some time. You will have read in your newspapers about the assassination of the Austrian Archduke Franz Ferdinand in Sarajevo. Following that assassination, Austria has declared war on Servia, and Russia has come to Servia's defence, with the result that yesterday Germany declared war on Russia. With this very serious state of affairs it seems likely that soon all of Europe will be involved."

During the pause which followed, Alice was aware of a sick feeling in the pit of her stomach, a mixture of fear and excitement. It was serious, then; not just the usual fuss and rumours, although she couldn't quite see why the murder of an Austrian Archduke in a town no-one had ever heard of should need to involve the British Army. The Sedleys had had a son killed in the Boer War, an event of which Mrs Sedley sometimes spoke with great bitterness, and Alice dreaded above all else that Jack, in a surge of enthusiasm, would decide

25

to join the colours. She knew that he was restless enough to do anything for a change, and for some excitement to break the routine of his days.

The rector went on to speak of the sacrifices which would be called for if the situation did worsen. "The German Army is mobilizing," he summed up; "a highly-trained and determined army which is already sweeping through neutral Luxembourg. We are at a momentous point in history," he finished dramatically, "and I know that I can rely on the people of Littlehays to hope, pray, and – if necessary – fight, for a swift conclusion to this conflict. We all have our part to play, and we must play it as equals, since we will all be equally affected if might is allowed to triumph at the cost of the weak and the unprepared. Whatever may lie before us, we can rest secure in the knowledge that God will strengthen the arm of those on the side of righteousness."

Alice exchanged a worried glance with Emily, aware as she did so that Jack beside her had unconsciously taken on a soldierly bearing, his shoulders squared and chin lifted. She tried unsuccessfully to catch his eye as the organist struck up the opening notes of the hymn, *Fight the good fight with all thy might*, wishing she could know what her brother was thinking. She wondered whether people in Germany were listening to similar church services, with clergymen asking them to be patriotic, and telling them that right was on their side.

At the end of the service, people emerged squinting into the bright sunshine which hurt their eyes after the dim stained-glass light of the church interior. Everyone was discussing the sermon, some anxious and fearful, but others talking animatedly and giving every impression of excitement at the news. Jack went off to join a group of friends, while Alice and Emily were greeted by Tom, Emily's husband, who had slipped in at the back of the church soon after the start of the service.

"Kept behind with a cow with milk fever," he explained.

"Stirring stuff, wasn't it?" He took Emily's arm and she clung on protectively as they walked along to the Church Hall to meet the two children, who had attended Sunday school. Emily would have no need to worry about him, at any rate, Alice thought. No-one would expect married men with children to join the Army. She stood for a moment feeling the sun warm on her back, and looking at the squat stone church, the gravestones which stood up starkly from the mown grass, and the centuries-old yew tree. The church and its surroundings always gave her the feeling that she and her worries were insignificant, that life went on regardless. Next year, and the year after that, the oats would ripen in the field beyond even if there were someone different to harvest them, and the turtle-doves would croon in the elm-trees, and the red–admiral butterflies would show their brilliant colours against the mauve buddleia at the edge of the churchyard. And this scene, so very English, epitomized all that the rector had said they should fight for. With a sigh, Alice turned away to follow her sister.

Edward Sidgwick, helping his mother into the doctor's dog–cart, raised his hat to Alice as she passed. He too was elated rather than depressed at the news, she noted. She wondered whether he would want to fight. They were a clever family; Edward was reading History at Cambridge University, and his older sister, now living in London, had also had a University education, an unusual thing for a woman. She was a Suffragette, to her father's frequent embarrassment; she had been arrested outside Buckingham Palace in May along with Mrs Pankhurst, but had been released soon afterwards. Alice could hardly remember a time when Suffragettes hadn't been in the news, but recently their activities had been eclipsed by the war rumours. To some of the villagers, far-removed from goings-on in London, the campaigning women were little more than a joke. "They want women's suffrage – well then, let them go on suffering," people would say.

Alice secretly admired the Suffragettes but she wondered what effect women getting the vote would really have, if they ever did get it. The men who had the vote wouldn't have voted for a war, would they, for all the current air of excitement? It was all beyond the control of the ordinary person.

She followed Jack and his friends along the lane, turning her thoughts towards the preparations for Sunday dinner.

Galliard

"Mr Philip won't be riding Galliard today, so you can take him out for an hour's quiet exercise," Sedley told Jack. "Watch him though – he's a bit of a handful, from what I hear."

Jack saddled and bridled the bay thoroughbred, hardly able to believe his luck. He mounted from the block, and rode under the archway and out into the lane, between verges lush with summer growth. It was too early in the day for the heat to be oppressive, although the faint haze suggested that it would be very hot later. Galliard walked out eagerly, mouthing his bit in anticipation, his stride long and free, so that Jack felt a sudden elation at his unexpected good fortune – to be riding a horse like this, and to call it work!

The gate into the hayfield was enticingly open, and the gentle gradient of the cropped grass was too much for Jack to resist. He looked round to check that he was out of sight of the house, and urged Galliard into a canter. The horse responded keenly, accelerating up the slope. Jack, used to the stolidity of Mr Morland's hunter or the fussiness of Miss Madeleine's grey mare, felt that this was a different kind of creature altogether; it was like sitting on a coiled spring, boundless energy beneath him ready to be released with a mere relaxing of his hands. They were already approaching the headland, bordered with its trimmed hedge, and Jack knew that he had no intention of stopping. He touched the horse's sides with his heels, Galliard sprang forward and they were over the low hedge as if it were no more than a log on the ground.

Wheeling, Jack realized that he was now in the field in which he had witnessed Philip's fall. The obstacle Philip had funked was at the bottom of the field. Jack had never tackled anything so large but he felt that on this horse he could attempt anything. Besides, he thought, trying to justify his intended action, jumping the fence would help restore the horse's confidence. He turned in a controlled circle, taking stock of the formidable hedge and remembering the drop on the landing side, then turned Galliard towards it, urging him on into a springy, balanced stride. The horse bounded forward in excitement but then seemed to hesitate. Jack, suspecting that he remembered what had happened before, pushed him on, judging his stride. One, two, three, and then Galliard threw himself forward, clearing the hedge in a huge, scopy jump that filled Jack with a surge of pure delight. For a second they seemed to hang in mid-air, before dropping down into the next field, pitching slightly on landing so that Jack was almost thrown over the horse's shoulder. Galliard found his footing quickly and cantered on over the dry grass. Jack leaned forward, patting the horse's neck, wisps of flying mane stinging his face.

"You did it, lad! I knew you could do it!"

He could feel the heat of the horse's sides through his trousers, and the reins were slippery with sweat, hard to hold. He pulled Galliard up with difficulty. He'd have to walk him quietly through the woods now, to dry him off before returning home.

"What do you think you're doing?"

The voice cut into Jack's thoughts, wiping the grin of triumph from his face. There in the lane at the top of the field was Geoffrey Montjoy's yellow Model-T Ford, with Geoffrey and Philip looking over the hedge. Cursing his stupidity for not checking more carefully that he hadn't been watched, Jack rode slowly toward them, trying to repress his pride at having succeeded where Philip had failed.

"I said what do you think you're doing?" Philip repeated.

Jack thought it was obvious but he replied politely, "Exercising your horse, sir."

Philip's face was as red with anger as Jack's was from exertion. "Quiet road exercise, was what I told Sedley. Who gave you permission to gallop about jumping hedges?"

"No-one, sir. I thought it would give the horse confidence, sir, to jump . . ."

Jack realized at once that this was the worst thing he could have said. Philip leaned over the hedge and grasped the bridle.

"Get off my horse at once. You can lead him back to the stableyard. When I want my horses trained I'll go to an expert. You realize you could have lamed or injured a valuable animal? I shall speak to Sedley immediately I get back, and he'll make sure you never ride the horse again."

"Sir." Jack dismounted, feeling suddenly weary.

"It was a marvellous jump," Geoffrey said mildly, but was instantly silenced by a glare from Philip.

Jack led Galliard along the hedge to the gateway which opened on to the lane.

"And you can be sure my father will hear about this," Philip shouted as he got back into the car.

Jack trudged on, his triumphant moment well and truly over. "He'll really do for me this time," he thought savagely. Then he remembered the war rumours. If he were to be dismissed from Greenstocks, he might find an escape route ready and waiting.

At War

"This sauce just *won't* come smooth," Mrs Sedley said irritably, bent red-faced over her mixing bowl and wooden spoon. "And I'm behind today as it is. I don't know what I've done wrong, I'm sure."

"We're low on milk now, as well," Harriet reported from the steps which led down to the cellar. "We'll have to send down to the farm for some more. I'll see if I can find Albert, shall I?"

"No, you can go yourself," Mrs Sedley replied, glancing up at the kitchen clock above the cooking range. "Alice and I can manage here. Albert's got enough to do and it's nearly time for his dinner-break." She rummaged in a drawer, looking for a whisk.

Harriet, with a humph of protest, snatched up the empty milk-can and flounced out of the kitchen, almost colliding with Albert, the elderly man who did the gardening and odd jobs around the house, as he came in for his midday meal.

"Steady on there, lass. It's too hot for dashing about."

Harriet's reply was inaudible. Albert, sitting down at the long kitchen table, extracted a large off-white handkerchief from the pocket of his moleskin breeches and mopped his brow with it.

Mrs Sedley, whisking energetically, glanced up. "We'll be a few minutes yet, Albert. Alice hasn't served the luncheon yet."

"Not to worry. I'm glad to get the weight off me feet," Albert replied, stuffing the handkerchief back into his pocket. "Heard the news today, then?"

"Yes, we have," Mrs Sedley replied shortly.

Alice took the warm bread rolls from the oven and arranged them in a serving-basket. All day, she had felt a sense of unreality. The rumours of yesterday had been confirmed – Great Britain was at war with Germany – and yet here they all were getting worked up about lumpy sauce and milk shortages, exactly as if nothing had happened. She wondered what it would take to upset the unshakeable routine of Greenstocks.

"They're saying down at the stables as young Master Philip's going to enlist," Albert remarked.

"That doesn't surprise me." Mrs Sedley, satisfied at last with her sauce, was pouring it into a china boat. "It's what Mr Morland's wanted for him all along – wanted him to join the regular Army when he left school, only Mr Philip wouldn't. And he hadn't really decided anything else about his future, wasting his time around here pretending to help out on the estate. Here, Alice, you can start taking the first course in now."

The atmosphere was taut in the dining-room, conversation dwindling as Alice opened the door with her tray of soup. Miss Madeleine was not at home today; Philip looked ill-at-ease, his mother tight-lipped and anxious. It occurred to Alice that maybe he didn't want to join the Army; perhaps his father had talked him into it.

Back in the kitchen, Harriet had returned from the farm and had heard the rumours about Philip. "I think he'll look so handsome in uniform," she was saying, setting places for the servants' lunch. "I can't wait to see him."

"There's more to it than that," Mrs Sedley remarked, and Alice wondered whether she was thinking of her dead son.

"Aye, he won't be the only one," Albert said, taking a sip of his beer and wiping the froth from his lips. "Mr Green from the Post Office, his son's already been called. He's in the Reservists."

"Your Jack's going to go, isn't he?" Harriet said to Alice.

"I don't know," Alice answered, trying not to betray her concern.

"Young Jack will, if I know him," Albert said. "He won't want to stay at home when there's fighting to be done."

"Here, Alice, take these in and stop fretting," Mrs Sedley put in, handing over a steaming vegetable dish. "Don't you worry about your Jack. They only want trained men. It said so in yesterday's papers."

"Only trained men?" Alice repeated, on her way out of the door. "But the rector said . . ."

"Only trained men – that's what it says," Mrs Sedley repeated firmly. "It's different for Mr Philip. He's got an uncle in the regiment, who'll arrange something for him, I don't doubt. But your Jack won't be needed."

Re-entering the dining-room, Alice was unable to suppress a smile of gratitude. Mr Morland remarked on it at once. "You're looking very cheerful today, Alice. Haven't you heard the news?"

"Oh, yes, Mr Morland. Sorry, Sir." Flustered, she backed out of the room, trying to compose her features into a more suitably serious expression.

After lunch, while Alice was in the dining-room putting away the napkin-rings and table–mats, there was a knock at the front door. She opened it to find Edward Sidgwick standing in the porch, with his father's pony and trap waiting in the driveway.

"Alice! I hoped I'd see you here." He doffed his tweed cap exaggeratedly. "Special delivery – for Mrs Morland." He held out a small bottle of pills and handed it to her.

"Oh, thank you! Dr Sidgwick usually brings it himself. He's not ill, is he?"

"No, but I'm helping him out this week with some routine deliveries. I've just finished, as it happens. Like to come for a spin?"

"Oh!" Alice was taken aback; Edward called fairly often at

home, usually bringing books to lend her, but she felt uneasy at conducting a conversation on the Morlands' doorstep. "But I'm working!"

"I thought you had a half-day?"

"Yes, on Thursdays."

"I'll see you tomorrow, then, at about the same time?" Not waiting for an answer, Edward was back in the driver's seat in one agile movement. He picked up the reins, clicked his tongue at the grey pony, and was trotting out of the driveway, one hand raised in farewell, before Alice had a chance to collect her thoughts. She stood at the open door for a moment, embarrassed in case anyone had overheard the exchange, and uncertain whether or not he had intended to make a definite arrangement. She collected some unused cutlery from the dining-room and returned to the kitchen.

"Was that the doctor's son?" demanded Harriet, who never missed a thing. "I saw you talking to him at church on Sunday."

"Yes, it was." To her dismay, Alice felt herself colouring up. "He was just delivering Mrs Morland's pills."

"They say he's sweet on Mary Springfield, from the draper's."

"Do they?" Alice replied as nonchalantly as she could. Edward was perfectly entitled to be interested in anyone he liked, she told herself.

That evening Jack went rabbiting in the woods above Greenstocks. Alice was picking blackcurrants in the small garden behind the cottage as he left, and they had the usual argument.

"Oh Jack, must you go? In the Morlands' woods?"

"I won't get caught." Jack stuffed his nets into his trouser pockets, took the sand-coloured jill ferret from her cage outside the back door and put her into a sacking bag.

"You *think* you won't."

"I know I won't. The gamekeeper'll be having his supper."
He pushed the bag with the ferret in it down inside the front
of his jacket.

"He'll surprise you one day. Is it really worth it? A fine or
even a prison sentence, just for a rabbit or two?"

"You won't mind when I bring back a nice rabbit for the
pot."

"I'd rather do without," Alice retorted. "So would Ma."

"Don't worry. I won't be long."

Alice always tried to stop him, but he knew that she understood his motivation as well as he did himself. He went more
from a sense of defiance than from an urge to provide for his
family. The element of risk pleased him, adding spice to his
outings; if the Morlands gave him permission to take game
from their land, the activity would cease to have any appeal
for him. Besides, Alice wouldn't be annoyed with him for
long, he knew; he could always get round her.

The gate clicked behind him, and he strode through the
thistly pasture behind the cottage, heading for a faint path
which wound up into the woods. By the warren at the top of
the hill, he pegged his nets across the rabbit holes, slipped the
ferret into one of the entrances, and waited. He heard the
pounding of feet seconds before a rabbit burst out of the warren and was caught in the net, struggling. He was on to it at
once. Crouching, he hardened the edge of his hand and struck
the rabbit cleanly behind the ears. The body was soft and limp;
he laid it on the ground and reset the net.

When he had caught a second rabbit, he waited for the ferret to emerge and picked her up carefully by the scruff of the
neck, avoiding being bitten. The strong musky scent of her fur
rose to his nostrils as he slipped her back into the bag and
replaced it in the front of his jacket. She would be angry, filled
with blood-lust and deprived of her reward, but he would give
her some of the meat later. He unpegged his nets and folded
them, then picked up the rabbits by their hind-legs.

He paused at the edge of the wood, where hawthorn and elder grew thickly. The air was still warm, only a faint breeze cooling his face. A haze hung over the barley fields and meadows, giving the twilit landscape a tired, dusty look. Jack looked down the sloping fields towards Greenstocks, standing square and stolid among its neat gardens and trees. Beyond the house, the hunters were moving about slowly in the growing dusk. All the land Jack could see, from the dry earth beneath his feet to the distant plantation, belonged to the Morlands, and Jack often thought that he and Alice belonged to them too.

"But not for much longer," he told himself. He turned back through the undergrowth, snails cracking underfoot and brambles catching at his corduroy trousers. He and Philip would both be in the Army before long, far away from Greenstocks. Philip's privileged background would be certain to give him advantages, even so, but Jack was unsure about the details.

"I suppose Mr Philip won't be a regular soldier, like everyone else," he remarked to Sedley next afternoon, as they cleaned the saddlery. This was a job Jack always rather enjoyed. It was less strenuous than most of his duties, providing a welcome period of relaxation after the hay-carting he had been doing earlier, and the mild effort needed was rewarded by the sight of gleaming leather and shining bits and stirrups in the orderly tranquillity of the harness-room.

"Good gracious no, not the likes of him," Sedley replied, rubbing vigorously at a brass-mounted browband. "He'll apply for a temporary commission. His uncle's a Colonel, you know."

"I thought as Mr Philip hadn't done army training or anything . . ." Jack paused, frowning over the complicated reassembly of a double bridle.

"No, he'll go in as an officer." Sedley spat into the saddle-soap. "Probably go off on a training course and get his commission in a few weeks. They need trained officers quickly, see."

Jack fell silent, giving the bits a final polish. He tried to imagine what Mr Philip would be like as an officer, in charge of other men. The picture was not a convincing one. The ideal given by the rector of everyone fighting as equals was not intended literally, then: there would be inequalities on the battlefield just as there were everywhere else. It hadn't seemed like that when he and his local friends, the boys he had been at school with, had talked of enlisting. They had thought only of the adventure, the opportunity to prove themselves, the glamour and excitement of it. "I know I'd be a better soldier than him," he told himself, thinking of Philip's failure of courage when attempting to jump the hedge. What would he be like under gunfire? All the same, it gave Jack some satisfaction to think that his path was hardly likely to cross Philip's again – for the duration of the war, at any rate. Since the hedge-jumping incident Philip seemed to have gone out of his way to find fault with Jack – criticizing Galliard's turnout, and telling Sedley that the horse seemed nervous and must have been handled roughly in his stable. Sedley, fortunately, knew well enough that it was Philip's handling rather than Jack's which was likely to have upset the horse, and took the matter no further. Mr Morland had given Jack a stern talk-ing–to, rather than the dismissal he had feared – though the confirmation of war looked like making such considerations irrelevant.

Sedley interrupted Jack's train of thought. "There goes that young Edward Sidgwick, down to the house again," he remarked. "He was here yesterday, as well."

"Hmm." Jack wasn't interested, but a few moments later, looking up at the clatter of hooves as the pony-trap passed by on the outward sweep of the drive, he saw that Edward had a passenger.

"Isn't that young Alice?" Sedley asked. "Didn't know she was walking out with young Sidgwick."

"It's France's war and Belgium's, not ours," Alice was saying, as the grey pony trotted smartly along the tree—lined lanes in the dappled sunshine. "I don't see why we have to get involved."

"But, you see, we're Allies," Edward explained. "And Allied countries have to help each other in a crisis like this one. The Germans haven't tried to invade England yet, but they would do if they got the chance. They've already broken more than one treaty. And if we don't help France and Belgium now, why should we expect any help from them if Germany should invade us later?"

"Yes, I see," Alice conceded.

"And people are saying that if we don't enlist now we'll only end up as conscripts in the Prussian army. It's ourselves we're fighting for, not just for the French and the Belgians. But Germany simply can't win. She's at war with four countries now – us, France, Belgium and Russia." Edward stopped talking to slow the pony to a walk to negotiate an errand-boy on a bicycle.

"You talk as if you're planning to join the Army," Alice remarked, clasping the side of the trap as the pony sprang forward into a trot again.

"Of course I am." Edward turned to look at her in surprise. "I think most of the young men in the village are."

"But . . ." Alice faltered. "I thought it said in the papers yesterday that no untrained men would be needed. That's what Mrs Sedley told me. So I thought that people like you and Jack . . ."

Edward looked still more surprised. "But there's a notice in *The Times* today saying that young unmarried men between eighteen and thirty are wanted. Besides, I think Jack has definitely made his mind up to enlist. He told me so on Sunday."

Alice said nothing, silenced by the realization that her relief of the last twenty-four hours had been misplaced.

Edward, noticing her concern, said, "Is he eighteen yet?"

"Next week," Alice said. "Our birthday's on the twelfth."

"Would you come into the drawing-room for a moment, Alice?" Mrs Morland said next morning when Alice was clearing away the breakfast things.

"Yes, ma'am." Alice was puzzled, supposing that her employer was about to point out an imperfectly dusted shelf or a missed corner. Mrs Morland led the way without speaking, and closed the door behind them, her expression stern.

"Alice, I suppose your mother realizes that you've been seeing Edward Sidgwick alone?"

"Yes, Mrs Morland!"

"And does she allow it?"

"Of course, ma'am. We've known Edward for years; he's a friend of the family." Alice was surprised at the question, it never having crossed her mind that anyone could possibly object to her friendship with Edward.

Mrs Morland still looked displeased. "Well, it's up to you how you spend your time off, but I'm afraid I can't allow Edward to call for you here. I don't consider it proper for a maidservant here to be walking out alone with a young man, I'm afraid, and to do it so indiscreetly."

Alice felt herself blushing. "But I'm not *walking out* with Edward!" she protested. "We're just friends – we have been for years –"

"That may be, but other people may think differently. I'm afraid Mr Sidgwick's sister must be affecting him, with her London ways; he should know better. I'm not forbidding you to see Edward, Alice, just warning you to think of your reputation, and not to ask him to call here for you. I don't think his parents would be very pleased if they heard of it."

She nodded, indicating that the interview was at an end. Alice went back to her duties, her cheeks burning. She felt indignant that her friendship with Edward should be a matter for public discussion, and even more so when she considered the fact that Madeleine went out riding and driving with young men with perfect freedom. As for her *reputation* . . . why ever should her reputation be damaged by a short drive with a family friend?

She tidied and dusted the dining-room with furious energy. "Just wait till I tell Jack," she thought. She knew what he would say, and could already hear him saying it.

Partings

"So your Jack won't be with you for much longer, then?" Mr Richardson remarked, dumping the box of groceries on the kitchen table.

"That's right," Mrs Smallwood replied proudly. "He's staying on at Greenstocks till he gets his calling-up papers. He signed up the day after his eighteenth birthday – one of the first boys in the village to take the King's shilling, and the youngest too."

"Aye, he's a good lad, young Jack," Mr Richardson said. "I'm right out of dried peas, Mrs Smallwood, so I've put in a box of lentils instead. That'll be one and sevenpence ha'penny, thank you."

Alice counted out the money from the jar on the mantelpiece. She felt perturbed by her mother's reaction; she was proud of Jack herself, but her pride was tempered by fear that he might not return. "It is a war they're going to fight," she thought. "Doesn't she think what it might mean? Her only son?"

However, other people in Littlehays shared Mrs Smallwood's mood of excited anticipation. Alice had overheard young men talking about "giving the Germans a bashing", as if they were talking about a cricket match, or some special outing devised for their entertainment. But already there were reports of casualties, and rumours were flying of what the Germans were said to have done in Belgium, killing and maiming women and children. "They'd do the same here, if they got the chance," people told each other. There were warnings to look out for spies, and it was reported that a group of Germans had tried to poison the water in a reservoir in north

London. They had been caught and shot, it was said.

The Smallwoods listened to the spy warnings, but thought it extremely unlikely that any German spies could be lurking in their own small village, where everyone knew everyone else.

"They must mean in London," Jack remarked to Sedley. "There can't be any spies here."

Sedley just grunted, heaving a sack of oats up to the edge of the cornbin. He slit the top of the sack with his pocket-knife and up-ended it, so that the oats poured down into the bin with a faint hissing sound, raising a fine hazy dust that hung in a shaft of sunlight. He had enrolled as a Special Constable, and Jack supposed that he would have received special instructions to be on the alert for spies. Sedley had told him that there were fifty thousand aliens in the country, so presumably he envisaged this as a fairly heavy responsibility. Jack grinned to himself as he stooped to lift a second sack, thinking of Sedley, armed with a truncheon, marching a hefty band of murderous Huns into the local Constabulary.

Having enlisted, Jack was now experiencing mixed feelings about it. On the one hand, he was eager to go, to face a new challenge, to be in a situation in which he would depend on his own wits and physical capability. On the other hand, he felt pangs of regret that he would soon be leaving Greenstocks — which, to him, meant the stables and farm, for he had little to do with the house. The familiar routines, for all their repetitiveness, often gave him a feeling of well-being and contentment. He liked the orderliness of the stableyard, the horses with their coats shining from hours of grooming, the neat harness-room with the saddles and bridles on which he and Sedley lavished so much care, the warm mustiness of the feed room. All that would soon be changing. Officers had been in the area looking for suitable horses for the Army, and all the Greenstocks horses were to go except for Miss Madeleine's grey mare, which was too small. Hearing of this, Jack felt alarmed for the gentle horses, who knew nothing of this man-made war; he hoped they would receive the care they were accustomed to.

Jack's calling-up papers arrived at the end of that week. On Saturday evening, when he had finished work, he called for Harriet at the kitchen, hoping for the chance of walking home with her.

Harriet came to the door with hands soapy and reddened from washing-up. "I haven't finished yet. You can wait if you want," she told him.

"Come on inside, Jack. Sit down and have a glass of beer," Mrs Sedley invited. "Your last night, is it?"

"Last but one. I go to the barracks on Monday."

Mrs Sedley handed him beer in a cool pewter mug. "Your Alice'll miss you, and your ma."

But would Harriet, Jack wondered, watching her neat figure in the dark uniform as she reached up to replace the clean plates in the rack. He knew that she was conscious of being watched, but she avoided catching his eye, not hurrying about her work. She might be vaguely sorry that several of the young men in the village would be going away, but she wouldn't miss him in particular, he was sure. He sipped his beer, disappointed.

Alice came in from the dining-room carrying a loaded tray, and looked across the table at Jack in surprise. "Hello! Are you waiting for Harriet?"

Jack nodded, and Mrs Sedley said kindly, "I should think we can finish off between the two of us, can't we, Alice? You go off a bit early, Harriet."

"Yes. There's not much more to do," Alice agreed.

"Oh, all right," Harriet said ungraciously. She took off her cap and apron and hung them on a hook behind the door. Jack drank down the rest of his beer quickly, and got up to go.

"Call in tomorrow, if you can, to say goodbye," Mrs Sedley told him.

"Yes, I will. Thank you for the beer."

It was growing dusk outside. Harriet and Jack walked, a little apart, down the back lane and across the footpath to the village. Jack wanted to ask her if she would write to him during his absence, but did not know how to begin.

"I thought I'd better give my ferret to Alfie," he said instead, referring to Harriet's younger brother.

"All right. He's going to have your job at the stables, did you know? To work with the farm horses."

"Yes. Sedley told me this morning."

Jack hadn't liked to think that he could be so easily replaced by a boy three years younger who knew little about stable routines, but Sedley had told him gruffly, "I shall miss having you around the place, Jack lad. I've trained you well, and you've quite a way with the horses."

Everyone would miss him, it seemed, except Harriet. She had expressed no regret at his imminent departure, had given no sense that it was anything out of the ordinary. They were nearly at the village now; he must say something before they got to Harriet's cottage.

"I'll send you letters, while I'm away. You will write back to me, won't you?" he said, almost desperately.

"I'm not much good at writing." She had a way of looking at him that was half-inviting, half-mocking. "I should go back to school, my mum says."

"But you will be – be my girl, won't you, while I'm away, and when I get back?" he persisted.

Harriet didn't answer. Instead, she came close to him and kissed him, brushing her mouth quickly against his. He caught her arm and pulled her closer.

"Harriet –" He kissed her clumsily, so that their noses bumped. She returned his embrace for a few moments, then pulled away, laughing.

"Yes, I'll be your girl, if you like. I've got to go in now. I'll see you again tomorrow if you want. Come round after church if there's time. And don't forget to bring the ferret."

Jack was left standing in the lane, wondering, as always when he was with Harriet, whether she really did care for him a little, in spite of her offhand ways.

"You must be proud of your brother," Madeleine remarked, as Alice lit the lamps in her room. "I know I'm proud of mine. Will you be going to see Jack off, when he goes out to France?"

"I don't know, miss. That'll be a long time off yet. He only went to the barracks on Monday," Alice replied. The gas lamp flared into life with a faint hiss, illuminating Madeleine's rose-coloured room with a soft glow. Madeleine looked very beautiful, Alice thought, watching as she brushed her long silky hair in front of the mirror, her hands white and soft against the dark ruby red of her evening dress. Alice ruefully looked at her own hands, chapped and reddened with work, with fingernails cut short.

"I expect he's looking forward to going out," Madeleine said. "I went to the boat train with Mr Grove, when he left. It was all so exciting . . ." She gave a few more thoughtful strokes of the brush, lifting her hair and letting it fall like a blonde waterfall.

"Shall I pin your hair up now, miss?"

"Yes. Would you do it the way you did on Saturday?"

Alice took the gold-backed brush and began gently brushing the smooth hair back from Madeleine's brow. "Are you dining at home tonight, miss?"

Madeleine appeared to be in a wistful mood. Her eyes, reflected in the mirror, had a dreamy, abstracted look, brought quickly back into focus at Alice's question. "No, I shall be dining out, at the Montjoys'," she replied.

According to kitchen gossip, an engagement would shortly be announced between Madeleine and Geoffrey Montjoy. Geoffrey would be safely out of the war, at any rate, since he had a heart defect and was unfit for active service. But Alice wondered whether Madeleine was more interested in the good-looking young lieutenant.

War seemed to have changed little at Greenstocks, beyond the fact that Mrs Morland had organized a sewing and knitting group for local women with time on their hands. Madeleine alternated between excitement and total indifference to the fact that the country was at war. She passed her time in much the same ways as she always had: shopping in London, visiting friends, riding out on her grey mare, and driving with Geoffrey in his Model-T Ford. Alice had become accustomed, over the years, to Madeleine's abrupt changes of mood. One day Madeleine would treat her with the complete indifference that was a servant's due; the next, she would entrust her with confidences and gossip as if she were a trusted friend. Alice had learned to be cautious, to say nothing until she had gauged the older girl's mood. She privately thought Madeleine's life rather aimless, with nothing to do but amuse herself until she found a husband. Brought up to regard hard work as the norm, Alice could not imagine what it must be like to have all day to do as one pleased.

Madeleine surveyed her finished hair-style in the three-panelled mirror of her dressing-table. "Thank you, Alice. That looks lovely." She stood up, running her hands down the smooth velvet of her skirts. "Oh – I've something to give you." She rummaged in a drawer, and produced something soft in a *Dickins & Jones* wrapper. "Here. I bought this in London, but now I don't think it suits me. I thought it might fit you – we're much the same size."

Alice, amazed, opened the bag to reveal a cream-coloured muslin and lace blouse with a high neck and long sleeves. She fingered the lace panels rather nervously. The blouse was exquisite, far better than anything else in her meagre wardrobe.

"You mean you want me to have it?"

"Of course." Madeleine, already bored by her generosity, was selecting a string of beads to match her dress.

"Oh, thank you, miss!" Alice didn't know what else to say. Her thanks seemed quite inadequate. Madeleine had given her small presents before, usually cast-offs, but nothing as lavish as this. Alice thought that the blouse must have cost at least three shillings, and she wondered how Miss Madeleine could bear to spend so much money on a garment and then give it away on a sudden whim. She didn't know whether she was more impressed by Madeleine's kindness, or shocked by her capriciousness.

She showed the blouse to her mother before leaving for Greenstocks next morning. Mrs Smallwood's thin fingers with their swollen knuckles stroked the expensive lace, giving Alice a sharp pang of regret as she remembered that her mother still had the same shabby winter coat she had worn for years. There was not much money to spare for clothes.

"It's beautiful," Mrs Smallwood said with a faint sigh. "I suppose you'll need some better clothes if you're going to be walking out with young Edward."

"Oh, Ma." Alice felt herself reddening; her mother was making the same assumption as Mrs Morland. "Edward's just a friend, to all of us."

"Oh, yes?" her mother said. "I haven't noticed him calling on Jack as often as he does for you."

"What do you mean? He and Jack like each other –" Alice began, then realized that her mother was teasing.

She, Jack and Edward had played together as children, in the days when her father had been alive and had run the village draper's, and she had not been so conscious of the class difference between her family and Edward's. But then her father had died, and Edward had gone away to Bancroft's School in Woodford, and by the time he returned she and Jack had gone into service. Edward's parents were planning an academic career for him, while the most Alice could hope for was a position as a lady's maid, and Jack might rise to the status of Head Groom if he waited long enough.

Alice knew that the family circumstances would have been different if her father hadn't died so young. He had wanted better things for them, and Alice, who had been clever at school, would have stayed on to become a pupil-teacher, instead of leaving as soon as she had passed her Labour Certificate, to bring in some money. Mrs Smallwood had never been ambitious, and relative poverty combined with ill-health had brought about a lowering of her sights, a desire not to look too far into the future. Alice felt that her family's position in the village was an odd one. They belonged neither with the middle-class families, nor with the farm labourers who lived in the ramshackle cottages in the same lane – families whose children were sent out gleaning when the harvest was finished, or stone-picking in the fields to earn a few pennies. Mrs Smallwood was proud of Alice's education, which marked her out from the many villagers who could barely read or write. Alice had been determined to keep up her reading after she had left school, and this had been largely thanks to Edward, who had seen to it that she was supplied with books.

"Jack won't be going to France for a good while yet," Edward told her when she next saw him. He had called at the cottage to bring a book of poems by John Clare which he had promised to lend her, and they had decided to walk up the lane to Spinney Hill to look at the sunset. "He'll be in a training camp for several months, learning rifle drill and marching and that sort of thing."

"Perhaps he won't get there at all, then," Alice said, relieved, "if it's all likely to be over by Christmas, as they say."

Edward said nothing, stopping to lean on the top bar of the gate, and Alice knew that he did not believe in the rumours. He was waiting to be called up himself now, having applied for a temporary commission in the regular Army. Because of his background and education, he would be an officer, like Mr Grove and Mr Philip. It was another sign of the difference between them, Alice knew. Edward would not be out-of-place dining with the Morlands; courting Miss Madeleine, perhaps, instead of walking along the twilit lane with a domestic servant. Alice knew that she would miss him, when he had gone; there was something comfortingly dependable about him. She leaned on the gate beside him, trying not to think about what might happen.

The sun had gone down in an extravagance of fiery red, streaked with sooty black, like dark fingers trying to blot out the light. Flocks of starlings swept over the elm trees, making clouds of grey against the pink glow. The stubble of the harvested field swept down to the valley in clean lines; reflected sky picked out the winding thread of the river, and far beyond lay the blue-grey haze that was London. The warmth of the evening had gone with the sun, and Alice shivered suddenly, pulling her shawl more closely around her.

Edward, noticing, said, "Come on. It's late. We'd better be getting back." He took her arm as he spoke, but made no move to continue walking, instead turning to face her. "You will let me write to you, won't you, when I go away?" he said softly.

He was standing very close to her, making her feel suddenly self-conscious. His eyes were a clear blue, with dark lashes: "He'll look lovely in uniform, that's what Harriet would say," she found herself thinking. She said aloud, "Of course, Edward I'd like that very much. I – I shall miss you."

"I'll miss you, Alice," Edward replied, very seriously. They walked slowly in silence for a few moments, still arm-in-arm, Alice not wanting to break the mood by saying more. She had attributed Edward's recent attentions to kindness, no more, never seriously thinking that the friendship between them could become anything else. She felt now that there was a new tension between them, a subtly different kind of emotion, made more poignant by the fact that Edward would soon have to go away, bringing their new closeness to an abrupt end.

Alice became aware that a noise behind them, which had been vaguely intruding upon her thoughts, was becoming more insistent. She turned round to look, and pulled away from Edward sharply.

"Edward! Isn't that –?"

There was really no need to ask, for no-one else in the neighbourhood owned a dark green Daimler. Alice's first impulse was to run into the woods and hide, but reason told her that this would be pointless, since the occupants of the car had had plenty of time to observe that she and Edward were walking together arm-in-arm. A glance at Edward's face showed that he didn't see any reason for concern, but then the Morlands weren't his employers.

"Oh dear," Alice said unguardedly, "now I'll get another lecture –"

"A lecture? Whatever for?"

The car had amost reached them now, and Alice could see that the driver was Sedley, with three passengers. Mr Morland, and two ladies in hats and veils. Alice took them to be Mrs Morland and Madeleine, but the larger of the two ladies lifted her veil as the car drew level, and gave them a cool stare. Edward's expression changed abruptly. Alice recognized the lady as Mrs Sidgwick, Edward's mother; she looked decidedly displeased at what she saw.

"Oh dear, it'll probably be Edward getting the lecture this time," Alice thought uncomfortably. She wished everyone would stop interfering and leave them alone, to enjoy what little time they had left.

Training Camp

"It's not what I expected," Jack remarked disappointedly to Jimmy Taplin as they filled cans of water for washing-up. "It doesn't seem much like being in the Army, does it?"

"It'll feel more like it when we get our uniforms," Jimmy said, sloshing water as he lifted two steaming cans.

"I suppose so. But they keep telling us we'll get our uniforms *soon* and our rifles *soon* and our helmets *soon*. *Soon* still seems a long way off."

"I shouldn't worry. Time enough for all that," Jimmy said complacently. "And at least you're not at the beck and call of Philip high-and-mighty Morland any more."

"No, there is that. With a bit of luck he'll stay on in the Army after this lot, and get himself sent to India or somewhere."

But Jack still had a sense of anti-climax, after enlisting with the others in a surge of patriotism and self-sacrifice, and leaving the village as if bound straight for the battlefield. He didn't know quite what he'd expected on the day he'd reported to barracks, but it wasn't this oddly assorted bunch of boys and men playing at soldiers. Jack suspected he wouldn't feel like a proper soldier until he was dressed like one; meanwhile, they marched and paraded in their ordinary clothes, and practised rifle drills with wooden sticks, giving everything an air of pantomime. In spite of the newness of it all, the war seemed far away. The recruits lived in a sort of village of tents which had sprung up over half a hillside, reminding Jack more of the fairground he had visited on Bank Holiday Monday than of military orderliness.

He had been pleased to find old friends in his platoon, Dick Twyford and Ted Briggs, who had been in his class at school, and Jimmy from the Hunt kennels. The Hunt horses, like the Greenstocks ones, had all been taken for the Army.

"You're not the youngest bloke here after all," Jimmy told him now as they plunged greasy plates into the water. "That Will chap – fair-haired bloke that looks like a girl – he's even younger. Under age, Dick says."

"He looks it. I asked him if he was eighteen, the other day, and he wouldn't answer."

"He's fed up of people asking him, I bet."

Jack turned his attention to the scrubbing of an egg-encrusted saucepan. The whole washing-up operation was a fairly futile business, since everything was done in one large bowl full of cooling greasy water, and the plates were hardly any cleaner at the finish than at the start. He couldn't help thinking of the spotless kitchen and scullery presided over by Mrs Sedley at Greenstocks – every saucepan and plate and jug in its proper place, gleaming and polished. Mrs Sedley would soon lick this company into shape, he thought with a private grin.

Later, when Jack happened to find himself in conversation with the fair boy at the end of parade, Will admitted that he was in fact barely seventeen. All his friends were joining up, and he hadn't been able to face the prospect of staying at home while the war went on without him. "I never thought I'd get away with it, but I lied about me age and gave 'em all the details for me brother, who's nineteen," he told Jack.

"And were they taken in?"

Will gave a lopsided grin. "Reckon they don't believe in asking too many questions," he said simply.

Getting over his initial sense of disappointment, Jack settled into the routines, compensated by a sense of well-being; he enjoyed the discipline, the regular exercise and fresh air, ample food, and – most of all – the companionship. Used to a far more solitary life, with only Sedley and the horses for company during working hours, he liked the fact that there was always someone to laugh and joke with.

Already hard and fit from physical work, Jack adapted quickly to the demands of his new life. The day began at five-thirty in the morning, when the recruits, awakened by a bugle call, would emerge from their tents. Sustained by a mug of coffee and biscuit, they would set out on a run along the country lanes. This in itself was enough to exhaust those young men who had worked in shops and banks, sitting down for most of the day; complaining of aching muscles and sore feet, they would be almost too tired to eat the breakfast served on their return. For the rest of the day, they practised marching, forming and re-forming, wheeling, advancing and retiring, and bayonet-drill, which Jack found faintly blood-curdling. He could not make himself believe that the stuffed sack which they were instructed to assail with such alarming cries might one day be a human being.

"Blimey – he'll bust a gut one day, the way he shouts and bawls," Jimmy remarked, referring to the Sergeant in charge of the platoon, who was encouraging Will to stab at a sack more ferociously.

"He's all right though, Sergeant Jones, isn't he?" Jack said. "Not as fierce as he sounds."

Jimmy laughed shortly. "You wait till you let your feet get blistered. He'll practically have you up before a firing squad. According to him it's a treasonable offence."

"Well, it must be a bloody awful job, inspecting everyone's feet," Jack said, preparing for a renewed assault on the row of sacks. "Especially the other day, after we'd done that long march in sweltering sun. I wouldn't have swapped places with the poor blighter."

An enraged bellow interrupted their conversation. "Smallwood, Taplin, what do you think this is, a debating society? Get yourselves over here at the double!"

"'*Dear Ma and Alice,*"' Alice read aloud. "'*It is good fun here at camp. There are plenty of good lads and we all keep very fit. Do you remember Mr Downes who used to be at the chandlers, well he has a son here George who is a very nice chap, we do a lot of marching but they feed us well. Jack.*'"
Alice looked again at the front of the postcard before handing it to her mother. "He doesn't really say much, does he?"

"Maybe they're not allowed to. You hear such a lot about spies." Mrs Smallwood smiled fondly at the postcard, reaching up from her chair to stand it in pride of place on the mantel-shelf. "I'm pleased Jack signed up, at any rate. You know Mrs Stringer? She's got three sons, all fit and of age, and not one of them has enlisted."

"It's the upper classes as well," Alice said. "Look at that Mr Montjoy, that Miss Madeleine's seeing. I know he's not fit, but he could still volunteer for non-combatant duties. And Mrs Morland and Madeleine – what are they doing? Making baby clothes for soldiers' and sailors' wives. Now why should they need more baby clothes than at any other time, I'd like to know?"

"At least it's something," Mrs Smallwood said placatingly. "There's plenty in their position wouldn't lift a finger, I know."

Alice was not convinced. She wished that she could do more herself, besides just spending her free time knitting socks, but the family couldn't afford for her to give up her job at Greenstocks and do voluntary work. Edward had told her that Lorna, his sister of Suffragette fame, had immediately given up her campaigning activities on the outbreak of war, and had trained as a VAD nurse. Alice considered this far more worthwhile than making baby clothes.

Edward himself had gone to Officers' Training Camp a few days after the evening of his walk with Alice. She hadn't liked to ask him whether his mother had said anything about seeing them together in the lane, but in any case it seemed unimportant now, with Edward gone. Although they had promised to write to each other, Alice was aware that their relationship was at such an early stage, and built on such tenuous foundations, that it could be swept away by the war. There were people with far worse burdens to bear, she knew – like Rosie Taplin whose wedding to the farrier's apprentice had had to be cancelled. And there was constant news of casualties from the fighting on the Marne and the Aisne, and around Ypres. As November approached, people stopped saying that the war would be over by Christmas.

There had been a recruitment meeting in the church hall, and by now most of the younger men in the village had enlisted. Alice felt the absence of both Jack and Edward acutely, and with so many others gone the village had a deserted feeling to it, with many empty places in church on Sundays serving as a reminder.

Shortly before Christmas, the villagers found a new focus of attention. Sedley, the first of the Greenstocks staff to hear about it through his duties as Special Constable, told Harriet's brother, who told Harriet, who passed it on to the others, bursting into the kitchen excited at being the bearer of news.

"Did you know Hillbank House has been sold at last?"

Hillbank House, a large and once gracious property standing in its own extensive garden, had been empty for some months. It looked down on the village from its vantage point on Badger's Hill, and everyone was used to seeing the blank stares of its windows since the previous occupant, an elderly man living alone with his servants, had died.

"Who's bought it, then?" asked Mrs Sedley, kneading dough.

"Some people from London, Sedley says – artists and suchlike. And they've got a maid with them –" Harriet paused for maximum effect – "a *German*!"

"A German!" Mrs Sedley repeated. "What does Sedley say about that?"

Harriet tossed her head disapprovingly. "Not enough, if

you ask me. With all this talk about spies, all he's done is to take down particulars. And Mrs Richardson says this German woman has even had the cheek to go into the shop. It's a disgrace – Jack and all the others going off to kill Germans, and one of them living in our own village!"

"Whatever can these new people be like?" Mrs Sedley remarked, pounding energetically at her dough. "It makes you wonder, don't it, why they've moved away from London?"

Part Two: 1915

Lorna

The Morlands usually celebrated the New Year with a big, lavish dinner-party. This year, feeling that this would not quite be in keeping with wartime seriousness, they restricted themselves to a quiet dinner with a few friends, to see in 1915. The Sidgwicks were among the guests, causing Alice another painful reminder of the difference in status between herself and Edward. If he hadn't been away at training camp, he would have been dining with the others.

To Alice's embarrassment, Dr Sidgwick turned and smiled at her as she entered with the first course. "Good evening, Alice. Your mother is well, I hope. And how did Jack enjoy his leave?"

"Very much, thank you, sir," Alice faltered, conscious of Mrs Sidgwick's aloof glance. She had the same good looks as her son, but her expression made her look tough and unapproachable. Alice wondered whether the Sidgwicks knew that she and Edward had been corresponding regularly. He had sent her a photograph of himself in his officer's uniform, which made him look extremely handsome; she kept the photograph beside her bed, and wished she had one of herself to send him in return. He was hoping to be sent to France very shortly.

"Lovely to have a bit of a do," Mrs Sedley remarked as Alice returned to the kitchen. "Makes a change from all those sewing groups and their cups of tea, don't it?"

"It *is* nice," Alice agreed. "Like the old days – before the war, I mean." For all her lack of personal involvement in the war, the days before it began seemed far-off.

"Over by Christmas, they said at the start. Never mind,

love. We'll have ourselves a New Year's drink later on, shall we, and hope that the war'll be long finished by this time next year?"

But the next few weeks brought little to suggest an early victory, with three people killed in a Zeppelin raid on Yarmouth, and fears of similar raids on London. The war was beginning to seem dangerously close.

The new inhabitants of Hillbank House continued to arouse interest. It was said that there were five people living there – two men and two women in their late twenties or early thirties, apparently quite affluent, and the elderly German woman who was thought to have been the governess of one or more of them. None of the five was ever seen in church, and there was a good deal of speculation as to the nature of the relationships between them.

"Two couples, and none of them even married," Mrs Richardson, the post–mistress, told Alice with a disapproving sniff, when she went to post letters to Edward and Jack. "And those two men of fighting age, not even doing a proper job of work, from all accounts!"

"Rosie Taplin, she gave one of 'em a white feather when she saw him in the village," said Mrs Riley, who was waiting behind Alice to be served. "She says he just took it from her, cool as you like, says 'Thank you m'dear,' with a little bow, and walks off holding it!"

Alice, like the rest of the villagers, was curious about the new arrivals. One spring evening on her way home from Greenstocks, she met the German governess walking slowly along Goose Lane, holding a bunch of primroses. The elderly woman was dressed in a black skirt and a shawl pinned by a little blue floral brooch; she wore small round spectacles, and her thin, lined face looked tired and downcast. Her glance flicked up to meet Alice's and then quickly dropped again. Alice wished her good evening, feeling a wave of sympathy. The woman might be a German, but that didn't make the war her fault. She must be lonely and unhappy, in a foreign country where most people were hostile to her. Maybe she was worried about friends or relatives involved in the fighting; she would probably prefer to be at home in Germany. According to Harriet, she never went down to the village any more, since a group of boys had thrown stones at her and jeered.

The woman murmured something in reply to Alice's greeting, and continued on her solitary way. Alice walked on homewards, enjoying the sounds of the mild spring evening, a thrush singing from a treetop and the babyish voices of lambs in the fields. It was a pity to spoil such an evening with thoughts of war; everything was busy with new life, not with death. The hedgerows were misted with the first shoots of green hawthorn, and decked with pointed beech buds like little golden flames; the glossy blue-bell leaves were thick in the woods beside the lane. It must be the same in the battlefields of France and Belgium, Alice thought, the delicate primroses trampled beneath soldiers' boots, and men dying amidst the luxuriant new vegetation.

A few days later she received a letter addressed in Edward's familiar spiky black handwriting. *"I am hoping to go to France sooner than I expected,"* he wrote. *"I heard yesterday that officers are urgently needed in the 5th Epping Foresters, who are about to go, so I have applied for a transfer. I should be leaving in about twelve days' time. Unfortunately I do not think there is any possibility of getting leave beforehand, but of course I will write to you as often as I can. I have just received a letter from Lorna, who thinks she may be returning home for a few days. I have asked her to call on you if she can."*

Mrs Smallwood, looking up from her knitting, saw the expression on Alice's face as she folded the letter and put it back into its envelope. "Oh, Alice love, it's not bad news, is it?"

"No – not really," Alice said. "It's Edward. He's going out to France very soon now. I know it's silly, but I was hoping the

63

war would end before he or Jack actually got out there."

"Neither of them will be happy until they've done their bit," her mother said.

Alice sighed, wishing she could do *her* bit; knitting and sewing occupied her few spare moments, but it wasn't enough, when Jack and Edward were risking their lives. She went upstairs to read Edward's letter again and to put it with the others in the flowered cardboard box she kept beside her bed, together with his photograph. She sometimes felt that without these letters, she would have wondered whether she had imagined the beginnings of romance; the times she had spent with Edward seemed so distant in comparison with all that had happened since.

"Oh, Edward, I wish you were here now," she told the photograph wistfully, and gazed at it for several moments, trying to recreate the Edward she knew in the handsome, distant face. Then, remembering what he had written about Lorna, she went downstairs again to tell her mother.

As the days passed and there was no sign of Lorna, Alice assumed that she had either changed her plans, or been unwilling to take up Edward's suggestion. Alice felt, on the whole, relieved. She felt very much in awe of the vivacious girl she only dimly remembered. Lorna, four years older than Edward, had been too grown-up for the childish games shared by her brother and the younger Smallwoods, and had gone away to boarding school while Alice was still quite young. Since leaving University, she had lived in London with various members of the Women's Social and Political Union, to which she seemed to have devoted most of her energies.

One morning, while dusting Madeleine's bed-room, Alice noticed a Model-T Ford in the driveway outside. At first she thought it must be Geoffrey Montjoy's, but before long she could hear girlish laughter from the drawing-room below.

"See who the visitor is?" Harriet asked, passing along the hall-way with a mop and bucket. "It's Lorna Sidgwick – that

Suffragette. She's come to visit Miss Madeleine."

Alice tried not to feel resentful. She went into Mrs Morland's room and picked up a crumpled silk wrap from the floor. Of course – Lorna moved in Madeleine's social circles, not her domestic servant's. It had been naïve of Edward to assume that his sister would want to call on her. Alice imagined Lorna laughing at the mere suggestion, teasing Edward about his affection for a servant-girl.

Later, when Alice was in the kitchen changing into a clean white apron and cap to serve luncheon, Mrs Sedley opened the inner door in response to a confident knocking.

"Yes, miss, Alice is here," Alice heard her say.

At the door stood someone who must be Lorna, tall and attractive, with Edward's blue eyes and dark hair. She held out her hand and shook Alice's firmly.

"I'm so glad you're here. I know we must have met many times before, but so long ago that you might not remember me. I'm Lorna Sidgwick. Edward's told me so much about you."

Alice was unsure how to react, not used to introductions in the kitchen doorway. "How do you do, miss," she replied formally.

"Oh, please call me Lorna," the older girl continued. "Edward tells me that you usually have a half-day on Thursdays, so I wondered if you'd care to come for a drive tomorrow? I do want to get to know you a little. I've been lent a car for the few days of my stay."

Alice, very conscious of Harriet and Mrs Sedley listening behind her, faltered, "Yes, thank you, Miss – miss Lorna –"

"Good. I'll pick you up here, then, at half-past two. Will you be free by then?"

The arrangements made, Lorna left briskly, leaving Alice standing in the doorway, rather stunned. She turned slowly to face the others.

"Didn't know you was on friendly terms with the upper

65

classes! *Would you care to come for a drive?*" Harriet mimicked. "She'll be inviting you to garden parties next!"

"It's not like that. I've hardly seen her before," Alice protested. Why had she agreed to go? What could she find to talk about to Lorna, with her University education and London ways and altogether greater experience of life? Alice had never even been in a motorcar.

"There. He must be serious about you," Mrs Smallwood said, when Alice told her about the proposed outing.

"Oh, Ma," Alice objected, secretly pleased. "I was going to do the baking," she added. "I don't suppose we'll go for a long drive, though, and I'll be able to do it when I get back."

"Don't you worry your head about it," Mrs Smallwood said. "It's not every day you get the chance to go for an outing in a motorcar. The baking can wait."

Alice need not have worried about what to say to Lorna, for she found the older girl easy-going and determined to put her at her ease. When she had overcome the embarrassment of getting into the car in front of the curious gazes of Harriet from the kitchen and Miss Madeleine from the dining-room, they set off along the greening lanes. Alice, alarmed by the speed at first and clutching at her hat to prevent it from being blown clean off, was soon reassured by Lorna's confident handling of the car.

"Have you heard from Jack recently?" Lorna asked, and Alice told her all she knew. Both having brothers in the Army immediately established mutual interest, and soon they were talking easily.

They drove southwards, through the busy market town of Epping and on past its tree-lined common, bordered with timbered cottages and grazed by cattle. Driving on into the fringes of the forest, Lorna explained, "I thought we could have tea at the Forest Arms, if you'd like that?"

The Forest Arms was a large red-tiled hotel set in a clearing in the trees near High Beach, with a garden bright with daffodils and scarlet tulips. Several motorcars and horse-drawn carriages were waiting in the forecourt. It felt most odd to Alice to be going in at the front door instead of by the servants' entrance which would have seemed more appropriate, and sitting down with Lorna in the elegant tea-room, with its velvet curtains and lace tablecloths and a little vase of tulips and forget-me-nots at each table. Lorna ordered the tea, while Alice glanced around the room, feeling rather an interloper and hoping she wouldn't recognize any of the Morlands' friends. She liked Lorna very much, she decided, with her open manner and total lack of regard for convention.

Lorna poured pale scented tea into bone-china cups. "Edward tells me," she remarked, "that you wished you could do some real war-work."

"Oh, I do!" Alice agreed. "It's all very well knitting socks and helmets, but I wish I could do something more important – like you're doing." She took the cup of tea Lorna passed her. "But I know I'm not old enough to work in a military hospital, and besides there's our mother to look after. I couldn't leave her alone, with her weak heart."

"Yes, I see your difficulty. But had you considered working at a local hospital? Perhaps part-time, if you didn't want to give up your work with the Morlands."

Alice was doubtful. "Well, I would like to do that, but I don't know of any hospital near enough."

"Perhaps you haven't heard that Broadlands Hall is to be converted into a Red Cross hospital? Many country houses will become hospitals, you see, now that the others are so full. Broadlands Hall is near enough for you to get to, isn't it? They'll be needing part-time help, even if you couldn't spend all your days there. But Mrs Morland wouldn't mind, I'm sure – she'd probably consider it part of her own war effort, to lose you for a few hours each week. Would you like me to help you make the arrangements?"

"Yes, I would. It's very kind of you."

"Not at all. Have you got a bicycle? If not, I can lend you mine – I shan't be needing it while I'm in London –"

Lorna's forceful personality swept aside all difficulties as if they didn't exist. Alice looked at her admiringly, thinking of the new possibilities suddenly available.

Departures

Rumours of a move became increasingly detailed as they swept through the battalion.

"We're off to France at last, lads!"

"About bloody time. I was thinking it'd be all over by the time we got there."

"Going straight to the Front, they say."

"Time to give old Fritz a bashing, eh, instead of ruddy sacks of straw?"

Such rumours had previously led to nothing more than a march to another training camp for more trench-digging or bayonet drill, or a parade before some visiting Colonel, but nevertheless Jack felt a stirring of excitement.

"Tell you what, Jack," Jimmy remarked while they were preparing for kit inspection, "I shall enjoy meeting those French mademyselles, won't you?"

Since the uniforms had arrived, several of the young recruits had already discovered an unexpected benefit of being ready to die for King and Country, in the sympathetic attentions offered by young girls in towns where soldiers were billeted.

Jack polished vigorously at a boot which was reluctant to shine. "Don't know about that. I can't speak French."

"Oh, you only need a bit of the old parly-voo," Jimmy replied confidently. "You stick with me. I'll make sure you're all right."

Jack rather wished that Harriet was around to be impressed by his uniform and soldierly bearing. Perhaps he'd have the chance to see her on his next leave, he thought, awed by the sudden realization that by then he would almost certainly have seen some real fighting, if the rumours were anything to go by.

At the end of parade that afternoon, it was confirmed that the battalion was to march to Chelmsford next morning, and to continue from there by train to London and Folkestone.

"That's it then! Our last night in England!" Jimmy said delightedly as he, Jack and Will made their way to their billet in the village. "We'll have to think of some suitable way to spend it, eh lads?"

"Don't make it sound so final," Will Fletcher said plaintively.

They made an early start next day. It was a perfect May morning; the sun rose in a clear sky and slowly dispelled the low-lying mists, its rays slanting through foliage, back-lighting fresh green leaves and downy catkins. Marching along in the column of soldiers, Jack felt a pang of nostalgia. It was unfair that he should be given such an idyllic day to remember England by, with cows grazing knee-deep in lush grass and buttercups, and a cuckoo calling from a distant wood. He would almost have preferred cold, wet weather.

By the time they reached the next town, people were going about their morning tasks, shopkeepers opening blinds and delivery boys riding bicycles or driving pony-traps. Several people shouted cheers and encouragement as the troops marched along. In Chelmsford itself, people lined the pavements to cheer and clap, and some young women rushed forward to present flowers or even kisses to the surprised soldiers.

"Sorry, my sweet – I've got a pressing engagement with a chap called Fritz," Jimmy said, disentangling himself from an ardent embrace. "Strewth," he added, with a grin at Jack, "it's a hard life in the army, isn't it?"

There was almost a holiday atmosphere as they boarded the train, cramming into the crowded compartments and stuffing their packs wherever they could find space.

"Goodbye, Essex," Jack thought as he looked out of the window at the grass meadows which would soon be ready for mowing. He wouldn't be cutting the hay this year, at any rate. The thought gave him an odd feeling, bringing back the nostalgia he had felt earlier that morning and which had evaporated with the cheerfulness of the march and the crowd's admiration. Greenstocks, Sedley, the horses – they were all part of his past now, a finished chapter.

At Charing Cross, Jack felt quite dazed by the crowds, the noise and the confusion. People seemed to be hurrying everywhere, soldiers and civilians alike, pushing their way through the marching columns. A flower-girl thrust a bunch of violets under Jack's nose. In the background, troops waited in a haze of steam. Jack's company joined the boat train, pushing along a crowded platform where many painful separations were taking place. Wives, girlfriends and mothers clung to their loved ones until the last possible moment. Several of the women were openly weeping, and Jack was surprised to see a tall young man in officer's uniform furtively wiping a tear from his eye; other men were kissing their wives passionately, to the cheers of interested Tommies watching from the carriages. It must be dreadful for a man and wife to share their last moments together so publicly, Jack thought, glad that he needn't think about such emotional matters, and could join in the unconcerned joking and laughter of Jimmy and the others.

It was evening by the time they finally embarked on the troop ship at Folkestone. The ship was as crowded as the trains had been, a tide of khaki swamping the decks. A hospital ship had docked alongside, and Jack could see men on crutches and others with bandaged heads looking across at the departing troops, while more seriously wounded men, in wheelchairs and on stretchers, were being unloaded from the ship by medical orderlies and nurses. Jack turned away from this grim reminder of the reality of war to look back at the crowds of civilians, who waved and cheered as the ship eventually pulled away into the calm waters of the Channel. The wide, foaming tracks of churned water curved behind the ship as the coastline dwindled to a blurred smudge on the horizon and at last became indistinguishable from the sky.

Jimmy interrupted Jack's reflective mood by nudging his elbow and offering him a cigarette. "Cheer up, old son. Feeling homesick, eh? Don't you worry, we'll polish off old Fritz and be back home before you can say Kaiser Bill."

Alice, calling at Emily's cottage before church, told her sister of her plans to work at the hospital.

"I've found out that they need full-time probationer nurses at Broadlands Hall, as well as people to help out odd hours. I'd do full-time work if only I could, but there's Ma to think of . . ."

"But why doesn't she come and stay with us?" Emily suggested. "There'll be more company for her, now that Jack's gone and you'll be out even more than usual. She'd like to see more of the children, I'm sure. Mary, hurry up, or Sammy'll be late for Sunday school," she called up the stairs.

"*I'm* ready," Mary's voice came back. "Sammy's lost his cap."

"It's down here on the dresser," Emily called back.

"But I don't want to give you extra work," Alice said. "And wouldn't Tom mind?"

Sammy clattered down the stairs, and Emily combed his hair briskly before clamping his cap into place. "Don't you worry about the extra work," she told Alice. "Mary's quite old enough to make herself useful around the house, and she and Sammy can share the small room again. No, Tom won't mind. We were saying the other day we didn't like her being at home by herself during the day, what with these Zeppelins coming over. Mrs Miller told me that her niece in Southend saw one with her own eyes!"

"I'm glad we don't live on the coast. It must be hard to sleep at nights," Alice said. "You're lucky to have Tom at home. It must be a comfort for you and the children."

"Yes, but I don't know how much longer that'll last. There's talk of conscription for all men of army age, whether they're married or not. Course, farm workers might not be included, but knowing Tom he'll want to go if it gets to that stage."

"Perhaps the war will be over before they bring in conscription," Alice said, with little conviction.

"Anyway, we'll go round home and ask Ma what she thinks after church. Are you ready then, you two? Have you got your twopence, Mary?"

In spite of Alice's doubts, Mrs Smallwood agreed readily to the suggestion of moving in with Emily and Tom.

"It makes sense," she told Alice. "If you're going to live in at the hospital we may as well close up the cottage, and save on the rent. We can put the money towards Emily's housekeeping."

"Are you sure you don't mind?" Alice said, feeling twinges of guilt. "I'll call in to see you as often as I can, when I have time off."

"Does Mrs Morland know you're going to stop working up at the house?" Emily asked.

"No, I haven't told her yet. I'll wait until I've definitely got a place. I'm going to see the Red Cross organizer on Thursday."

By the end of that week, Alice's arrangements were made. She was due to start work at Broadlands Hall within a few days, and on Friday she gave notice to the Morlands.

"We're very sorry to lose you, Alice," Mrs Morland said, "but of course you must do your war work. I'm sure Harriet will be able to cope here."

Her tone implied that Alice was being rather inconsiderate, but Alice thought of Madeleine staying at home and doing nothing much, and replied, "Yes, I'm sure she'll manage."

She had dressed her hair in a more severe style than usual for the Red Cross interview to make herself look older. She disliked lying, but she gave her age as twenty-two, and the organizer wrote it down without apparent surprise. This deception was necessary because, after talking with Lorna, Alice had made long-term plans to transfer to a proper Army hospital when she had had sufficient training. Lorna had lent her a bicycle, and she learned to ride it by wobbling up and down the village street. It was not long ago that cycling for women had been considered indecent, but now Alice hitched up her skirts without fear of disgracing herself in the eyes of the village community. Having learned to control her balance, she pedalled off to Broadlands Hall with her belongings in a bag slung over her shoulder. The bicycle would be useful for her trips back to the village when she had an afternoon or an evening off.

She had never been inside such a grand house before, and once inside the lodge gates it took her several minutes' more cycling before she reached the house itself, with its countless windows looking over a sloping lawn. There was little time to assimilate her first impressions of the interior – a long picture gallery, lined with oil paintings and hung with chandeliers, and incongruously lined with rows and rows of beds – before she found herself in uniform and trying to look knowledgeable and helpful.

She had arrived at Broadlands Hall at the same time as a batch of wounded men, and the ward was in the midst of a wave of activity. A cheerful well-spoken VAD nurse called Grace took charge of her and led her into the kitchen. "We'll put some water on for tea and Bovril," she told Alice. "They'll be exhausted, poor things. Most of them will just want to sleep and sleep."

Alice felt rather relieved to have been given a mundane domestic job to start with, rather than being summoned to the bedside of some horribly wounded man.

"You'll soon get used to the routines," Grace told her kind-ly, sensing her concern. "There's a lot to learn, I know. Most of the men here are convalescents – the more serious cases are in the regular hospitals, although they're getting so full now ... This lot have been sent straight on – there was no room for them in the military hospital. Could you take this in and make a start on serving? I'll get the next urn going."

Alice wheeled the urn and cups into the ward on a trolley, and shyly approached the man in the first bed to ask what he would like to drink. He was lying on his back, staring at the ceiling. When she spoke to him, he turned his head to look at her, face expressionless and eyes blank.

"No good asking him, Miss," the man in the next bed called out cheerfully. "He's Belgian, see – don't speak the lingo. Give him a cup of tea."

Alice placed a cup of tea beside the Belgian's bed, but he made no sign of having seen it. She felt a surge of pity for him, alone among strangers in a strange country.

"Don't worry, miss. He'll be right as rain when he's had a bit of a rest. Plenty of sugar in mine, please." The man grinned at her as she handed him his cup, and she smiled back gratefully. Continuing down the ward, she saw that Grace was right – few of the newcomers were as alert as the man who had just spoken to her. Many were sleeping deeply, while others, though awake, seemed barely conscious of the activity around them.

When she returned to the kitchen, a Sister came in with an armful of used bedding and carried it through to the adjoining laundry. "There's more to come," she told Alice. "I'll leave you with this lot and get the men sorted out – they haven't all got pyjamas yet, some of them have been sent straight on. You can make a start on the washing when you've finished with the drinks. Can you get the copper going?"

"Yes, of course."

By the time the Sister returned with her second bundle of laundry, Alice had lit the fire under the copper and had started washing up the tea things. The Sister looked on approvingly. "You're a lot more practical than some of the young ladies we get, I must say. Some of them think it's nothing but smoothing fevered brows."

Alice felt pleased to find that her domestic experience was an advantage. But working in the hospital was a far cry from Greenstocks, where social gradations were so clearly defined – here the men in the ward called her "Miss" in exactly the same way that they addressed Grace and the other real nurses. The Red Cross uniform gave her a sort of classlessness, she decided, finding the experience a novel one.

"Have you got anyone in the Army?" Grace asked her later as they scrubbed the sheets.

"Yes, my –" Alice remembered her lie just in time; she would have to be careful what she said in casual conversations "– younger brother."

New Impressions

Boulogne was bustling with activity. Pleasure boats, pressed into service as troop ships, jostled for position with the local fishing smacks; the quay and main street were crowded with all kinds of vehicles, motorized and horse-drawn. Tall hotels lined the sea-front, many of them with English names, Jack noticed, somewhat disappointed. Peasant women in black skirts carried baskets of fruit and vegetables and bunches of flowers, and small boys clamoured round the troops as they were marched to the railway station, asking in broken English for cigarettes or sweets.

"They look just the same as the nippers back home, don't they?" Dick Twyford remarked, next to Jack in the column. "Non, non," he pronounced emphatically to a skinny boy who was tugging at his sleeve.

"Well, what on earth do you expect them to look like?" Jack said.

"Oh, I dunno – just different. Anyway, what the hell are we going to this Base Camp place for? I thought we'd done enough square-bashing back home."

"I should think we have. Still, it's a chance to see a bit of the French countryside, going on a train ride."

However, the railway transport proved to be less than luxurious, and Jack soon saw that there would be no chance of looking out of windows. The men were to travel in cattle trucks, each one labelled:

HOMMES 40
CHEVAUX 8

"It means forty men, eight horses, doesn't it?" someone

remarked. "That puts us in our place, all right."

"As long as it doesn't mean forty men *and* eight horses," Jimmy muttered.

They piled into the trucks and then had to wait some considerable time before departure. There was little room to move or relax, and the journey to Étaples seemed interminable.

"This is a sight better, I'll say," Jack said, filling his lungs with air when at last they disembarked. After the cramped and stuffy compartment, it was a relief to be out in the open, breathing the fresh air laden with salt from the nearby sea, and preparing to march towards the camp.

The landscape was one of sand dunes, pine trees and open sky. The camp, not far from the railway station, was in a picturesque spot overlooking a wide, sandy estuary, with thick woods on the opposite bank. Jack looked around him with approval, feeling that his army career was entering a new and important phase. Boulogne had seemed busy, but this place was alive with military activity. Sentries guarded entrances to various depots; brass-hats in staff cars were driven through the crowds of troops, and columns of men could be seen parading and marching for almost as far as the eye could see, beyond a maze of tents.

"Blimey, this is a bit more like it," Jimmy said, looking rather awe-stricken. "A bit different from the training camp back home. Wait till I write to me Ma and Rosie about all this. They won't half be impressed."

"I hope they're thinking of feeding us soon," Jack said, sniffing deeply and trying to identify the various aromas emanating from a canteen hut. "It was hours ago we got our last meal."

"My mate came out here a couple of months back," someone else said, "and he wrote they got the best dinner here they'd ever had, the night they arrived."

After the troops had been shown to their tents, they were served an ample hot dinner in one of the canteens, and then left free to wander around the camp, investigating the various halls, clubs and bars which provided entertainment and refreshment during off-duty hours. The camp seemed to contain men from every regiment in the British Army – Yorkshiremen, Cockneys, Seaforth Highlanders in kilts – and Jack's ears quickly became attuned to a wide variety of regional accents.

"Your first time out, son?" asked an older man waiting beside Jack to be served with a drink.

"Yes. We came out yesterday. What about you?"

"Been out since last August – Regular Army. Sent here for a spell away from the line. It's no holiday here, though, lad – you'll soon find out."

"Dear Ma and Alice," Jack wrote a few days later. *"Here we are at* Étaples *(you say it Eetaps) it is a very pretty spot here near the river and the sea but damn hard work, they keep us on the go, also you keep getting white dust or sand in your eyes and hair, it is always windy. We are doing some extra training before we go up the line, same as we did at home only harder work, they are very strict here. We have a new platoon commander Lietenant Gray, we call him Dolly but not to his face. He went to Bancroft's School same as Edward, and knows him. There must be thousands of troops here always marching and parading and on assort courses, it is called the Bull Ring but I don't know why. There are little market stalls sometimes where you can buy things from French women who come in. Also there is a Cinema. There was a London Bus once, it looked very odd. We are going up the line very soon now they say so when I write to you next time I should be a proper soldier. I hope you are both well, also that Alice has been able to get the nursing work she wanted. I will write to you again when I can and hope you can write back, have you had a letter from Edward, I hope he is getting on well. And if you see Harriet can you ask her if she got the letters I sent, I have had no reply. All my love Jack."*

Alice bent to look at her reflection in a small mirror as she pinned her hair underneath her cap. Grace, who was sitting on her narrow bed writing on a note-pad, looked up at her.

"Is it time? I must just finish this, to catch the post . . ." Grace's fiancé was an Artillery Officer in the Buffs; they were hoping to be married when he next came home on leave. She sealed the letter quickly, and addressed the envelope. "Have you got any to send? I'll take them over for you, if you have."

"Yes, two. Thank you."

Alice handed over the two envelopes. Grace glanced briefly at the addresses and then up at Alice.

"It must be awful for you, with two people to worry about. I've only got Roland."

"Yes, it is," Alice said with feeling. "But at least we're kept so busy here that it keeps our minds away from worrying."

"True." Grace stood up, yawned and stretched, and took her coat from the hook on the hut door.

Alice already felt that her Greenstocks days were far in the past. She came off duty each evening with an aching back and sore feet, ate her meal in the nurses' canteen, and retired to the small hut she shared with Grace, to sleep exhaustedly – so heavily that she was not awoken by the nearby flight of a Zeppelin one night in mid-August. Some of the patients who could walk unaided had gone out into the grounds and seen it flying overhead, and it had been the main topic of conversation next morning. Everything seemed quiet on the ward today, Alice noted, glancing round. The men were just waking, and those who were able were starting to wash and shave. Two tired and heavy-eyed nurses were waiting to be relieved.

"A fairly quiet night," the duty Sister reported, "apart from that new man having bad dreams and calling out. He's sleeping now."

"Poor fellow," Grace said sympathetically.

"You can help me with the dressings," Sister Jarvis said

briskly, "and Nurse Smallwood, help Sister Talbot."

Alice went to collect the dressings trolley, mentally bracing herself for the task. At first, her days had been spent exclusively in tasks such as washing and rolling bandages, scrubbing floors and serving meals; now, she was also assisting with wound dressings, administering medicines, and helping mobile patients to walk out to the gardens for fresh air. Helping with the dressings was the job she dreaded most, hating the dreadful sights revealed when bandages and gauze pads were peeled back, but she tried to take herself firmly in hand, telling herself that she would certainly see far worse sights if she achieved her ambition of working in a military hospital. She knew, from the haggard, strained faces of many of the men and the conversations she overheard, that their war experience was far from the heroic adventure portrayed in *The Illustrated London News*.

"It's so dreadful to think of them going back, to face it all again, as soon as they're fit," she remarked to Sister Talbot.

The older woman gave a barely perceptible shrug. "We've got too much to do to worry about that."

The trained nurses seemed to hide any compassion they may have felt for the men behind a professional veneer of brisk efficiency. Alice, who saw Jack's or Edward's features in every new face, found this hard to emulate.

She had little time for conversation with the other nursing staff, apart from those in her ward. Later that afternoon, when she was taking a patient out to the garden in a wheelchair, she saw two nurses who looked faintly familiar. She was unable to remember where she had seen them before, and thought no more about it until Lorna wrote to tell her that she would be coming back to the village for a brief visit.

"*I shall be spending three or four days at home,*" Lorna wrote, "*and I do hope your working hours will permit us to meet, so that we can exchange news of Edward. Of course, I shall also want to hear all about your nursing experiences, and to tell you of mine."*

Alice wrote to let Lorna know when her next half-day would be, and Lorna sent a further letter saying that she would collect Alice at Broadlands Hall and take her to meet some friends. Alice was rather mystified by this, but by the day of Lorna's visit she had more exciting thoughts to occupy her mind – she had received a letter from Edward saying that he hoped to be home on leave in three weeks' time.

Lorna, arriving punctually in the doctor's pony trap, jumped down and hugged Alice. She looked tired and thin, but her blue eyes were as vivacious as Alice remembered.

"Did you have a letter from Edward this morning?" Alice asked as soon as they had exchanged greetings.

"Yes! Isn't it a pity it wasn't this week? I hope to be able to meet him in London, though, before he comes on home." She clucked at the sturdy grey pony, who set off at a steady trot.

"I'm taking you to tea at Hillbank House – with my friends, the Braithwaites and the McLarens. Have you met them?"

"Hillbank House – you mean the new people who moved in last year?" Alice was shocked, remembering the village rumours and the German governess.

"Yes. Of course they'll be regarded as 'new' for at least ten years in a village like Littlehays," Lorna replied, amused.

"I've never met them, no. They hardly come down to the village, or the church."

"They wouldn't go to church – they're agnostics, you see. I met them in London, at the house of a mutual friend. I know you'll like them. You may have seen Dorothy and Mathilda before. They're both VAD nurses at Broadlands Hall."

"Oh!" Alice remembered the two vaguely recognized faces in the garden. She tried to match up this new information with the local speculation about the German governess and the two unmarried men who showed no interest in enlisting.

And they were *agnostic* – was that the same as being an atheist? Either way, it was unheard of in the small community of Littlehays, where the church was in many ways the focal point of village life. Alice wanted to ask Lorna for clarification, but was hesitant to do so.

"The two men – they're still at home, then – they haven't joined up?" she ventured.

"No. That's because they're pacifists, but then there are other married men in the village who haven't enlisted, surely?"

"Oh – but I thought – they said in the village that none of them were married."

"Village gossip. I don't think the local people can accept the idea of two couples sharing one house, and the fact that neither couple has children makes it seem even less conventional. But village people can be very narrow-minded, Alice." Lorna guided the pony through the narrow gates of Hillbank House.

It was hard to believe that it had been empty and neglected for so long. The garden had been tidied and replanted since the new occupants had moved in, and was in full summer splendour, plants blooming in cottage-garden profusion, which Alice thought preferable to the tailored formality of the grounds at Broadlands Hall. A lady in her late twenties, with a mass of soft brown hair pinned up loosely, greeted them at the door, and took them into a cool hallway.

"Mathilda's at the hospital, I'm afraid," she told them. "We weren't able to have the same half-day, unfortunately. I'm Dorothy McLaren," she told Alice, shaking her hand warmly. "We've seen each other at Broadlands Hall, I believe."

Alice was introduced to Geoffrey McLaren, Dorothy's husband; Richard Braithwaite, her brother, and the elderly German lady, whose name was Frau Edith Zellern.

"Richard and I were brought up in Bavaria," Dorothy explained to Alice, "and Edith was companion to my mother for many years, and then tutor to us. When our family moved back to England ten years ago, Edith came with us."

Frau Zellern shook hands and wished the guests good-day with only the slightest hint of a German accent. Alice, very conscious of the strangeness of the situation, felt relieved when she politely took her leave and went upstairs. The rest of the party went into the main downstairs room, which was light and uncluttered, with pale muslin curtains, a hessian rug on the floor and cream-washed walls, bare apart from a few small earth-toned drawings. French windows opened to the gardens behind the house, with views downhill towards the village.

"I'm afraid it's very difficult for Edith at present," Dorothy said, serving cool lemon drinks. "Anti-German feeling is becoming more and more pronounced, and going to ridiculous extremes. We heard that a Dachshund dog had been stoned to death in Colchester."

"Oh, how stupid people are!" Lorna exclaimed angrily.

"Edith no longer dares to leave the house alone," said Geoffrey. "Some of the village boys threw stones at her last time she went to the village. Now, with the Zeppelin raids and the spy rumours, she's afraid to appear in public."

"You heard of the Zeppelin raid on Chelmsford, Lorna? Miraculously no-one was hurt, even though five bombs were dropped. That particular Zeppelin was seen passing overhead not far from here – did you see it, Alice? Some of the patients at the hospital said they did – and people have been saying that a car was signalling to it with its headlights. I'm sure it's nothing more than gossip," Dorothy said, "but I think most of the villagers would like to have poor Edith arrested and shot, and us with her – even though she hasn't been out of the house for days, and she certainly can't drive a motor–car!"

"Ironic, isn't it," said Richard, "that we moved away from London in search of rural tranquillity, and now find ourselves almost in the danger zone – first the fears of invasion from the sea and now the Zeppelins as well."

"Your brother is in the army, isn't he?" Geoffrey said, to bring Alice into the conversation. "Have you heard from him recently?"

"Yes, but he doesn't say much in his letters."

"Edward writes to us regularly; he's billeted near Béthune now," Lorna added. Alice felt strange to be talking to people whose pacifist views separated them from young men like Edward and Jack; what did these new acquaintances think, she wondered, of men who had accepted the call to arms without question? She wanted to know more about their beliefs, but hesitated to raise the subject; people in the village talked of pacifists as if they suffered from some queer disease. Lorna, however, had no such reservations, asking, "What will you do if conscription is brought in?"

"I'll probably enlist in the Royal Army Medical Corps," Geoffrey said. "Dorothy and Mathilda are already taking the middle line, of course, by working as nurses, and so is Richard, by running the Belgian refugee hostel."

The conversation moved on to the dock strikes in London before the war, the harsh conditions now prevailing in the East End, and the poetry of Rupert Brooke. After tea, Geoffrey read out some poems he had written himself: allegories of war, sprinkled with allusions to Greek mythology, which Alice found hard to understand. She had found it a most interesting afternoon, even though she had been unable to contribute much to the conversation; Richard and the McLarens had been most kind to her, she thought, and she left with an invitation to come again any time she was free. She felt that these new friends and Lorna came from a new, enlightened age, compared with which Littlehays and all its concerns seemed positively medieval. The light, airy rooms of Hillbank House were perfectly suited to the freedom of thought which prevailed there, whereas in the village you were simply expected to think as everyone else did and to do as you were told. She was less happy with the abstract ideas of agnosticism and pacifism, and asked Lorna for her views on the way home.

"It is a difficult choice, of course," Lorna said. "Whether to help to relieve suffering where you can, by becoming a nurse, or whether to distance yourself completely from war and all it stands for. That's one of the reasons for the split between Christabel and Sylvia Pankhurst, and I honestly don't know which view I feel more sympathy for – I can see the force of both. Christabel is in favour of women supporting the war effort – the suffrage campaign must wait, and women must work towards the winning of the war. But Sylvia says that women should always represent peace – this surge of militarism is betraying the women's movement. I suppose, as Geoffrey said, I'm taking the middle ground."

"I really don't see what else there is to do," Alice agreed. "I understand their point of view, about it being wrong to kill, but that would only work if all the soldiers on both sides thought the same, and threw down their weapons. The war isn't going to stop, is it, as long as there *are* people willing to fight?"

"I know. The alternative seems to be to let ourselves be overcome. And yet, when you think of the young men praying in church and then going out to kill people in battle . . . I think, when our young men volunteer, our thoughts are so taken up with fears of them *being* killed that we forget they're out there *to* kill – to kill men who are other people's sons and brothers and husbands. And how will that change them? We can't expect them to come home and carry on living their lives exactly as before, when it's all over. War will have changed them, just as working in the hospitals and being involved in our own way will have changed us."

"There's no easy answer, is there?" Alice said. "It's hard for us to stand back and look at the issues coolly, isn't it, when our brothers are out there?"

86

"Yes. Oh dear, we are getting serious. Let's talk about something more frivolous and girlish," Lorna said, giving the pony a little flick with her whip. "Didn't you love that dress Dorothy was wearing? She designs and makes all her own clothes . . ."

To The Front

"That's it, lads. Out you get," bellowed the Sergeant.

"Are we here? Where are we?" mumbled Dick Twyford, who had been dozing beside Jack on the seat they shared in the bus.

Jack was growing accustomed to long journeys, crowded conditions – in stifling heat or chilling damp according to the weather – and interminable waiting. It seemed an age ago that they had left the farmhouse and barns where they had been billeted, and been jammed into a troop train which, apparently rarely travelling at more than walking pace, had taken hours to bring them to their destination. It had been the early hours of the morning when they had stumbled out of their trucks, dazed with sleep and fatigue, into an arc-lit goods-yard, to board the grey-painted London buses which waited beyond. Climbing in, Jack heard the intermittent dull crump of heavy guns in the distance.

"This bus is a bit lame in its off fore," Jimmy commented as the bus rocked away down an uneven road, dipping and swaying like a ship at sea. "Either that or I'm still feeling the effects of that van blonk we had the other day."

The windows were boarded up, and Jack resigned himself to spasmodic dozing, aware in his semi-conscious state of other traffic outside and the boom of the guns becoming louder ahead. Now, tipped out on to a road pitted with shell-holes, he took stock of his surroundings. The road was busy in both directions with motor convoys, ambulances and staff cars, while a dispatch-rider on a motor-cycle wove his way through the slower vehicles. Ahead, where the guns sounded alarmingly close, white flares looped into the sky, illuminating the vehicles, the white faces of the men and the poplar trees which lined the road.

Brought swiftly back to alertness by the cold night air, the men shouldered their packs and prepared to continue on foot. Jack hardly knew whether he felt more thrilled or more daunted by this nearness to the war zone, and the thought that he could be in the trenches within a matter of hours. The Western Front, which had dominated his imagination for the last year, would soon become a reality.

Among the traffic returning to the railhead was a straggling column of men in dishevelled, mud-spattered uniforms, their faces haggard and strained.

"You'll be all right up ahead," one of them told the newcomers, "it's a nice quiet sector."

Jack, noticing arms in slings, blood-stained uniforms and the grey unshaven faces of some of the men, doubted whether these words were intended seriously. They were passing through a deserted village, which had evidently come under heavy bombardment, to judge by the smashed roofs and the piles of bricks and masonry which sprawled across the road. Beyond the village, a slight incline brought them to a point at which every man ahead of Jack seemed to pause and catch his breath. From this vantage point, a huge area of the Front was spread out like a relief map, a vast area lit at intervals by the arching and fizzling flares, the sky pierced by the shaft of a revolving searchlight scanning the darkness for aircraft. The heavy guns sounded thunderous now, their insistent booming accompanied by flashes of fiery red.

"Pretty, ain't it?" Jimmy remarked laconically. Jack grinned, falling into step again. He felt illogically reassured by Jimmy's stoical acceptance of new circumstances, however extraordinary.

Piles of chalky soil ahead marked the beginning of the trench network, and the men ahead of Jack were already disappearing below ground level. The first shallow trench became gradually deeper and narrower, so that Jack soon felt he was completely underground. He could see no more than three or four men ahead as they made their way through an endless maze of intersections and crossroads, some incongruously labelled "Piccadilly Circus", "Regent Street" or "St Pancras Station". He had imagined that they must be close to the front line by this time, but the men ahead of him were pressing further and further on, stumbling over sacks, loops of wire and piles of sandbags. Fighting off waves of drowsiness, he longed for the chance to lie down and sleep.

As soon as she was relieved at the end of her spell of duty, Alice went straight to the entrance hall to see if any mail had arrived for her. The sight of an envelope addressed in Edward's characteristic spiky handwriting was enough to make her forget her tiredness and hunger. She snatched it from the rack and opened it hurriedly.

"Dear Alice," she read, *"I am so looking forward to seeing you next week. Lorna has written to me of your meeting while she was staying at home. She thinks very highly of you, and I am delighted to hear of your friendship. It seems an inordinately long time since I was at home, and I long to spend some quiet hours with you — if your work permits — and to go on some of our favourite walks. I can picture Littlehays very clearly; the harvest is probably in by now, and there will be blackberries in the hedgerows and chestnuts ripening on the village green . . . next week I will be seeing it in reality instead of in my mind. I am counting the hours until my return.*

I have been in and out of the line several times now, but have not been exposed to any real danger. My corporal was wounded in the shoulder. but is recovering well. It is very pleasant to be out of the line just now, in this fine weather; this is a rural landscape rather like ours, with golden cornstooks in the fields, and orchards decked with ripening fruit.

Thank you so much for your letters; it really does brighten my day to receive one. I know how hard you are working

*at the hospital and it must be difficult for you to find the time
to sit down and write to me; please do not deprive yourself of
rest on my account, even though I should be very sorry not to
hear from you. I am pleased to hear of your news from Jack.*

*Thank you too for sending me the peppermints and cake;
they reached me in good condition. I have been reading
Tennyson, and will give you the book when I return, although
I know you will have little enough time to read it.*

*It is so good to know that I will soon be able to give you
my news in person; the thought will keep me going through
the next few days. Till then, with my fondest wishes,*

Edward."

"From your young man?" Grace enquired, arriving at Alice's
side to check the letter rack for herself.

"Oh . . . please don't call Edward my young man. He's just
a friend of the family," Alice explained.

"Oh yes, of course. A friend of the family who writes to
you every single day," Grace teased.

It had been a busy shift. Every bed in the hospital was in
use, and huts had been erected in the grounds to make more
room. Convoys were arriving almost daily, and the Sister in
Alice's ward said that many of the men were really too seriously ill to have been moved. Extra VAD volunteers were
brought in, several of them completely inexperienced and
needing constant supervision, making Alice feel like an old
hand.

"They want to send us thirty more men," Sister Talbot had
told Alice as they carried mattresses out to the new huts.
"Where they expect us to put them, I don't know. We'll be
using the greenhouses at this rate."

"Are the Army hospitals so full?" Alice asked.

"No, they're empty," the Sister said darkly. "There's a new
offensive in the offing. They're clearing the wards of everyone
who can loosely be termed convalescent, and sending them

out to the Red Cross hospitals. They'll need every bed available, in a few days' time, for the new casualties."

Alice worried about Jack, not knowing where the planned offensive was to take place or where he was, but thanked God that at least Edward would be safely out of it. She hoped that he would be on the boat for home by the time the offensive began. But the next post brought her a quickly scribbled note which dashed her hopes.

"Sorry – all leave cancelled – will not be able to come home next week after all – will write. Edward."

Near Loos

"A quiet sector of the line, that codger said?" Jimmy bellowed when the roars and crashes from the heavy guns slackened for a moment.

"This *is* quiet compared with what it's like farther down," Jack shouted back. He guessed that the soldier on the road had meant in terms of lack of activity from either the British or the German trenches, rather than in a literal sense. Further down the line, towards Loos, a deafening bombardment began soon after the company's arrival and continued for two days.

"Blimey. I should think they can hear that in London," Jack shouted to Stephen Cartwright, one of the two East Londoners who had joined the platoon shortly after the battalion had left Étaples.

"It nearly shatters your eardrums. What's it like for the poor blighters down there?" Stephen shouted.

"It'll be worse for them when it stops. They'll be going over the top then," contributed Charlie, the other newcomer, a married man in his late twenties.

"Thank God it's not us – yet."

Jack couldn't imagine how anyone could tolerate the ceaseless din at any closer range. He felt that the pauses, even at this distance, only added to the strain, making him brace himself for the next thunderous explosion. Surely the German trenches must have been completely wiped out? How could anything survive the endless battering, which made the earth shudder as if some giant strode over the landscape, and the sky tremble as if it would shatter into fragments and rain down into the trenches?

He was beginning to adjust to the routine now, becoming

accustomed to the odd mixture of apprehension and boredom. B Company alternated between the front line and the support trenches behind, spending three days and nights in each. Night-time was the busiest period – the time for trench-repairs, wire maintenance, patrols and carrying parties. After stand-to, when everyone had to stand at the front of the firing-trench with rifle at the ready in case of a "morning hate" from the Germans, the men cooked themselves a breakfast of bacon, tea and biscuits with plum-and-apple jam. Later, Lieutenant Gray and Sergeant Jones inspected the length of trench manned by the platoon, usually stopping to have a word with each private. Gray was generally considered to be a good fellow, taking the trouble to get to know his men – often enquiring after Jack's sister or Charlie's wife and small children – and not too rigid about the more trivial points of discipline. Sometimes a senior officer would come up to check that everything was satisfactory, nodding curtly at the men and telling Lieutenant Gray that the parapet needed reinforcing here or the duckboard replacing there.

When the tour of inspection was over, the men passed their days in cleaning rifles, brewing up tea, writing letters home, and snatching sleep in odd moments. Jack quickly learned to sleep whenever the chance presented itself, and to be awake and alert within seconds when disturbed by the screaming whine of the shells which came over at frequent intervals, occasionally bursting near enough to send earth sputtering into the trench. Spending all the daylight hours below ground level, Jack had seen no sign of German troops, although they were only a few hundred yards away, presumably spending their days in the same sort of routine. If anyone were rash enough to show his head above the parapet, the German presence was quickly made known in the form of a bullet ripping into the sand-bags, or passing over the trench with a crack like a whip. Their snipers were ever-alert.

It was a sniper who provided Jack with his first glimpse of

death at close range. Half-dozing, slumped against a pile of sacks, he was awakened by the explosive crack of rifle-fire, a yell from further along the trench, and shouts of "Stretcher bearer!"

"Some poor blighter's copped that one," Dick Twyford muttered.

The stretcher bearers hurried past Jack and his friends, returning minutes later with their burden. Jack unwisely looked at the victim and turned away abruptly, trying to stop himself from vomiting; it was the first time he had seen such striking evidence of what a bullet from a high-velocity rifle could do to frail human flesh. Jack later found out that he had known the dead man, Albert Brigstock, who had been a wheelwright in Finchingfield in civilian life. The random nature of the extermination shocked Jack, the realization that one unpredictable instant had changed Albert from a cheerful Essex labourer into a corpse on a stretcher, one more name to be added to the casualty lists.

Stephen nudged Jack out of his daydream and mimed that he was going to brew up some tea, and Jack followed him into the dugout.

Stephen, who had worked with brewery horses in the City, was the same age as Jack, endowed with a glowing, golden-skinned beauty and an air of physical well-being. He and Jack had become friendly, spending idle hours talking about the horses they had cared for in civilian life. Stephen, like Jack, lived with a widowed mother and a sister. He had shown Jack a photograph of his sister, Sarah, who was working in munitions in the East End.

"I wish she didn't have to do it," he told Jack. "They work in the most awful conditions, and long hours – I reckon they're worse off than we are here."

The girl gazed out from the photograph with eyes as wide and clear as Stephen's; the resemblance between brother and sister was striking. She looked so young and pretty that Jack found it hard to imagine her toiling in a begrimed shell factory.

"That's right. It's criminal, the way women are being exploited," Charlie Jenkins, the older man, said. "No decent society ought to stand for it."

Charlie had worked in the East End docks, and talked of unions, strikes and lockouts, giving Jack visions of a way of life entirely different from his own. He felt quite unable to envisage himself and Alice approaching Mr Morland, union cards in hand, to demand fairer wages, improved conditions and shorter working hours. Mr Morland would have apoplexy, Jack thought, amused at the idea. He had heard about the industrial unrest before the war, but it seemed that Littlehays had slumbered in its complacency while events elsewhere had moved on. Charlie's other main topic of conversation was the incompetence of the generals. "Lives are being squandered in this war," he told Jack. "What happened at Gallipoli? What happened at Neuve Chapelle? Same as'll happen up the line here in a day or two. Mass slaughter, and they'll report it in the papers as a victory."

Jack had not met with such cynicism before, and he felt disturbed by it, preferring to talk to Stephen about the brewery horses. A few days later, though, when they retired from the front line to billets in Béthune, they met up with survivors from the fighting around Loos, and Jack was reminded sharply of Charlie's words.

"Caught in our own bloody gas!"

"Blokes choking to death . . ."

"What do you mean?"

"They released the stuff as instructed, with no wind, and it just drifted around our own trenches . . ."

Jack was shaken by these reports, having believed that poison gas was an evil weapon used exclusively by the Germans, and finding it difficult to reconcile this picture of chaos with the orderly advances he had practised at home and at Base

Camp. He realized that he had been lucky so far, not to have been under fire, but in a sense he found the hanging about even more difficult to bear; he wanted to go over the top. Only then would he know how he would acquit himself in battle, whether he'd be able to keep his nerve and follow his instructions, or whether he'd funk it and make a fool of himself or get shot for cowardice.

Meanwhile, he decided, it wouldn't do to think too far ahead. Far better to concentrate on the present, enjoying the pleasant late summer evenings and drinking with his friends in the many cafes and estaminets which vied for soldiers' attentions. Jimmy had already discovered another diversion in the form of a pretty, dark-haired French girl, the daughter of one of the café owners.

"Trust old Jimmy to be first to get himself fixed up," Dick remarked enviously, watching his friend sitting with the girl in the shadowy interior of the café. "Wish I'd seen her first."

"We could try over the road. There's usually some local girls hanging around there, waiting to be picked up," Harry Larkins suggested. "I've heard they'll take you upstairs for a few francs . . ."

"Might as well try our luck."

They got up to go, discussing the merits of the various girls they had noticed earlier. Jack stayed in the cafe with Will and Charlie and Stephen, lingering over their cigarettes and listening with amusement to Jimmy's attempts to communicate in French. He mildly envied his friend's good fortune, but had no real appetite for such an encounter himself, preferring to think of Harriet at home. He wanted to prove himself as a soldier first, before seeking other forms of initiation into manhood.

After Church

Alice sat on a bench in the churchyard, watching the pale sun setting hazily over the autumn trees. Edward was beside her, but she had an uncomfortable sense that the distance between them was greater now than while he had been in France. He was smoking a cigarette, something she had not know him to do before, and staring gloomily at a bunch of withered chrysanthemums by a gravestone. Alice wanted to say something to restore the intimacy they had reached through their letters, but he seemed so deep in thought that she was unwilling to intrude.

Alice had been unsure how to greet the thin, tired stranger who met her outside Broadlands Hall, and their first few remarks had been polite to the point of formality. Now she tried to ignore her bitter disappointment, knowing that Edward could hardly be expected to shrug off the strain of war the instant he set foot in his home surroundings. But in three days' time he would be gone again; Alice was painfully aware of the wasted minutes passing.

Edward finished his cigarette and rose to his feet. "Shall we walk on?"

He had said in his letters that he wanted to tell Alice all his news, but now seemed reluctant to do so. She knew enough from her contact with men at the hospital to realize that he was suffering from the emotional after-effects of the fighting at Loos. Men reacted in different ways: some wanted to talk and talk, as if reliving their experiences would help to purge the horrors from their memories, while others retreated into silence. From Edward's brief descriptions, Alice knew that he had been in the thick of the assault, and had seen men and officers of his company killed and wounded in alarming numbers. She felt grateful that her hospital work at least provided her with some insight into his withdrawn condition; it must be very difficult, she thought, for relatives who had no such foreknowledge, and expected their sons or husbands to come home as conquering heroes, bursting with thrilling adventure stories.

After they had walked in silence for a while, Edward seemed to make a conscious effort to throw off his downcast mood. "My mother asked if you'd come to tea with us on your afternoon off tomorrow," he remarked. "Can I tell her you'll come?"

"Oh." Alice was rather taken aback. "Does that mean she . . . I mean, do you – do you want me to come?"

"Of course I do. I know you think Mother disapproves of you – of our seeing each other," Edward said, rather awkwardly. "But she knows that I've been writing to you regularly, and about your friendship with Lorna. She wants you to come."

"I thought she wanted . . . you know . . . someone better for you," Alice ventured, not wanting to take too much for granted.

"Alice, don't say such things! Why must you belittle yourself?" Edward gave her an affectionate, amused look, slipping his arm through hers and squeezing her fingers against his side, and for the time being she forgot her doubts.

Next day, she dressed her hair as elegantly as she could and put on the blouse Madeleine had given her, wondering what the tea-time conversation could possibly consist of. For Edward's sake, she didn't want to talk about the war or the hospital, and there was really very little common ground between Mrs Sidgwick and herself.

"Now, don't worry!" Edward said when he came to meet her. "You look lovely," he added, taking in the details of the blouse and the hairstyle.

Alice felt apprehensive as a young maid she didn't recognize opened the front door and showed them into the drawing-room. It was smaller than the one at Greenstocks, cluttered with ornaments and photographs and embroidered screens. Dr Sidgwick rose to his feet and greeted Alice cordially.

"How's mother, my dear? And how is young Jack getting on?"

Mrs Sidgwick was more formidable in both appearance and manner. She was almost as tall as Edward, but her blue eyes were lighter and less warm than his, with pale lashes instead of his dark ones. Alice tried unsuccessfully not to feel intimidated as she returned Mrs Sidgwick's greetings and sat down on a sofa in the bay window. "She can't really be pleased about Edward seeing me," she thought. "She probably hopes he'll come to his senses after the war, when he gets back to ordinary life."

The maid brought in tea, and Mrs Sidgwick passed round cups of tea and plates of sandwiches. The conversation, at first, was largely of local people and events: Mr Studley at Three Gates Farm had bought some of the new black-and-white Friesian cows; the Fifth Essex Territorials had gone out to the Dardanelles; recruiting officers were signing up local men under Lord Derby's scheme. "They've been round at the munitions works – plenty of fit young men there," Dr Sidgwick remarked. "With more and more women signing up for munitions, it frees men for the Army. Not all of them want to be released, of course – they're doing very nicely as they are."

"Women are taking over all sorts of work nowadays – going off to the factories – delivering coal, so I hear, in London," said Mrs Sidgwick. "There are even women working on some of the farms locally. I found it quite hard to find a maid to replace Doris when she went off to work in munitions. It really is quite remarkable, how everyone's supporting the war effort."

"Not always from the purest of motives," Edward said quietly. "There are plenty of people lining their own pockets. Some of the wealthy farmers and factory owners and aircraft manufacturers would be quite happy for the war to go on for ten years."

"What nonsense, Edward. How could we possibly fight the war without them?" his mother said, vigorously stirring her tea.

"Edward says you're applying for a transfer to a London military hospital, Alice," Dr Sidgwick said, rather obviously changing the subject, and passing her a plate of scones.

"Yes, I want to go where nurses are most needed. There are quite a lot of VAD volunteers at Broadlands Hall, mostly part-time, but the hospitals in London are short of staff. I'm hoping to be transferred in a few weeks' time."

"I should have thought your mother would have liked you to stay nearer home," Mrs Sidgwick remarked. "Especially with your brother away. And there's plenty of voluntary work for you to do locally. Madeleine Morland is helping out at a troops' canteen, and of course there's the War Supplies Department – Mrs Morland helps me with that."

Alice caught Edward's eye, leaving unspoken the obvious point that her family couldn't afford the luxury of voluntary work.

"Well, I think it's marvellous of Alice," Edward said loyally. "She knows from Lorna that the work will be much harder in a military hospital, but she's made up her mind to do it."

"One of those young men from Hillbank House is running a Belgian refugee hostel," Mrs Morland continued. "Do you know that German woman is still living with them? Even with all these spy rumours and Zeppelin raids! I don't see why she wasn't repatriated at the start of the war."

"But she's just an old lady," Alice said, surprised that Mrs Sidgwick had listened to the village gossip. "Surely no–one seriously believes she's a spy!"

Mrs Sidgwick gave her a sharp look. "But my dear, surely you've heard that someone in or near the village was signalling to the Zeppelin with car headlights?"

"But Frau Zellern can't drive a car!"

Mrs Sidgwick's eyebrows shot up. "Oh, you know her personally, then? I didn't think she came down to the village."

"I've been to Hillbank House – with Lorna," Alice said rashly. "The Braithwaites and the McLarens are friends of hers. I met Frau Zellern when we were there. She's a quiet old lady who has no family of her own."

"*Lorna* knows those people?" Dr Sidgwick queried.

"Yes, she met them in London."

"Lorna told me about them when I saw her on Thursday, on my way down," Edward said. "It would have been heartless to send the poor woman back to Germany, and it's ridiculous to think that she had anything to do with the Zeppelin raids."

"I wouldn't be surprised if she were compulsorily repatriated if the war goes on much longer," his father remarked.

Mrs Sidgwick still looked doubtful. "It didn't have to be headlights from a car. A torch shone from an upstairs window would have been enough. You saw Lorna in London, then?" she asked Edward.

"Yes. She's thinking of putting her name down for overseas service."

"Oh, dear. I did hope she'd stay in London for the duration of the war. She could be sent anywhere – the Dardanelles, the Middle East . . . How was she looking?"

"Oh . . . tired, but reasonably fit. She's had hardly any time off recently, with so many urgent casualties from Loos . . ."

Every conversational opening seemed to lead them into areas which were best not discussed. Alice was glad when the tea things were cleared away, and she and Edward had a little time alone together in the garden. He seemed more relaxed away from his parents, taking her arm as they walked under the apple trees and watched the stars beginning to appear in the twilit sky.

He told her an amusing story about a man in his platoon who loved darning socks during odd moments in the trenches. "He enjoys it so much that he darns for the whole platoon, and it really spoils his day if no-one has any holey socks to give him. One or two of the men deliberately make holes in theirs, to keep him happy. Most of the socks in the platoon must be more darn than original sock by now. He does a beautiful job, apparently." He reached up to pick an apple, and polished it on the sleeve of his jacket. "I'm surprised these trees haven't been requisitioned by the Army for its infernal plum-and-apple jam. We despair of ever getting anything else. These chrysanthemums are flowering late, aren't they? I'll see if I can cut a bunch for your mother."

He was beginning to seem a little more like his usual self, Alice noticed with relief, his eyes beginning to lose the strained look they had had when he first came home. He looked positively cheerful as he darted round the garden in the dusk, selecting the least faded blooms. Later he walked with Alice round to the farm cottage where Tom and Emily lived, so that Mrs Smallwood could be presented with the flowers immediately.

On their way, they passed Harriet walking out arm-in-arm with a local youth, George Franks, who was working at Marconi's.

"Oh dear," Alice said when they had exchanged greetings and walked on. "I wonder if Jack knows about that. He's been writing to Harriet, I know. I don't know whether she writes back."

"Harriet must be a fool, then, not to stand by Jack if she has the chance. I wish I had him in my platoon," Edward said. "It's hard for the young men at the Front, thinking that their sweethearts may be deserting them for those who are staying at home and earning good money."

"I wish Jack wasn't so fond of her," Alice burst out. "I know it sounds unkind, but I hate to think of him hoping, all this time, when she doesn't care . . . she didn't even mind that I'd seen her with someone else! Now I don't know whether I should tell Jack or not."

Edward considered for a few moments before replying, "I don't think I would. It would only make him unhappy, and things may resolve themselves . . ." He stopped walking and lifted a hand to stroke her hair. "I'm luckier, aren't I?" he murmured. "Thank you so much for coming this afternoon, Alice. I hope it wasn't too much of an ordeal."

"Well, I –" Alice hesitated, but he continued, "It *was* an ordeal, I know. I'm sorry Mother's so difficult, but you mustn't think it's your fault; it's just her way." He looked at her rather doubtfully. "When will I see you again? Can you get any time off tomorrow?"

"I'll come to church if I can, but I'll probably have to go straight back afterwards."

Next morning, she arranged to work the early morning shift, but finished rather late, and arrived in church during the first hymn. She slipped into the usual pew next to Emily, Mary and Tom; Edward was at the front with his parents. When the vicar prayed for all the fighting men of the village, she added her own fervent prayers for Edward and Jack, glancing between her clasped fingers at the tall, square-shouldered figure on which so many of her hopes rested.

"I expect you'll be wanting to see your young man," Emily said as they walked out into fitful sunshine at the end of the service. "Has he got much longer?"

"Only till tomorrow."

"Oh, you are lucky, Alice." Mary turned to stare at Edward as he came out of the church porch with his parents. "Edward is so *handsome* in his uniform . . ."

Emily caught her arm and pulled her away. "Get along with you! You're much too young to be ogling young men. Come on, let's leave Alice and Edward what time they've got to themselves."

"I'm *not* too young!" Alice heard Mary's voice raised in protest as she followed her mother towards the lych gate. "There's only five years difference between me and Alice. Nancy Simmons is younger than me and she . . ." Her voice faded into the general chatter of emerging churchgoers.

Edward exchanged a few remarks with the Morlands, then disengaged himself from them and his parents, and hurried over to join Alice.

"I feel I must get away from here," he said abruptly. "Will you walk with me for a little while?"

"Yes, of course," Alice agreed, concerned at his taut manner.

Ignoring the curious glances of onlookers and the rather put-out expression on Mrs Sidgwick's face, they left the churchyard and walked slowly down to the low arched bridge over the river, where golden-green streamers of willow swayed in the leisurely current and cattle trampled the muddy banks as they came down to drink. The hedgerows at the field edge were bright with hawthorn berries and twining garlands of bryony, frosted here and there with old-man's-beard. The tranquillity of the scene seemed to soothe Edward. After contemplating the languid river for a few moments without speaking, he said, "I'm sorry – I'm not very good company, am I?"

"You know I don't mind," Alice said, thinking that it was the prospect of returning to France which had so subdued him.

"I don't think I can endure another church service," he exclaimed. "The sententious moralizing – the attempts to jus-tify the senseless slaughter of war as if it springs from some divine inspiration . . . I can't tell you how much it means to me that you understand so much when others can't. My aunt and uncle, who called in last night, talked as if the war is some sort of rugby match, in which I might, if I'm lucky, be rewarded with a distinction of some kind. How can one explain to people like that? Do they have no imagination at all? – I'm sorry, Alice," he broke off suddenly. "You shouldn't let me go on at you like this. I can't think why I'm wasting the short time we have together."

"I'd far rather you told me what you really feel, rather than keeping it to yourself," Alice told him.

"There's no-one else I could contemplate talking to like this. Damn!" He looked at his wrist-watch with an impatient gesture. "I shall have to go back – my parents have invited yet another aunt to lunch. But I must see you again before I go – will you have any time free tomorrow?"

"I'll try to arrange something, even if it's only half an hour. I've had so little time off in the last few weeks that I'm sure Sister will agree."

"I suppose we'd better walk back, then," Edward said reluctantly.

"Yes, all right."

But they had only walked a few steps away from the bridge when Edward stopped suddenly in the middle of the lane and took both Alice's hands, turning her to face him. He seemed about to speak but then checked himself, frowning.

"What is it?"

"Alice –" He held her at arm's length, watching her closely. "I know this isn't the time or the place, and I never intended to ask you such a thing until the war was over, but – do you think you might consider marrying me?"

In Broadlands Grounds

The trees in the parkland behind Broadlands Hall were in the full beauty of autumn, the warm colours appearing to glow in the dusk as if giving back the light absorbed during the day. Alice and Edward walked hand-in-hand up a slight rise towards a stand of beeches. A faint dampness veiled the ground, so that their progress was marked by a darker trail through the misted grass.

"You don't have to make up your mind immediately," Edward said. "I want you to be quite sure before we come to any definite agreement. But I do know that my own feelings won't change."

"Nor mine. But you do understand, don't you? It isn't that I don't want to marry you – please don't think that! It's all the other things that make it so complicated."

"It's perfectly simple," Edward said, lifting her hand and kissing her fingers. "I love you, and I want to marry you. But you can have all the time you want before you give me an answer."

They stood beneath the copper beeches, looking into the field beyond the park fence. A horse-team was ploughing, turning over the damp earth like a shining wave, with gulls wheeling and swooping in its wake. Alice could hear the creak of the harness and the shouted commands of the ploughman as he turned the team at the headland. "I'll always remember this walk," she found herself thinking, alarmed by this premonition of finality.

She had managed to snatch only an hour away from the ward; very soon now, Edward would be leaving to catch the boat-train. It seemed dreadful to let him go without giving him the simple answer he wanted, but it was for his sake that she hesitated. She was anxious that he should not commit himself to an engagement now, with his judgment very probably impaired by the stress of being on active service, only to find himself regretting it later. It was ironic, she found herself thinking. Of course the idea of being married to Edward had entered her thoughts during the long months of their separation, but in the form of mere romantic daydreams rather than serious speculation. In her fantasies, she would have found no difficulty in responding to Edward's suggestion with declarations of love and loyalty; now, she found that considering the prospect in real life was less simple than she had supposed.

The faint sunset glow over the hills was fading; their short time together was almost at an end. They walked back to the house and parted unwillingly, Alice trying not to think of all that could happen before Edward was next able to return home. She returned to her ward, still hearing his whispered endearments and feeling the warmth of his lips on hers, and suspecting that her odd mood of light-headedness mixed with aching sadness must be apparent to everyone she met. She fought off an urge to run down the road after him, to shout at him to come back and to tell him that of course she would marry him.

Later in the week she visited Emily and her mother, finding Emily distraught because Tom had signed up under Lord Derby's scheme.

"He'll be killed – I know he'll be killed. Why didn't he wait till they bring in conscription?" Emily demanded.

Alice did her best to comfort her sister. "He's only on a reserve list – he might not have to go out for months, perhaps not at all."

Emily sniffed and dabbed at her eyes. "Yes, I suppose I'm crossing my bridges before I get to them. It's bad enough having our Jack out there. And you must be feeling the loss now Edward's gone back. He seems to be serious about you," she added, cheering up slightly.

"I've thought that all along," Mrs Smallwood said smugly.

"Oh – well." Alice felt awkward at having to conceal her new dilemma. Although she and Edward had agreed that they would not mention the possibility of their engagement to either family, she found it hard to fend off her mother's questions with evasive answers, tempted, in spite of her promise, to seek another point of view.

She left to cycle back to Broadlands Hall, wondering what her mother and sister would say about her hesitation – probably, she thought, they'd tell her to take her chances, ignoring any doubts she might have about the social gap between herself and Edward. But she was certain that Edward's parents, particularly his mother, would oppose the suggestion fiercely, wanting their son to make a more advantageous marriage.

"Oh, curse it," Alice thought as she cycled through the dusk, disturbing a pheasant which flew up from the roadside covert with a rattling screech, so that she wobbled and almost fell off her bicycle. The common-sense arguments assembled themselves in formidable ranks in her mind, but her desires refused to be dominated by mere logic. "Surely if we love each other, we can overcome all those problems?" she thought.

The next day, shortly before going on duty, she received a letter from Edward.

"I returned to find the battalion out of the line, and billeted in a quiet village. We are staying in a large farmhouse; I have a small room upstairs, which looks out over an apple orchard. As I sit at the window now, I can see white geese grazing beneath the trees, and some of the men picking fruit with the farmer's wife and daughter. A church bell is tolling in the village. It could easily be Essex, apart from the women's peasant skirts. It has been raining, and everything smells very fresh and clean; the war seems very distant.

I have been reading the Thomas Hardy poems which Lorna sent out to me. I have written out one of them for you; the

description of the horse-team ploughing will always remind
me of our walk together on that last evening.

I feel now that perhaps I was wrong to suggest an engage-
ment; not because of any change in my feelings for you – I
assure you of that! – but because it is unfair of me to want to
commit you to a relationship which could suddenly be ended.
I should have kept to my original resolve, and waited until the
war was over before asking you to marry me. We both know
that the chances of my being killed or seriously injured are
high; it is pure selfishness to ask you to tie yourself to one in
such a position. For my own part, I think I loved you before I
came out to France, and hope that my telling you this will put
aside any doubts you have on that score; but I shall quite under-
stand if you decide against an engagement or even to end our
relationship altogether."

Alice put the letter into the pocket of her dress, and went
on to the ward to begin taking temperatures and pulses. She
was impatient to write back at once, filled with remorse;
Edward had misunderstood, she thought, if he thought her
reticence sprang from fears of future loss. She already faced
the possibility of his death; how could that fear become any
greater if she were his fiancée or wife? She wrote to him as
soon as she came off duty, frowning over her writing paper
and wrestling with her difficulty in expressing such complex
thoughts in writing.

"I wish I had been more able to explain my thoughts to you
clearly – it was for your sake, not my own, that I hesitated. I
want to be absolutely sure that you know what you are doing,
and that you really do want to be married to me, not just now
but after the war, and have thought of all the disadvantages
to you. As for the risk that you may not return, I have to think
of that already, and marriage could not make it any worse. I
have been thinking this over very carefully, and if it would bring
you happiness – as I know it would to me – then perhaps we
should take our chance while we can, and face any problems

together. I feel very proud and honoured that you have even considered asking me to be your wife, and if you have not changed your mind then I will be engaged to you and will marry you whenever you think best."

The next day's post brought her the official letter she had been waiting for, but had almost forgotten in the excitement and anxiety over recent events. It informed her that she was to attend an interview at Devonshire House in London, and that if successful she would be required to start work almost immediately at a London hospital.

"So you are really going, then?" Grace asked, when Alice showed her the letter.

"Yes, if they give me a place."

"I shall be sorry to see you go. We've got on well together."

"Yes, we have. I shall be sorry too. And thank you for all you've done for me, helping me to learn how to cope."

Another parting – Alice was getting used to partings. But when, a few days later, she moved into a nurses' hostel in a tree-lined suburban road, she felt a wave of nostalgia for the Broadlands Hall days which were now behind her. Her immediate future was to be spent in the 1st General Hospital in south London, in surroundings with which neither Jack nor Edward had any connection, and as she unpacked her bag in the shared room in the hostel she was aware of a disturbing feeling that she had relegated them to the past.

Trench Raid

The officers' horses were tethered by the roadside, standing miserably with tails clamped to the wind and rain.

"Why do they insist on clipping them for the winter? It's madness, when they spend half their time standing about in the sleet and rain, with no shelter more often than not," Jack said angrily to Stephen as they marched past in a column.

"I know. And they don't look as if they get enough to eat either. It's not surprising they're in such a state."

"When I think of the horses at Greenstocks – the luxury they lived in . . ."

"I wish I was in the horse lines," Stephen said wistfully. "Do you think we could ask for a transfer?"

"Not a chance. They'd think we were after a nice cushy job."

As autumn had turned to winter, Jack had lost count of the number of times he had been in and out of the line. Although they had not taken part in a major offensive, he and his friends began to feel like seasoned campaigners in comparison with the new, even younger boys who were filtering into the company. He had learned to adopt a stoical attitude in the face of all conceivable kinds of discomfort. When in the front line, he grew used to being filthy for days on end, his feet damp and painful with chilblains; he began to forget that tea ever tasted of anything other than petrol, and that there were other kinds of food than bully beef and Maconochie stew. He had spent wet nights on carrying parties, wading and stumbling throught the gluey mud of the trenches, loaded with ammunition boxes or cumbersome bundles of pit-props; he had stood numb with cold on sentry duty, only the pain of his frozen limbs preventing him from succumbing to waves of tiredness. Men had been court-martialled and shot for falling asleep on sentry duty.

Throughout it all, to his own surprise, he found that he could keep up a reasonable semblance of cheerfulness. If you never expected anything other than rain, mud, noise and bad organization, he decided, you weren't likely to be disappointed, and he and Jimmy could usually joke their way through any tedious or fraught situation. The stretch of line they arrived in this time was much the same as any other, with mud, sagging wire and burst sandbags. The men had hardly settled themselves in before Sergeant Jones came round with the news that there was to be a night-time raid on the German trenches opposite.

"Captain Hutchins' orders," he reported briskly.

"Well, he's chosen a bloody nice spell of weather for it," Jimmy remarked, emerging from a dripping dugout into the steady drizzle.

After morning stand-to, a group of officers and men were gathered together to be briefed by the company commander. Both Jack and Jimmy were to go with Lieutenant Gray in the raiding party, which was to consist of some twenty men from three different platoons, while Will and Charlie were to be among those giving covering fire from the front-line trench. The German wire was to be strafed during the day, so that the raiders should be able to walk straight through.

Captain Hutchins' instructions were matter-of-fact. "Our aim is to bomb German trenches and dug-outs, and to take prisoners."

"Good for morale," Charlie observed drily when the briefing was over. "The morale of the staff back at the Base, that is. Sounds nice and easy, doesn't it?"

"I wouldn't mind so much if I had your job," Jimmy said. "Staying down in the trench. What did I do to get chosen for this little stunt? Has someone got it in for me? Everyone knows you're our best shot," he told Charlie.

"Well, there's times when that pays off, evidently."

Jack thought it quite likely that an officer as considerate as Lieutenant Gray would avoid sending a married man with children into danger when there were plenty of others who could go instead. None of them were under any illusions as to the risk factor in this sort of show. The plan had been described in straightforward terms as if it were no more than an exercise on the training ground, but Jack was awed by the realization that he would be crossing No-Man's-Land for the first time, and, even more dauntingly, coming face to face with German troops, in a situation where it would almost certainly be a case of killing or being killed. "I might be dead in a few hours' time," he thought, watching the sky darken. Stephen, who had brewed up some tea, passed him a tin mug. It seemed bizarre to be standing in the trench in the rain, calmly drinking tea and contemplating death.

Just before midnight, the raiding party assembled in the front-line trench. The twenty men, all with faces smeared with mud, had been divided into four groups of five, each led by an officer or corporal; Lieutenant Anderson, commanding officer of No 6 Platoon, had been instructed to see them off and to count them back in again, and was waiting with them now, holding a dim electric torch to show them their way over the top. Jack felt a tight knot of fear and excitement in his stomach, as he looked up at the dark sky, where thick clouds were blowing over towards the east. The fresh wind drove a spattering of rain into his face. He could hear the distant roll of the heavy guns further up towards the Belgian border and Ypres, and, nearer at hand but not close enough to worry about, the ratatatatat of machine-gun fire. It would all be over in half an hour or so. He would either be safely back in the trench, or . . .

The two scouts, who had been sent on to check that the wire in front of the trench had been cut, wriggled over the parapet, their uniforms coated with dark, semi-liquid mud. "Lovely gap straight in front. You can't miss it," one of them told Lieutenant Gray.

"Marked?"

"Yes, sir. Lime sprinkled on the ground on the far side."

"I think we'll be getting on our way, then. Ready, men?"

"Ready, sir."

"Good luck," Lieutenant Anderson said quietly. Gray was already scrambling up the facing wall of the parapet, pushed by the men behind. Jack gave Jimmy, in front of him, a heave and was hoisted over in his turn, almost glad to be moving at last after all the hours of waiting. The men in front of him were crawling on all fours into the gloom; he followed, carefully keeping his rifle out of the mud. It would take them all night at this rate, he reckoned, already feeling like some wounded animal squirming on the ground. Occasional flares in the distance revealed veils of rain, an expanse of mud pitted with shell-holes and craters, and thickets of barbed-wire entanglements. It took a moment or two to readjust to the darkness after the flare fizzled out. If any of those came any closer, Jack thought, the crawling men would be spotlit as surely as actors on a stage, sitting targets for the Germans opposite. He heard a burst of rifle fire somewhere, and an answering volley from the other side; the machine-gun chattered on in the background. Gray was already at the gap in the wire, waiting for the men of his party to catch up.

"All right?" he whispered.

"Yes, sir."

Through the wire and on into No-Man's-Land . . . Jack concentrated all his efforts on following Jimmy in front, not relishing the thought of becoming separated and blundering about on his own. Gray was leading them on a circuitous route, avoiding the shell-holes, Jack supposed, though God knew how he could see them. The cold, clammy dampness oozed between the fingers of his woollen gloves, and he tried not to think of what might be there besides mud. He was conscious of the weight of the bombs in his haversack, and pictured the sleeping Germans in their snug dugouts about to be awoken just in time to die . . . He mustn't think of that yet – just get to the German wire . . .

"Blast it!" Gray muttered, close ahead. "Wire's intact – we must be too far to our left . . . Try further along."

After a minute or two, groping along beside the wire in the darkness, Jack heard a muttered conversation between Gray and Corporal Smith, and gathered that the next party along had also been unable to find a gap. The strafing must have failed to cut the wire.

"Bring the wire-cutters. Everyone else, stay down, rifles trained."

These commands were given in a whisper, yet to Jack's taut nerves it seemed that they must be echoing into the nearby trenches as if shouted through a loud-hailer. He lay on his front in the mud, eyes trained on nothing but the blackness ahead. The wire-cutters were produced; the clack as the first strand of wire was severed sounded to Jack as loud as machine-gun fire. It would take them hours to cut the wire, surely, and every snick was accompanied by the risk of drawing enemy fire.

A flare suddenly fizzed up close at hand. Jack saw the parapet of the trench ahead, much closer than he had supposed, with the hunched figure of a man visible behind it. The German sentry could hardly have failed to see the men working at the wire. "This is it," Jack thought. "We're sitting ducks."

He had hardly had time to frame the thought when he heard the command "Retire!" followed by a volley of rifle fire from the German trench. One of the men further along had been hit; Jack could hear a quickly stifled groan some way to his right. He hesitated. "Retire! Now!" Gray hissed at him. Someone must have thrown some bombs into the trench – he

116

could hear the explosions close at hand, and shouts. He followed Jimmy, half-running as best he could in the slithery mud, bent double, and flinging himself to the ground as another flare went up, bathing the scene in white light. Finding that he was still unhurt, Jack got to his feet and ran on. He dodged and zigzagged, relying on the flashes of light to show him where to go. A shell burst close at hand, and he heard the singing of splinters as they passed his ears – God, that had been a close one! But it was just a few more yards now . . . Jimmy, ahead of him, was through the gap in the wire. Jack floundered and slid after his friend, and flung himself through the gap, barbs tearing at his trousers as he blundered into some loose strands of wire. His lungs were bursting, breath rasping as he reached the parapet and tumbled over it, caught awkwardly by the men waiting in the trench. He'd never imagined that a front-line trench could seem so welcoming.

"Twelve . . . thirteen . . . fourteen . . ." Anderson counted. "Where's Gray?"

"Didn't see him, sir, after he told us to retire," Jimmy gasped.

After a few minutes, one more man came in staggering and clutching a bloodstained arm.

"Mr Gray's hit bad, sir. Saw him helping in a wounded man – that last shell got both of them, I think, sir. They're in the crater quite close to our wire – couldn't help them on my own, sir."

"Right," said Anderson. "I'll go out myself and see if we can get them in. See to this man, Tompkins, and get the stretcher-bearers up here. You can come with me, Smallwood. Got your breath back?"

"Yes, sir."

Jimmy patted him on the shoulder sympathetically as he prepared to climb up over the parapet again, cursing his bad luck in being chosen for a second excursion just when he had thought he was safe.

"Don't be long, mate. We'll get some tea brewed for you."

"I'll need something a bloody sight stronger than that."

The fireworks were nearly over, just the occasional shell looping casually across, but there was still enough light for Jack to make out more than he had been able to see the first time. The commonly-used phrase "theatre of war" now struck him as appropriate; it *was* theatrical, with the dramatic flashes and sparks of light, the background rumbling of the big guns, and the sense of having been unwillingly thrust out on centre stage in front of the spotlights, inadequately rehearsed.

Lieutenant Anderson was making his way purposefully towards the gap, dodging and weaving as he negotiated the shell-holes. Jack could hear groans as soon as they reached the lip of the deep, water-filled crater; a man was crawling up through the soft earth of the side as best he could, dragging one leg behind him.

Lieutenant Anderson scrambled down to him, followed by Jack. "All right. We're here to help you in. Can you make it?"

The man's teeth were clenched with pain as he answered. "Yes, sir. Mr Gray's down there, but I think he's dead. He was hit at least twice, sir."

"Oh God. I'll go down and make sure. Wait here, Smallwood."

He slithered down towards the black gleam of the water. Jack waited with the wounded man, who slumped face-down on the ground, shivering with cold. He was from No. 6 Platoon, no-one Jack knew. His ankle seemed to be broken, but there was no other sign of injury, and there was nothing Jack could do for him until they moved on out of immediate danger. He found that he was trembling himself, weak with an accumulation of the stress of the last half-hour and the shock of the news about Lieutenant Gray. He hoped the wounded man had been mistaken; perhaps Gray was merely injured or unconscious.

Minutes later Anderson crawled up to rejoin him.

"He is dead, I'm afraid. We'll get him in later when there's less going on – first we must see to Webber here. Oh, Christ –" He checked himself, shrugging fatalistically, and Jack caught a glimpse of his pale, stricken face in the light of a distant flare. Anderson, for all his air of authority, was only a year or so older than Jack, about the same age as Gray, with whom he had been friendly. The raid had achieved nothing whatsoever, Jack realized; the only result had been one more death on the Western Front, one more name for the lists, one more telegram to be sent home. They began to cross the treacherous few yards back to the trench, hauling Webber between them.

Part Three: 1916

On the Ward

"The first day of 1916. I wonder what we'll be doing this time next year?" Jack remarked.

The restaurant was decked with Christmas decorations and crowded with soldiers and their families, a mixture of those who had just arrived at Victoria and those who, like Jack, were waiting to catch the next boat train. Alice touched the wooden table superstitiously. "Surely the war can't last out another whole year? People said it would be over by *last* Christmas."

"I don't know," Jack said cheerfully, sipping his beer. "You get so used to it, it's hard to remember any other kind of life. I'd feel strange now, going back to working at Greenstocks, wouldn't you?"

"Mmm." Alice looked at him fondly across the table. He seemed taller than she remembered, with a new air of confidence. It struck her that he was a very personable young man; his tawny hair, weathered skin and frank brown eyes were as attractive in their way as Edward's darker good looks, and she noticed several girls giving him appreciative glances. Alice was breaking hospital rules by lunching out with her brother – nurses, who were classed as officers, weren't supposed to consort with other ranks – but she had no intention of missing her only chance to see Jack before he returned to France.

"It was a pity you couldn't have got leave for Christmas," she told him. "Ma and Emily were hoping you'd be at home."

"It was good to get home for New Year, at any rate, even though it was only a short leave. And we made the best of Christmas Day, as much as we could in the front line. Captain

Hutchins said that last Christmas, blokes walked out into No-Man's-Land and shook hands with the Germans and gave them cigarettes. There was none of that this year."

"It was nice in the hospital," Alice said, "with decorations, and all the gifts people sent in, nuts and fruit and sweets for the men."

"I'm sorry Edward didn't get home. He sent me a card and some cigarettes, did I tell you?" Jack finished his beer and glanced up at the clock above the bar; there was not much time left.

"I wouldn't have been able to get home to see him anyway. And at least he wrote to me that he was in a quiet sector, so I didn't have to worry too much."

Alice was relieved to see Jack looking so well, showing few signs of strain. Unlike Edward, he had talked freely about his experiences; she understood that the companionship of the men in his platoon, new friends as well as old ones, helped to compensate for the hardships. Jack made her laugh with his impersonations of various brass-hats, and his only indication that life in the trenches was anything other than good fun with the occasional risky moment was when he spoke of the death of Lieutenant Gray, whom he had mentioned in his letters. Alice was saddened by this news, alarmed to hear of the danger Jack had been in on the night of the raid – although he spoke of it flippantly – but, above all, glad to see him in such good spirits.

However, her mood faded abruptly as she watched him walk away down the platform at Victoria to join his train. She stood amidst the crowds, watching the departing train until it was out of sight, and then made her way back to the 1st London General Hospital in a subdued and pessimistic frame of mind – most unsuitable for the first day of a new year, she thought, trying to shake herself out of it.

On her return, she found that the ward still retained some of its Christmas conviviality, with its coloured streamers and the gramophone playing a Scott Joplin piano rag. A convalescent patient grabbed her as soon as she walked in – "Come on, nurse, give us a whirl!" – and spun her around to the music, amidst wolf-whistles.

Alice struggled to free herself, seeing the ward Sister emerging from a screened bedside.

"You're rather late, Nurse Smallwood," Sister Woodhams said disapprovingly, passing by with a tray of dressings. "Jenkins has been waiting to go off-duty. Balderson, you shouldn't be dancing around in bare feet."

Alice looked up at the ward clock; she was only a few minutes late. "I'm sorry, Sister. I've been seeing my brother off at Victoria."

"Her brother – that's what they all say," said Balderson, before being silenced by a glare from the Sister. He saluted briskly behind her back and winked as he caught Alice's eye.

Life in the ward was not usually so light-hearted. With large numbers of staff to organize and serious casualties to attend to, the Sisters were far stricter than the ones at Broadlands Hall, and the work was exhausting. Alice's working day included a considerable walk between the hostel and hospital each morning and evening; her legs and feet ached from the constant walking and standing, and her hands were always red and chapped from immersion in hot water, lysol and disinfectant.

On her second morning in the ward, another new nurse had fainted while helping with a wound dressing, and Sister Woodhams had called Alice over to take her place.

"It's not a very pretty sight, I know," the man said ruefully. He was already sweating, and Sister Woodhams had done no more than uncover his wound. "Don't you faint as well, or we'll have the floor littered with young ladies."

"Nurse Smallwood won't faint," Sister Woodhams said firmly.

Alice wished she felt as sure. The man had a horribly lacerated thigh, with a large area of raw flesh exposed, and two tubes inserted into it for drainage. The whole thing looked more like a mangled joint of meat than a human limb. The warm, sickly odour of pus made Alice's head reel, and she had to force herself to stand calmly, reassuring the patient as best she could, proffering the kidney-dish and passing the instruments while the Sister irrigated the wound and removed and replaced the drainage tubes. The whole process was agonizing, and the poor man could hardly stop himself from crying out. Alice was greatly relieved when she was sent to fetch the hot fomentation, and the wound could be bandaged up again and the man left to rest. He was worn out with pain.

"You seem to be fairly useful, at any rate," Sister Woodhams said, almost grudgingly, and from then on Alice assisted her regularly on her round of dressings. Alice found it hard to face the dreadful sights which awaited her daily, but she knew she had no choice but to face the pain and disfigurement which the men themselves bore with such stoicism. Even so it was difficult to put this resolve into practice, and she often returned to her room in the hostel feeling completely drained, both physically and mentally.

The men's physical wounds were bad enough, but Alice soon realized that mental scars went deeper still and were even more difficult to heal.

"Bates woke eyeryone again in the middle of the night with his screaming," the nurse on night duty sometimes told Alice when she came into the ward in the morning. Her tone suggested that Corporal Bates was an irascible child who ought to know better.

Bates was a non-commissioned officer in his early twenties, who had been seriously wounded in the fighting around Loos. "His wound would have healed by now, if he'd been treated more quickly," Sister Woodhams told Alice. "There were so many casualties, he was left lying at the regimental aid-post and then kept waiting again at the casualty clearing station before he was put on a train to Boulogne. And then there was no room at the base hospital, so he was taken on a stretcher to wait for the next hospital ship. When he got here, he was still in his filthy uniform and his wound still with just a field-dressing slapped on. He had a deep wound full of mud – it's not surprising it had time to fester. There's still a chance he might lose the leg."

"But that's appalling!" Alice said, deeply shocked. "It's tragic for a man to lose an arm or leg under any circumstances – to lose one because of sheer bad organization is unthink-able!"

"If you'd been out to France, and seen what they're trying to cope with over there, you'd see why it happens. No–one ever imagined there'd be so many casualties," the older woman replied simply.

The wound in Bates' leg seemed to be responding slowly to frequent painful treatments with hypochlorous acid solution, but nothing could be done to stop his nightmares. According to the night nurse, he woke up screaming something incom-prehensible, often several times a night. One afternoon, the man in the next bed called Alice over.

"He's off, nurse. Better wake him before he starts yelling and screaming. Some of the boys are getting fed up with it."

Alice looked at Corporal Bates, who had apparently fallen into a light doze, and was shuddering and muttering. The touch of her hand on his shoulder had been enough to wake him, but she had been shocked by the look of blind animal ter-ror in his eyes as he stared at her uncomprehendingly for sev-eral seconds, before slowly focusing on the beds opposite and coming back to the present. She soothed him, rearranged his bedclothes and offered him a cup of tea, feeling completely inadequate to deal with whatever horrors possessed his mind, and were evidently more real to him than his actual sur-roundings.

"I remember at first I used to wish that you or Jack might

turn up in my ward, lightly wounded, but enough to keep you out of action," she wrote to Edward. "But it seems naive, now that I've seen for myself how the men suffer, to wish injury on either of you, just for my own stupid satisfaction."

In mid-February she packed her bag in preparation for a few days off, which she had managed to arrange to coincide with Edward's leave.

"Oh, are you going home?" asked Margaret, the nurse with whom Alice shared a room in the hostel, seeing the belongings spread out on the bed.

"Yes, just for three days."

"Oh, you lucky thing. I shall have to wait ages now, having been at home for Christmas. I can't wait to get home and have a decent *bath*. You'd think it wouldn't be beyond the hospital's resources to provide us with hot water. Goodness knows, we need it."

Alice met Edward's leave train next morning, and shortly afterwards they were seated together in a railway carriage bound for Essex and home. The compartment was crowded at first, but when the two passengers seated opposite got out at Theydon Bois, Edward took both Alice's hands in his and gave her a long, approving look.

"VAD must stand for Vivacious And Delightful, in your case," he said finally.

"Oh – I thought it meant Very Arduous Drudgery."

Edward laughed in appreciation of her quick response. "I'd love to have a photograph of you in your uniform – you look so charming in it . . . Alice," he said, suddenly more serious, "did you mean what you said in your letters – shall we really be married?"

"Yes, of course – if you're really sure *you* want it."

Edward said nothing, but the way he looked at her left no room for doubt. By the time they got off the train they had decided that they would tell their parents of their decision at once, and had agreed that they would marry next spring or at the end of the war, whichever came sooner. Walking along the platform, Alice noticed tiny spears of snowdrops piercing the soil in the station master's garden, smelt the fresh, cold air laden with the aroma of wood-smoke, and realized how much her gruelling work in the hospital had dominated her consciousness and dragged down her spirits. It came as something of a surprise to find that she was still young and healthy, that it was nearly spring, and that she loved Edward and was loved by him.

Lieutenant Morland

The rain drove steadily into Jack's face as he marched. The flickering light of distant flares and star-shells revealed the line of helmets ahead of him, stretching away into the darkness. The horizon ahead was dimly lit with a pulsing, fiery glow, and the roll of the heavy guns provided a bass accompaniment to the rhythm of marching feet.

The troops had set off cheerfully enough two mornings previously, even though they knew they were heading for the front line again. The rolling countryside of Picardy was lush with spring growth, and the men sang vigorously at first as they passed between fields of young wheat and barley, along white dusty roads lined with poplars. The villages of whitewashed, thatched cottages, with groups of children staring by the roadside and flocks of geese hissing defiance, had reminded Jack of Essex. But the picturesque scenery, with its sense of pastoral life untouched by the war, was far behind them now. They were approaching the front, greeted by dismal heavy rain and stretches of large uneven cobbles on which boots slipped and slithered. The roads, which had been quiet during the hours of daylight, were now busy with every kind of transport: guns, ammunition, ambulances, troops going up the line or returning. Officers on horseback rode alongside the men, calling out "Stick to it, lad!" or "Step up, there!" at anyone who was flagging.

Jack had passed through initial tiredness, through the numbed, hypnotic state which followed it and during which his legs had seemed to carry on marching of their own accord, and into a mood of acute irritability. His feet were sore, his shoulders ached with the weight of his pack, and he had twisted an ankle on the lumpy cobbles through the last village; with every new gust of wind, driving cold rain into his streaming face, he felt his temper shorten. As they drew closer to the front, occasional five-nine shells looped lazily over, making him imagine the carnage if one landed in the middle of the road. At a road junction, when his column became hopelessly entangled with another trying to progress in a different direction, he felt ready to burst into tears of rage and frustration.

Arrival in the trenches provided little cause for celebration.

"Phwah! Smells like a bloody sewage farm," Jimmy said disgustedly. "What did the lazy blighters who were here before spend their time doing?"

"We'll have days of slog getting this lot in order." Jack looked round dispiritedly at the squalid scene revealed by the lantern-light; sagging revetments, wires pulled away from the walls, decaying remnants of food littering the dugouts. A large, well-fed rat scuttled away from the beam of light.

"Oh, Christ. I can't think about that now." Jimmy yawned hugely, searching for a dry spot in which to put his pack. "I'm so dead beat, I could sleep standing up."

The tired troops; apart from those on sentry duty or assigned to the more urgent repairs, were sent to find shelter where they could in the inadequate dugouts. It seemed to Jack that he had barely closed his eyes before he was awoken by the grey dawn light filtering through the torn sacking which formed a makeshift curtain, and Stephen's voice calling, "Rise and shine, men. Stand-to in five minutes."

"What's he sounding so ruddy happy about?" Jack forced his stiff limbs into action and heaved himself up from the pile of sacks he had been sleeping on.

"We're to be inspected by our new officer later today," Stephen told him as he stumbled out into the open trench. "Some new chap coming up from Brigade Headquarters."

Since the death of Lieutenant Gray, the platoon had been temporarily under the command of another young subaltern straight from Officer's Training Camp, but he had recently been transferred to another company – "leaving us motherless," as Stephen put it. Charlie had been promoted to Lance-Corporal.

"Who's this new bloke then?" Jack asked Stephen, noticing that the rain had stopped during the night but that the trench was ankle-deep in water in several places, and stank of excrement and lingering gas fumes.

"Dunno. Corporal Woolmer did tell me his name but I've forgotten it now."

"Well, he's going to think we're an idle lot. We shan't make much impression on this cesspit before he gets here."

"We can't do much in daylight, anyway. He'll have to make allowances."

"Let's hope he's a good bloke then – like poor old Dolly Gray. What are our chances of getting another like him?" Jack yawned, stretched and went back into the dugout to prod Jimmy into some semblance of life.

Towards evening, while the men were eating their meal, word was passed along that the new officer had arrived and would be coming round before stand-to. When the meal was over, Jack and the others tidied themselves as best they could and prepared to stand at attention. The new officer was being shown round by Corporal Woolmer, who introduced him briefly to each man; Jack could hear the voices in the next fire-bay.

"Privates Taplin and Smallwood, sir," Corporal Woolmer said, rounding the corner.

"Did you say Smallwood?" the young man behind him queried.

The voice, familiar but out-of-place, startled Jack. His eyes swivelled to the right and with a shock of recognition he found himself looking into the face of Philip Morland.

"Yes, sir, Private Smallwood and Private Taplin," Woolmer repeated.

"Sir." Jack recovered in time to maintain a blank expression, and saluted smartly.

Philip Morland looked taken aback for a moment, then a brief, sardonic smile flickered on his face, and he said, "Well. How are you, Smallwood?"

"Well, sir, thank you."

Philip said no more, and moved on down the trench. He was immaculately turned out, with every badge and button highly polished and riding boots gleaming, just as in the old days; the peaked officer's cap emphasized his naturally haughty expression. Jack, hardly able to believe that fate had brought him back into contact with his old enemy, managed by an effort of will to remain silent until Woolmer had led Philip out of earshot before giving vent to his feelings.

"God Almighty! Of all the officers in the whole blasted regiment I have to get landed with him!" he hissed at Jimmy.

Jimmy, to Jack's increased fury, found the situation amusing rather than distressing.

"You'll be able to polish up your impersonations. Give us all a bit of entertainment," he suggested.

"Entertainment! I'm glad you think it's funny. I certainly don't. Christ, I haven't seen him for nearly two years and I wouldn't have minded if I never saw him again," Jack fumed. "Of all the bloody awful luck . . . *why* did he have to come here when he could have gone anywhere on the whole blasted front or out to the Dardanelles . . ."

"You'll have to make the best of it. There's a war on, you know."

"Yes, I had noticed," Jack said bitterly.

He kicked at the side of the parapet, deeply aggrieved both by Jimmy's lack of sympathy and by the horribly neat irony of the situation. Philip's arrival would change everything. "Perhaps he'll get himself shot," he found himself thinking resentfully. "Either that or he'll send me out on some impossible raid, and I'll get done for."

Philip would go out of his way to give him a hard time, he felt sure, to demonstrate that he was still in charge just as surely as he had been at Greenstocks. That night, when he and Stephen were part of a group given the unenviable task of enlarging and neatening the latrine bay, he was certain that Philip's influence was already beginning to make itself felt. While they worked, he told Stephen about the old animosity between him and his former employer, finding Stephen, with his love of horses, a more willing ally than Jimmy.

"He sounds like a right four-letter man," Stephen said when Jack had told him about Galliard and the hedge-jumping episode.

"He is," Jack said feelingly. "That's why I'm doing this now. He'll make sure I get all the worst jobs – you wait and see."

"Well, I'm doing it as well, and he can't have anything against me. I've never seen him in my life before," Stephen pointed out reasonably. "Perhaps you're making too much of it, Jack. He might be different now. All that was before the war."

"Come on, you two. Stop chewing the fat and get on with it," Charlie called to them. "I don't know about you, but I don't fancy hanging around here any longer than I have to. This isn't the most pleasant place for a chat, and besides Fritz has a habit of aiming shells at the latrines."

The following few days did little to improve Jack's opinion of Philip and his abilities as a commanding officer. Philip was too unsure of himself to permit any informality between himself and the men; he enforced strict discipline at all times and insisted on Army regulations, however trivial, being adhered to at all times. Unlike Gray, he expected the men to jump to their feet and salute him when he approached, even when engaged in front-line duties.

"These men have been allowed to become slack," he was heard telling Corporal Woolmer.

On his second morning, Philip called for a full kit inspection. This was difficult, with the wet conditions underfoot, but groundsheets had to be found and all the equipment laid out and examined with a thoroughness Jack had not seen since leaving England. Jack was in trouble because he had no sewing thread in his housewife, while Jimmy was told that his hair was a good half-inch too long.

"I haven't had much time to consider my coiffure, sir," Jimmy said light-heartedly.

His attempt at a joke was met with a blank stare from Philip, who said coldly, "Don't answer back, Taplin. Just get it cut."

"I'll do it for you," Stephen offered when the inspection was over. He produced a comb and scissors from his pack, sat Jimmy on a pile of sacks and began trimming his hair with deft fingers used to plaiting horses' manes.

Charlie joined them in their dugout, where Jack was brewing up tea. "What a stickler that bloke is! I wonder what he's been doing all the war? Looks like a base-wallah to me."

"Knows the rule-book off by heart, but I wonder what he knows about things that count?" Jimmy remarked. "Ouch!" he complained as Stephen's comb caught a knotted strand of hair. "Careful – I'm not one of your ruddy Shire horses!"

"He obviously thinks it's the best way to show his authority over us, but he won't get our respect that way," Charlie continued.

Jack squatted on the floor, clumsily pouring tea into enamelled mugs, secretly pleased that the others were beginning to share his opinion of Philip Morland. "Tea up, all. You can have it with or without extra sugar, but petrol's compulsory."

Lawrence

Jack's letter arrived in an envelope bearing a hexagonal red stamp with the words "Passed Field Censor", and Alice found that all place names had been deleted from its contents.

"Dear Alice. We are back in the line near ——————— after resting in nice billets at ———————————. We have heard news of ——————— not much to know yet but I will let you have more news as soon as I can.

Your last letter took a long time to reach me as we have been on the move so much since we came up from ———————————. Anyway I am very pleased indeed to hear you are engaged to Edward, he is a very nice chap. You are lucky, and so is he and I know you will be happy. I bet Ma is well chuffed, she always liked Edward, and will be pleased you are going up in the world as well. You will have to let me know when you are getting married so I will try to get leave if I can, if the war is still on by then I mean.

I hope your work at the hospital is not too hard, it must be a bit different living in London than the village, I expect you miss it.

We have had one big surprise, that was when we got our new officer, you will never guess who it is, well it is Philip Morland. I never thought I'd see him again and was not too pleased as you will imagine. He is just like he was at home no sense of humour and not very much liked by the men, he is too strict not like poor Mr Gray who was a very different sort of bloke, I wish he hadn't gone west. Or if we had to have someone from home then what a shame it couldn't have turned out to be your Edward, he is a fine officer I am sure and just the sort the men like. Anyway we have to make the best of it and in this game you never know how long things will stay the same. Jimmy says he's so good at all the rules he will probably end up getting promoted to brass hat with a nice safe job.

Anyway this leaves me in good health and I hope you are the same, we are kept busy here because of ———————— *but when we get back to* ———————— *I will have more time to write to you. And please tell Edward I am very pleased about your news when you write to him. All my love, Jack."*

"It does seem to be awfully bad luck for you," Alice wrote back, *"but perhaps you will find that you and Mr Philip can put your diferences behind you – I do hope you will try, and that things will turn out better than they probably seem to you at present.*

I had just come back from a half-day out when I received your letter. London is full of talk about the Battle of Jutland – though it seems hard to know from the newspapers whether it was victory or defeat – and even more stunning, the news of Lord Kitchener's death. In case the news is slow to reach you, I am sending a newspaper cutting about the sinking of the HMS Hampshire. I can hardly believe that the man whose face we all know so well from the recruiting posters is no more . . ."

The Union Jack outside the War Office had been flying at half-mast when Alice returned from having tea in the Strand with Margaret. The afternoon had been dominated by the loss of the *Hampshire* off the Orkney islands, sunk by a floating mine. Billboards starkly proclaimed KITCHENER DROWNED, and people stood in the streets reading the evening paper or discussing the news in groups.

Usually, Alice enjoyed her weekly half-day outings, shopping or walking in the parks with Margaret or sometimes a group of nurses. For the first time in her life, in spite of her long and exhausting hours of work, she felt that she was independent. It was very different from her working days at Greenstocks. Times were changing, she realized, remembering conversations with Lorna. When the war was over, young women who had proved that they could cope with all kinds of demanding work would be unwilling to return to lives confined to the kitchen, nursery and drawing-room.

Edward continued to write regularly, referring to the fighting around Verdun and the pressure on the French Army which was trying so desperately to defend it. *"I don't know how much longer it can go on,"* he wrote. *"It seems that a new impetus must be launched elsewhere, to distract the Germans who otherwise look certain to break through."*

Edward's words struck an ominous note, reinforcing the current rumours that a "Big Push" would soon be taking place, and Alice worried increasingly for his safety and Jack's. A letter from her mother brought more bad news from Littlehays:

"There are hardly any young men in the village now, with all the conscripts sent out to France. Some of the farmers have managed to keep their sons, being as farming is a reserved occupation, but I must say the families who have sent out their sons and husbands are very bitter about these strapping young men staying at home. Hillbank House is up for sale again, the two men there have joined the RAMC, and the women have gone back to London to work in the East End. I don't know what's happened to the German woman. You will be very sorry to learn that young Albert Johnson, who was to have married Rosie Taplin, has been killed at Ypres. Mrs Johnson is taking it very bad and has hardly come out of her house since, and poor Rosie is hit bad as you can imagine . . ."

"Oh dear," Alice said aloud.

"What's the matter? Bad news?" Margaret asked, looking up from her own letter.

"Another boy killed from the village at home. He was going to marry a girl we all knew – her brother and my brother are friends."

"Oh, I'm sorry." Margaret made token expressions of regret, but such news was becoming commonplace by now.

And Alice was aware that her own reaction was partly selfish; she could imagine herself in Rosie's position only too clearly.

A conversation next morning gave her new cause for anxiety. "I hate it when people refer to the men by their injuries – you know, 'the shattered knee in bed four' or 'the gas case in the private room' as if they're bits of machinery to be repaired," she remarked to Margaret while they were walking to the hospital.

"It's inevitable, I suppose," Margaret said. "They come and go so quickly that it's not always possible to remember their names. And we wouldn't be able to carry on if we let ourselves get too fond of them. Which reminds me – Lawrence has got a thing about you, did you know?"

"Oh, surely not? You must be imagining it."

Her voice was temporarily drowned by the noise of a passing tram. When it had gone by, Margaret continued, "He watches you all the time, whenever you're in the ward. He's like a devoted Labrador."

Alice fell silent, uncomfortably aware of the truth in what Margaret said.

Corporal Lawrence had been in the ward for several weeks, making a slow recovery from numerous shrapnel wounds which had become infected. He was slim and dark-haired, slightly olive-skinned, with very beautiful dark brown eyes full of pain and exhaustion but still suggesting former liveliness. Alice had to help Sister Woodhams with his frequent dressings, which were horrible for him. He lay sweating, and clenching his teeth in an effort not to cry out with the pain, while the Sister probed his wounds with forceps, prising out tiny fragments of metal. Alice felt for him dreadfully, longing to hold him in her arms, anything, to help him through the ordeal; instead, she talked to him soothingly about whatever she could think of in a vain attempt to take his mind off it. Lawrence seemed to appreciate this, and sometimes, in quiet moments on the ward, he would talk to her about his home and family in Shropshire.

"I haven't upset you, have I?" Margaret said in surprise as they crossed the road by the hospital gates. "There's nothing unusual about patients having crushes on nurses. It's only natural. Nurse Wendover has got a positive army of admirers. You should hear some of the things they call out to her."

"I have heard," Alice said, smiling. But Lawrence wasn't like the cheeky young men who tried to be familiar with the nurses when Sister was out of earshot; he was quiet and withdrawn, almost brooding. "Anyway, even if you're right, Lawrence probably won't be in the ward much longer," she concluded. "They're going to start moving people out, Sister said."

Disturbed by what Margaret had said, Alice tried to avoid Lawrence for the next day or two, letting another nurse attend to him. But she was aware that his gaze followed her wherever she went on the ward, and she felt that she was deliberately hurting his feelings. It was stupid, she decided eventually, to expect to treat everyone impartially; human feelings didn't work like that. Corporal Lawrence was lonely and bored, that was all, and would doubtless have reacted in the same way to any young and reasonably presentable nurse. If talking to her gave him some small pleasure to lighten his pain-filled days, then surely she was mean to deprive him of it, she thought.

Her problem was abruptly solved two days later, when rumours of a Big Push were confirmed by instructions to clear the ward of all patients who could possibly be moved. Remembering Loos and the convoys of barely-recovering men sent out to Broadlands Hall, Alice knew what to expect. It seemed dreadful to think of the men now fit and healthy in billets in France, who would shortly be arriving on stretchers, part of the shattered debris of war, and of the others who would never return at all. The bombardment had already begun; the distant, threatening roll of the heavy guns could be heard in London, like approaching thunder.

Lawrence, in spite of his infected wounds which still needed three-hourly treatments, was sent with the rest to a hospital in the country.

"You've been an angel to me," he told Alice as he waited to be carried out to the waiting ambulance. "I'll never forget that."

"Good luck," she whispered, clasping his hand in farewell.

She cried bitterly that night. Whether her tears were for Lawrence, or for all the young men like him, she hardly knew.

The Second Wave

"Strewth, this really is going to be a big one," Jack remarked, looking at the expanse of neat tents which covered the hillside.

"You're telling me. Half the blooming British Army must be here." Jimmy stopped walking to light a cigarette.

"Exciting, isn't it?" Stephen said. "Nice of them to give us a few days' rest. I wouldn't have wanted to miss all this."

"Rest?" Jimmy laughed derisively, blowing a cloud of smoke. "I've nearly marched my way through the soles of my boots with all that parading and drilling. And we're on parade again at three."

"I hope we can find our way back through all this lot. We don't want to be court-martialled for desertion before the show even starts."

The area surrounding them was reminiscent of the base camp at Étaples, with nurses and medical corps, ambulances and Red Cross vans, staff cars, and troops in buses and on foot assembling in ever-increasing numbers. Besides the human traffic, horse-drawn artillery and the tractored howitzers in their camouflage colours were making their way along the dusty roads, and British planes patrolled the clear skies overhead. Casualty clearing stations were being set up in schools and village halls, making Jack wonder if he were destined to arrive in one in a few days' time.

"Charlie said he saw a carpenter's workshop by the quartermaster's stores churning out rows and rows of wooden crosses," he said to the others. "Cheerful thought, isn't it?"

"Oh, that Charlie," Jimmy countered. "He's a depressing sort of chap to have around. Always likes to look at the black side of everything."

Their instructions for the attack had been explained and rehearsed over and over again, with imaginary trenches indicated by tapes on the ground. "Z" day was scheduled for Thursday, by which time the preliminary bombardment would have smashed the German wire and killed the men in the trenches – "I doubt if you'll even find a rat alive," the battalion commander told them confidently. The British troops were to walk through at a steady pace, take possession of the German line and await further instructions and reinforcements for consolidating their position.

"Sounds like a cake walk, don't it?" Charlie said afterwards. "Let's hope they get it right this time. Remember what those blokes we met after the shambles at Loos told us?"

"For God's sake keep quiet, if you're going to do nothing but moan," Jimmy retaliated. "Being Lance-Jack hasn't done much for your morale."

Charlie just shrugged, and Dick Twyford said, "We're going to wipe the floor with the Fritzes this time. They won't know what's hit 'em."

The weather was warm and sunny, and the hedge-rows were lush with sweet-smelling honeysuckle. The banks of a nearby stream were fringed with water-mint and yellow flag irises; white butterflies fluttered over the grasses, and a willow-warbler poured forth its silvery, descending call. It was a strange setting for a battle, Jack thought, more appropriate for hay-making, or a game of village cricket. But for all the rural tranquillity of the surroundings, he was acutely aware of the strain of waiting.

When wet weather later that week resulted in the attack being postponed until Saturday, he didn't know whether he felt more relieved or exasperated.

"I wish we could get on with it," he grumbled to Stephen.

"I don't. I want to go home."

At last, shortly before dawn on Saturday, they were led into a support trench to wait in battle-assembly position. The bombardment of the German front line was a massive, nerve-shattering din which made the ground tremble as if in fear. Picking his way along the duckboards, Jack wondered that human ingenuity could create weapons which sounded like the wrath of an enraged Old Testament God . . . he wondered what it must be like for the Germans cowering in their trenches, if indeed any of them still survived after this onslaught – they must be as insignificant as pebbles in the path of a tidal wave, ground and smashed beyond recognition. He felt his nerves taut and strained in the terrible continuous din, but other men were in a worse state; some of them kept glancing up at the sky, faces distorted with fear, like petrified children.

Jack was conscious of the numbers packed in the trenches two or three deep, rows and rows of troops massed and ready, every man carrying a full pack and extra bandoliers of ammunition. Will Fletcher, next to him, looked pale green, as if he were likely to be sick at any moment, but further along the line some of the men were grinning and even smoking, confident of the easy victory they had been promised. Jack felt queasy himself, with limbs trembling and stomach a knot of tension. He was almost looking forward to zero hour, thinking that it would be a relief to get moving after this interminable drilling and waiting. How would Philip Morland shape up, Jack wondered, leading the platoon over the top? He was grateful now for his experience in the trench raid, and a few patrols and wiring parties since. "At least I've been under fire," he thought. "Some of those poor blighters don't know what it's like at all." Many of the men waiting with him were new drafts, and had never been in the trenches before, let alone in a major battle.

"Five minutes to go – check all bayonets fixed," the message came along.

The strafing was dying down now. Philip Morland, waiting to lead his men out when the first wave had gone over, kept looking at his watch and looking again, compulsively. There was an eerie quietness which rang in Jack's ears after the din of the bombardment. Incredulously, he heard a sky-lark singing above the trenches. The officers of A and C companies blew their whistles, and the men in front of Jack were scrambling up the ladders and out of sight. Philip glanced along the trench as his men moved forward, positioning themselves at the foot of the ladders. Jack, his heart pounding in his chest, found himself thinking of Lord Kitchener's message to the troops, which every soldier had in his pay book: ". . . *the Honour of the British Army depends on your individual conduct. It will be your duty to set an example of discipline and perfect steadiness under fire . . .*"

"Good luck," Stephen whispered on Jack's left, resting a hand on his arm.

"Good luck too. See you over there."

Renewed fire could be heard now, explosions of heavy shells, machine guns rattling – the Germans were retaliating, Jack realized – God, what was going on out there? Could the first wave really be strolling across as instructed, in the middle of that lot?

"Ready?" Philip yelled. He put his whistle to his lips and blew it, the sound barely audible, and waved his right arm as he hauled himself up the ladder. This was it . . . Jack gave Jimmy a shove, and pulled himself up, conscious of the dragging weight of his pack. Out in the open, double up through the gaps, lie down, wait for the lines to reform, all as instruc ted . . . Philip shouted to them to advance. Ahead, all was smoke, a terrific roar and clamour, explosions, machine-gun fire, screams and yells – God, this couldn't be right! This wasn't what they'd been told to expect – where were the orderly lines marching steadily across? Jack could see nothing but smoke, flame, fountains of earth. Machine-gun fire rattled out, and he saw someone near him throw up his arms and flop to the ground. Jimmy was slightly ahead, Philip Morland to his right. Jack was amazed to find that he was in control of his body, moving forward according to plan, his limbs operating independently of his confused brain. But the lines were already disintegrating, men falling, stumbling, yelling out . . . he saw Dick Twyford go down, clutching his chest . . . No time to stop, must keep in line, what was left of it . . . Someone was rugby-tackling him, grabbing at his leg. He looked down to see Will, lying on the ground beside him, looking up at him in desperation and crying in fear.

"I can't go on . . . I can't!" he sobbed.

"You've got to! Get up!" Jack yelled. "You can't stay here! Get up!"

But Will continued to sob, hiding his face, and Jack pulled himself free and ran on. Shells tore through the air overhead, one dropping short and bursting near Jack; the shock wave sent him staggering, earth spraying into his face. He was surprised to find himself unhurt, but something had gone terribly wrong – he was already passing dead men lying sprawled, could already hear the cries of the wounded. The haze was clearing ahead, and he caught his breath with a sob of amazement – the line ahead, already thinned out, was being felled like targets at a fairground shooting booth, man after man throwing up his arms and collapsing, six, seven, eight of them with one burst of machine-gun fire. A body lay near Jack with a deep bloodstain over the shoulder and back of the tunic, pack ripped open and spilling its contents over the ground – a crumpled shirt, mess-tin, clasp-knife; the details struck him with incongruous clarity.

"It can't be happening," he thought. "It can't be allowed to happen . . . the Germans are supposed to be dead . . ."

It was madness, they were being sent to certain death, running on towards the sheets of fire to take the place of the men ahead. He waited for the hail of bullets which must surely end his life at any second. He felt curiously unafraid. Every aspect of his life, everything he had done and everything he would have done in the future, was concentrated here in this maelstrom, about to be randomly extinguished. For a strange moment he felt as if he were watching himself, taking no more than passing interest in his fate. He heard Philip Morland shouting, trying to keep the men together. Two figures moved ahead of him like ghosts in the haze; there was a sudden shell-burst, a spattering of earth, and then nothing where the two men had been. He stared with horrified fascination.

"But I'm still alive," Jack thought. "Perhaps I'll be dead soon, and then I won't have to go any further . . ."

God only knew what lay ahead. The plan had obviously failed – he couldn't believe that he was going to walk calmly through the German wire and into a trench. Where was everyone? He could only see a few yards through the miasma; he could still hear Philip shouting, but could see none of the men who had been with him when he started – they were all spread out, or else dead. Bullets were zinging past him, one almost brushing his cheek. "Perhaps I'm dead already," he thought, "that's why nothing's hitting me." He was beginning to feel a strange sense of invulnerability; to have got this far unscathed seemed nothing short of miraculous. He had no idea how long he had been out there, it could have been min-utes or hours; the normal passage of time seemed completely irrelevant in this limbo world. He caught a glimpse of Jimmy over to his right, shouting something . . . He heard the *pit, pit* of rifle bullets thudding into the earth close to him, and there was just time to dodge to one side before another shell-burst lifted him off his feet and sent him sprawling. Earth showered over him again, and a fragment tore through the sleeve of his tunic; he felt a sharp pain in his arm, and a warm trickle. He had bitten his tongue too, he could taste the salt of blood in his mouth . . . but blood was everywhere, seeping into the grass where he lay, from men, and bits of men . . . "That last shell got us all. I must be dead, or mad," he thought again, sure that no-one could be seeing what he saw, and still be sane. He got up again and staggered forward. The hail of fire seemed to have travelled past him now, leaving a fog of dust and darkness in its wake, but the German wire must be somewhere ahead, unless it had been completely destroyed. Someone with a blooded face appeared in front, pointing and shouting, Jack couldn't hear what.

Dark shapes were looming ahead, drab, tangled, sprawled shapes; it was the German wire, uncut, hung with the bodies of dead and dying men. Jack halted in disbelief, with a vivid mental picture of the river at home after a flood, when the trees on its edge were left with debris tangled in their branches after the water had subsided. This was the human debris, all that was left of the first wave . . .

His reactions were too slow by now to move him out of range as another shell screamed by. It exploded behind him, and the blast hit him like a wall. His legs were giving way, the weight of his pack dragging him down. The ground seemed to rush up and hit him in the face, and he sank into darkness.

He came to his senses hours later, still lying by the wire in a warm, comfortable stupor, the furore still going on all around him but not seeming to affect him. He realized that he must have passed out – how long ago? But might as well go on lying there, he thought, a new wave of dizziness passing over him as he returned to consciousness; there seemed to be nothing else to do. He sank gratefully back into oblivion, and came to again to find someone shaking him and lifting him into a half-sitting position.

"Can you get back? Can you walk?"

Jack looked up groggily at the person helping him, and thought vaguely that he looked rather like Stephen, except that his face was bloody and begrimed, with bloodshot eyes looking wildly at him. He lurched to his feet and was promptly sick. His arm was stiff and sticky with dried blood, and he felt weak with shock and exhaustion. He must be injured, he supposed, remembering the shell that had knocked him over.

"But I'm still not dead," he realized with surprise.

"What time is it?" he asked when he had recovered slightly.

"It must be afternoon," Stephen said. "We're to make our way back with the wounded."

"What's happened to the others?"

"Some of them got through further to the right flank. Dick was killed ... and I saw Harry badly wounded ... Mr Morland was with Jimmy and some of the rest, but that was a long time ago."

Jack tried to walk, still sick with dizziness. With Stephen supporting him, he began to stumble slowly towards a group of wounded men further back, some of whom were crying out for help. The ground was littered with heaps of khaki, the shattered wreckage of men, like jetsam after a high tide.

"Oh, Jesus Christ, this isn't war, it's a bloody massacre," Stephen said, on the verge of tears.

They made their way slowly across the strewn ground, clinging together like two crippled old men.

Reckoning

Assembling for roll-call, the survivors exchanged shocked glances as they realized for the first time how few of them there were.

"Lamb?"

"Dead, sir."

"Are you sure?"

"Saw him for definite, sir. Machine-gunned over by the German wire, one of the first to get there."

The company Sergeant-Major wrote down brief details before continuing. "Larkins?"

"Badly wounded, sir. Taken to the Aid Post."

"Lawson?"

"Dead, sir."

It was a long, slow procedure, not because of the numbers of men present but because of the difficulty in establishing what had happened to those absent. The calling of some names produced conflicting reports, and the fates of their owners were discussed and argued over for several minutes; other names brought forth no response at all. Jack knew that, of his immediate friends, Dick Twyford and Ted Briggs had both been killed; Harry and Jimmy had been wounded, Harry seriously; Stephen, like Jack, had received superficial flesh wounds; Charlie and Philip Morland had both escaped without a scratch between them. No-one knew what had happened to Will, and Corporal Woolmer was also unaccounted for.

But these losses were slight compared with those of A and C Companies, of which only two officers and sixty men remained. Stretcher parties were still bringing in the wounded who lay out in No-Man's-Land, and battle was continuing along the forty-mile front. Jack, sent to the Aid Post to have his wounded arm dressed, had missed the renewed assault in which Jimmy had been injured. God Almighty, what must it have been like, he wondered, going out there for a second time, knowing what to expect?

The men around him looked as he felt, grey-faced and dull-eyed, faces emotionless. He listened without reaction as the deaths of Dick and Ted were reported. It was like the anaesthetized feeling he had experienced when out there under fire; his brain had absorbed too much to be able to cope with any more, and refused to acknowledge that two of his friends since childhood were dead.

They were taken back to a camp near Albert, on a ridge looking over the red-brick town, whose most notable feature was an ornate basilica with a tower surmounted by a huge gilt statue of the Virgin and Child. But the tower had been battered by shells and the Virgin now hung over the town at a drunken angle, as if bowed in anguish at the destruction of her surroundings.

"The French say that when the Virgin falls, the war will end," Charlie told Jack.

"I wish she'd bloody well get on with it then."

From his vantage point, Jack could see various buildings smashed to rubble and tangled masses of girders, above which the crumbling tower seemed to offer a gesture of defiance. Roadways leading into the town petered out into heaps of dust and rubbish littered with the broken remains of vehicles. The ridge didn't seem to be a very safe place for the resting troops – if the town could be shelled, then so could the camp – but in his present benumbed state, Jack felt that this was hardly worth bothering about. "What does it matter?" he thought dully. "If I don't get killed here, I'll get killed some other time. Why worry about it?"

"Here, I've brought you some tea," Stephen said, handing

him a chipped enamel mug. "Are you sure you won't have any breakfast? You ought to."

"No, I can't eat yet. Thanks." Jack put the mug down beside him on the grass. When he picked it up again a few moments later, a fly was drowning in the lukewarm tea, unable to free itself by gaining a foothold on the slippery enamel. He watched the struggling creature dispassionately for a few moments before offering it a blade of grass as an escape route. Within seconds it was methodically rubbing its back legs against its wings to clean them, preparing for flight. Jack was struck by the contrast between the insect's will to live, and his present lack of concern for his own survival. What was the point in worrying, when he had seen in the attack that a man's life counted for less than a fly's?

"Come on, mate," Charlie told him. "We've got kit inspection in half an hour."

"Yes, I'm coming." But Jack sat on, staring at the ground.

His mood of silent withdrawal was shared by the other men in his tent. They said little, spending their free moments sitting about smoking, each thinking his own thoughts. There was nothing they could have said to each other to make any sense of the last few days.

Jack wrote a brief note to Alice to tell her he was safe, but could not bring himself to write any more than that. Later, he would have to write to tell her about Dick and Ted, a task he was not looking forward to. Jimmy, who had apparently been confident that his wound was a Blighty one, had departed with high hopes of a spell at home; it was the first time that he and Jack had been separated since joining up, apart from the odd leave. Even Jimmy's stoical good humour must have been dented by the events of July 1st, Jack thought, but missed him nevertheless. He spent his free time now with Stephen and Charlie, glad of Stephen's unassuming kindness and Charlie's quiet cynicism.

The gaps in the company were being filled by new drafts,

men who had been held in reserve. They arrived fresh and clean in new uniforms, keen, cheerful, unable to understand the sullen expressions on the faces of the battle-scarred troops, or the curt responses to their attempts at conversation. "I was like that not so long ago," Jack thought. It was as though there was a vast, uncrossable gulf between the new men and the experienced ones, a gulf which mere words could not begin to bridge.

Will Fletcher had been sent back from the Casualty Clearing Station, unwounded, but vague as to what had happened to him in the advance. Shortly after his return, Jack was summoned by Philip Morland when the parade was dismissed. Philip was obviously ill-at-ease and therefore at his most haughty and abrupt.

"Did you see anything of Fletcher during the attack?"

"Yes, sir. He was beside me at first and then I lost sight of him," Jack answered, with discretion rather than perfect truth.

"How far towards the wire had he gone when you last saw him?"

"I can't really remember, sir. It was all a bit confusing, but I think he was a good way towards the German wire."

Philip looked at him closely. "You are telling the truth?"

"Yes, sir."

"You know that cowardice under fire is a very serious offence."

"Yes, sir."

Philip said nothing for a moment, continuing to stare steadily as if Jack were the one suspected of desertion. "Well, I shall have to make further enquiries," he concluded.

Dismissed, Jack went back to his tent to tell Stephen and Charlie what had happened. "For God's sake, if he gets on to you, tell him you saw Will right up by the wire," he told them. "We don't want the little blighter court-martialled."

"Poor little sod," Charlie said. "He was frightened out of his wits for days before the attack."

"I suppose I'm lucky it's not me he's after," Jack said. "Anyone could lie down in a shell hole and then come back when everything's finished. Who's to know?"

Jack felt, unreasonably, a little annoyed that Philip had acquitted himself reasonably well in the attack – as well as anyone could have done under those conditions. Charlie, who had been with him for most of the time, said that he had gathered the men together and brought them back when it became obvious that progress was impossible.

"Even if it's right – what he suspects about Will – you'd think he could have overlooked it," Stephen said, "in all the general confusion. No-one needs to know."

Charlie blew out a cloud of cigarette smoke. "I can't help wondering how the poor bloke'll cope next time."

Next time – it was a prospect no-one was eager to consider, but they all knew it was inevitable; the Somme offensive was continuing, and as soon as their company was up to strength they would be thrown back in.

Meanwhile, normal life was beginning to reassert itself. The practicalities of eating, washing and shaving, marching and parading gradually diverted thoughts from contemplation of what had passed. Jack's wound healed quickly and without infection. The weather continued to be warm and summery, and some of the men had found a large pond among trees which they said was perfect for bathing. Jack, Stephen and Charlie went down to investigate, relishing the thought of being properly clean again. The water supply in camp was inadequate for more than a quick sluice down, and after their days at the front they felt positively encrusted with stale sweat and dirt. In the front line they were not allowed to take their boots off, and Jack often thought that the state of continuous filthiness was enough to drain the last reserves of men already tried beyond endurance.

The pool was in a sheltered spot, out of view of the nearby road and fringed with trees which cast a dappled shade on the water. A few men were already splashing about and calling to each other, and someone had improvised a diving-board.

"Looks glorious, doesn't it?" Stephen approved.

They stripped themselves of their clothes and spread them out to air in the sunshine. Jack followed Stephen down the shelving muddy bank into the water, gasping with the shock of its delicious coolness against his skin. He ducked his head under the surface and came up spluttering and shaking his wet hair like a spaniel. Charlie dived in from the board, belly-flopping and sending sheets of water spraying into the faces of the other two.

"Leave some for us!" Stephen called out.

Jack turned to float on his back, looking up at the blue, mackerel-cloud-flecked sky. He felt relaxed for the first time since the attack, as if the water were cleansing him mentally as well as physically. He was learning to live for the moment, not to think about what had happened yesterday, or what might happen tomorrow, or the day after tomorrow. For now, he was content to enjoy this interlude in pleasant surroundings, with friends whom he had come to regard with something very like love. He watched Stephen wading slowly out of the shallows and walking round through the long grass to the diving board. The men were accustomed to seeing each other naked and to making all the usual sort of jokes about each other's shortcomings or peculiarities, but now Jack watched Stephen's progress through the dappled shade, aware only of his beauty; his slight, well-proportioned body and animal grace reminded Jack of a lithe young thoroughbred. He was aware that even now a shell could come screaming through the still air, shattering the idyll and reducing all of them to bloody fragments. Stephen, poised on the edge of the diving board, saw Jack looking at him and smiled, and Jack turned away abruptly, suddenly visualizing the pale slender body mangled and mutilated like those he had seen in No-Man's-Land. The vision was so vivid that he felt all his previous enjoyment draining from the afternoon. He got out of the water and began drying himself on his dirty towel.

He sat on the bank watching the other two, and after a while Stephen came and sat beside him.

"Grand, isn't it?"

Jack nodded. Stephen began to towel his wet hair, and Jack again found his gaze drawn to his swift, sure movements. How beautifully the human body was made! He had never thought before what a work of art an arm was, every tendon, muscle and artery perfectly integrated into the pleasing over-all shape, the wrist elegantly articulated in movement. Jack felt an almost irresistible urge to reach out and stroke Stephen's shapely, golden-haired forearm. He scrambled hastily to his feet instead. "God Almighty, what's the matter with me?" he wondered.

"Are you all right?" Stephen asked, typically considerate. "Not feeling ill?"

Jack couldn't begin to put his feelings into words, even if he had wanted to do so, which he most assuredly did not. "I'm fine, thanks," he said. "I think I'll go back in the water for a bit."

He dived off the board and swam across the pool with vigorous, clumsy strokes, joining Charlie and the other men, who were noisily engaged in a boisterous water-fight.

Some Other War

"Let's go out to the park this afternoon," Margaret suggested to Alice as they went off duty. "We won't get much time off once the convoys start arriving."

There was really little to do apart from wait – the ward was empty, the long rows of beds made up in ominous readiness for the convoys which would be arriving shortly. Newspaper bill-boards were already announcing VICTORY ON THE SOMME, but everyone at the hospital knew that victories were hard-earned.

The first wounded began to arrive on July 4th. Later, Alice read about the huge crowds which had gathered outside Charing Cross in those first days, buying flowers to throw in at the open ambulance doors, shouting congratulations at the wounded men. But the hot days wore on, and still the casualties arrived. More and more stretchers were carried in to the hospital; every bed was taken, every hut pressed into service. The Casualty Clearing Stations and base hospitals in France were so crowded that huge numbers of men were simply passed on to the next stage, and many arrived in London filthy with trench mud, and still with their first hastily-applied dressings.

Alice worked without a break for two weeks, often being called out at night to greet yet another convoy. She was amazed to find that she could be so exhausted yet somehow keep going until, retiring to her room at night, she hardly found the strength to get undressed for bed. She was too tired to weep for the men, for the procession of disfigured humanity which passed before her during waking hours and continued to do so in dreams. Remembering her early disapproval of the detached manner of trained nurses, she now saw that it was the only way to keep going. With so many new patients arriving and urgently needing attention, she simply couldn't afford time to consider her own feelings, which seemed less and less relevant.

She was immensely grateful to receive Jack's brief letter assuring her that he had come through. She was not sure whether Edward had even been involved in the fighting on the Somme until at last she received a short note from him dated July 7th:

"Wounded in head, not too serious, hope to be sent to England."

"Edward's wounded, and coming home!" she told Margaret, passing her on the ward.

It seemed awful to be so overjoyed that he was wounded, but at least he was safe. The relief of knowing that neither he nor Jack was among the worst casualties made her forget her tired limbs and sore feet, and she went off to wash dressing-trays feeling positively energetic.

Shortly afterwards, Dr Sidgwick wrote to tell her that Edward was in the 3rd London General Hospital at Wandsworth, and she went to see him there as soon as she could be spared from her duties. It felt odd to be walking into a ward in a strange part of London, only to find everything so familiar – the neat rows of beds, the men with bandaged heads, several with stumps instead of limbs, pyjama arms and legs pinned and folded over nothing . . . These unknown men aroused the pity which her duties usually suppressed into dormancy. Thank God Edward wasn't so badly off, she thought, searching for his face among the row of beds.

A very young-looking VAD nurse pointed him out. He was dozing, propped up in a half-sitting position, but woke when she touched his hand, his eyes focusing slowly on her face.

"Alice! I must be dreaming . . . oh, come here and let me look at you properly . . ."

She bent to embrace him, feeling his warm arms round her, and his lips against her cheek. "Oh, I'm so glad you're here," she mumbled into his shoulder. They drew apart, conscious of the interested gazes of the other patients, and she sat on a chair beside Edward's bed, holding his hand and stroking his thin fingers.

He looked at her for a long time without speaking, then said, "You look dreadfully tired – I'm sure you're working too hard . . . Have you heard from Jack – is he all right?"

"Yes, he is. He was slightly wounded in the first day of the fighting, but not at all seriously. But two of his friends from the village were killed, and others badly injured . . ."

She told Edward the contents of Jack's latest letter, not sure whether or not this was wise. He was saddened by the news of Ted Briggs and Dick, both of whom were village acquaintances. While she talked, Alice assessed his condition. His head was heavily bandaged, with none of his dark hair showing; she guessed that his injury was less trivial than he had led her to believe. His face looked tired and strained, and there were dark rings under his eyes, but he assured her that he was recovering well.

"I shall have a scar, they tell me, but the hair will grow to hide it."

"How did it happen?" she asked hesitantly. She was not sure whether it was wise to ask, remembering his previous reticence.

But Edward was more forthcoming this time, launching into a detailed account. "Well, luckily for me, my battalion was kept in reserve on July 1st, but they sent us out a few days later to Mametz Wood," he told her. "It was sheer madness. The wood was full of Germans with machine-gun posts; they had a clear view all around, and we knew we'd be mown down on the open ground before we got anywhere near the place. There had already been two attempts that day, and both had been forced back. We were waiting to attack in this sort of dried-up river bed – the only bit of cover between us and the wood, and you could hear the machine-gun bullets flying overhead and all around. We would have been dead men as soon as we left the ravine, and we were sure the Germans would soon realize where we were waiting, and send some shells over . . ."

He gave the impression that this was all more or less as expected, but the unusual feature of the episode had been that a Brigadier-General had gone up with the men to see the terrain for himself. "He said it was sheer lunacy, and he'd been trying to get the plan changed, because we'd have done much better to attack the wood under cover of darkness. We'd been told to advance again in twenty minutes . . ." He told her how the Brigadier had tried to get the advance called off, getting through to Division on a signaller's telephone, and from all accounts having a heated argument, eventually getting permission for the troops to retreat. "But he left us saying that it would be the end of his career. 'They want butchers, not brigadiers,' he said. I'll always remember that. The men are beginning to hate the staff more than they hate the Germans, but this was one who saw things from our point of view. I wish there were more like him," Edward finished. "I certainly owe my life to him – if he hadn't been there, we'd have been told to go ahead according to plan, and we'd have been wiped out."

"It's appalling, sending men in against all odds!" Alice said. "Surely there must be some alternative? But you still haven't told me how you were injured."

"Oh, just hit by flying shrapnel while we were getting the men out of the ravine. They'd started shelling by then. Luckily, I didn't have to walk far to the Aid Post, and I was taken straight down to the Casualty Clearing Station. But I'm lucky to be out of it. It sickens me to come back here and find the newspapers reporting victories, and people talking about giving the Kaiser a punch on the nose. It's different for you, working in a hospital and seeing the truth, but most people can't begin to understand what it's like out there."

Alice nodded in agreement. On her way to the hospital she had passed a column of new troops bound for the boat train; they had looked as eager as those of 1914, and pedestrians in the street had clapped and cheered them, and shouted out "Give Jerry one from me" and "Send 'em packing" just as they had two years ago.

"I couldn't even talk to my own parents about it, when they came to visit me," Edward continued. "There's no way of communicating – it's like coming back from the grave . . ." He was clearly worn out with the effort of talking, his eyelids drooping over dull eyes.

"Shh! You're tiring yourself," Alice said. "You should rest now."

But Edward carried on, "It isn't their fault. As far as the public and the newspapers are concerned, it's all heroism and derring-do, running the straight race and putting the foe to flight. It's as if the reality we know about – the bungled decisions, and the maiming and disfigurement, and the hopeless slaughter – all that, belongs to some other war . . ."

In the Apple Orchard

The harvest was half-over in the Greenstocks fields; the sheaves of corn were piled into stooks, casting long shadows across the stubble. The scene brought Jack vivid memories of scatched hands and thighs, the warm smell of ripe wheat grains, and the taste of cider drunk in the shade of the hedgerow. It was three years since he had worked on the harvest, he thought as he walked the last half-mile into the village. He wondered who was doing the harvesting this year, with nearly all the village men gone; the thought reminded him that he would have to visit Ted's and Dick's parents, an uninviting duty which he was not at all sure how to handle.

He made his way to Emily's house, where he would be staying, embarrassed to find himself greeted as a returning hero – Mrs Smallwood was in tears, Emily saying over and over again how proud she was of him, Sammy asking whether he had killed any Huns. Tom was still in training camp, and was expected to go out to the Front any day now. Jack hoped for Emily's sake that he would be sent anywhere than the Somme region, where the same battle-scarred land had been fought over for over two and a half dreary months.

The emotional greetings over, Jack found it strange to have time on his hands. On the first day of his leave he went to visit Jimmy in the Braintree VAD hospital, finding him in good spirits and on friendly terms with the prettiest of the nurses. His leg wound had become infected at first but was now responding to treatment.

"Timed it to perfection, I have," he said proudly. "Just bad enough to keep me at home for another month or three, by which time I hope you'll all have seen the last of the god-damned Somme. Give the old place my love if you get back there."

Jack told him the latest news of the platoon, and about Will's blue funk, and Philip Morland's suspicions.

"Poor kid's not cut out to be a soldier," Jimmy said. "If we ever have to do another show like that one, the kindest thing to do would be to put a bullet through his head."

"That goes for all of us, doesn't it?"

"You know," Jimmy said thoughtfully, "I reckon His Royal Highness might turn out to be windy after another stunt or two."

"You mean Philip?"

Jimmy nodded. "He did all right last time – I was with him the second time we went out – but I don't think it'll take much for him to crack up."

"Depends what you mean by windy. Aren't we all windy? I mean, how many shows do you think you can take, or anyone else for that matter?"

"Oh, well." Jimmy shrugged, tiring of the subject. "He came in to see me a couple of weeks ago, when he was home on leave."

"*Philip* did?" Jack repeated in amazement. "What on earth did you talk about?"

"Oh, this and that. He didn't stay long. I suppose he thought he ought to make the effort, as he was at home. I'd have preferred it if he'd brought his sister – she's a right classy piece." Jimmy yawned and stretched, and asked, "You didn't bring me any fags, I suppose?"

"Yes, I did. Here you are, you old scrounger."

"Thanks, mate. Got any matches?"

"Here." Jack produced a box from his pocket and handed them over. "You're allowed to smoke in here, then?"

Jimmy lit up and inhaled, offering the packet to Jack. "Home from home it is in here, I can tell you. Matter of fact it's a bloody sight more cheerful than it is at home at the moment, I reckon. You heard about Albert, Albert Johnson I mean, who was going to marry our Rosie?"

"Yes. Poor Rosie. She's taking it bad, then?"

"Mm." They smoked in silence for a few moments, and then Jimmy said, "What are you going to do with yourself then, while you're at home?"

"Dunno really. I ought to go and see Dick's parents, and Ted's. I'm not looking forward to that much."

"Going to see anything of Harriet?"

"I dunno. I heard she was seeing some other bloke."

"You mean that Franks bloke, who was working at Marconi's? He's at the front now, Rosie says."

Jack thought over this information on the bus journey home. Later, he went round to Greenstocks hoping to see Sedley, and found him out in the fields, embittered at having to work the farm horses. "Can't get farm staff for love nor money," he told Jack. "All you can get is women or Hun prisoners. I don't mind the women so much, but Huns is another thing. None of the farmers round here have taken any on yet, but they might have to, the way things are."

Jack would have liked the chance of exercising a horse, but there were none left at Greenstocks apart from the Shires, and Miss Madeleine's grey mare, which was in foal. He went to look at the stables for old time's sake, finding them neglected and untidy, with moss growing on the tiled roofs and thistles going to seed round the edges of the yard. A thin, scurfy cat miaowed at him from its perch on the water-trough.

"You're looking for young Harriet, I suppose," Sedley told him as he returned along the farm track. "She don't work here no more. She's over at the vegetable farm by Martlets crossroads."

Jack decided to get his duty visits over with before he sought out Harriet. That evening, he went to see Ted's parents and Dick's widowed mother, and gave them a somewhat embroidered version of the truth, which he thought would please them. They were all pitifully grateful for these small grains of comfort. Dick's mother wept copiously, embarrassing Jack, who had no idea how to cope with such outbursts of emotion. "Thank God he died as he wanted, doing his bit in a great battle," she sobbed. Jack, knowing full well that Dick had been shot dead within seconds of climbing over the parapet and had never even seen a German, agreed. He left at last, mightily glad to put these visits behind him. He thought that he really ought to go and see Rosie Taplin, and Harry's parents, but felt reluctant to bring himself into contact with any more grief.

Next day he went to see Harriet at Martlets Farm. He found her digging carrots, rather dashingly dressed in a blue pinafore, leggings and a straw hat. She greeted him with surprise, apparently pleased to see him.

"How do you like the work?" he asked. "You look very well on it, I must say."

"It's all right. Better than skivvying, at any rate. I'm not so keen on the muck-spreading –" She looked up at him, laughing. Her fair skin was lightly tanned, and she had a dusting of freckles over her nose. "You can stay and help a bit, if you like. It's nearly time for my dinner-break."

"All right."

Harriet fetched a spare fork, and they worked companionably for a while. Jack was glad to be doing something purposeful. The orderliness of the vegetable plots reminded him of the old days at Greenstocks; all Harriet's work, he supposed, looking at the well-weeded rows of carrots and peas, and the runner-beans trained neatly up sticks, with a few scarlet flowers remaining and the young beans plumping up, almost ready to be picked. The carrot plants were a fresh, delicate green, with feathery tops and greenish-white flowers, like cow parsley. The damp soil yielded easily, each forkful producing several sweet-smelling carrots, which they gathered up into sacks. While they worked, they exchanged gossip about people in the village and in Jack's platoon.

"And I wrote to you that Philip Morland is my platoon officer, didn't I?"

"Oh, yes." Harriet turned away to shake clods of earth from her fork.

"Jimmy said he was home on leave recently."

"Yes, I know. I saw him." She was blushing slightly, and Jack remembered that she had once had a liking for Philip – but surely she must have got over that by now, he thought? Nothing was likely to come of it, that much was certain. From what Jack had heard, she had other fish to fry.

"Do you ever see anything of that George Franks, these days?" he asked casually.

Harriet laughed, straightening up from her digging and pushing a loose strand of hair under her hat. "Not any more. I didn't know you knew about that."

"Oh, just village gossip."

She gave him a sidelong glance. "I'll meet you after work, if you're not doing anything."

"Yes, I'd like that."

Harriet went into the farmhouse for her dinner-break, and Jack went back to Emily's. Afterwards, he went out into the fields and coverts, to visit some of his old haunts. It was a mild September afternoon, with the hills and woods receding into blueness in the distance, the sun hazy through thin cloud. Some of the trees were already beginning to turn, showing the first flushes of gold and bronze; elderberries were ripening in the hedgerows, glossy black on wine-red stems. Walking along the ridge of Hill Spinney, by the edge of the wood, Jack began to feel uneasy, exposed. He couldn't help scanning the landscape, noting where a sniper might be concealed or a machine-gun post mounted, and half-expecting an abrupt burst of rifle fire from the wood. "Don't be so stupid," he told himself impatiently. But logic would not prevail, and he couldn't rid himself of the feeling of threat. He stuck to his planned route doggedly, but was glad to get back to the village.

He went to meet Harriet from work. The sun was setting in a glowing sky, with the scattered clouds purplish against the light and the trees bordering the lane thrown into silhouette. Harriet was waiting by the farm gate, smoking a cigarette, rather to Jack's surprise. She grinned at him as he approached, linking her arm through his and laughing at his obvious disapproval.

"Don't look so shocked. You smoke, don't you?"

"Yes, but I can't get used to the sight of women doing it."

"Why not?" Harriet took a long drag and blew an expert series of smoke rings. "Can you do that?"

"Here, let me try"

She giggled at his attempts. "No, look, you've got to hold your mouth like this . . . and breathe out like this . . . That's better! What do you want to do? Shall we go up to the Hardwick Arms?"

"To the pub? Have you been in there before?"

"Lots of times, with the other girls who work on the farm. My parents don't like it, but why shouldn't we? We work as hard as the men, and earn our own money. We're entitled to our pleasures, same as they are."

She was deliberately shocking him with her worldliness, Jack knew, wanting to demonstrate her new independence and modernity. "Let's walk for a bit first," he said, taking her arm again. "We can go to the pub later, if you want to."

They walked slowly along the lane between the orchards, where small unripe apples were already falling into the grass, and a thrush sang, hidden among the leaves. The warm air, moved by the lightest of breezes, carried with it the scent of the harvested fields. When they had walked out of sight of the farmhouse, Harriet slowed her pace and pulled Jack round to face her.

"Have you missed me, Jack?" she asked softly.

"You know I have. But you . . . you don't write to me . . ."

"I'm no good at writing letters. But I've thought about you, Jack, all the time."

She was teasing him again, taunting him. He knew she was lying. "Oh, yes? What about George Franks? Do you think about him all the time as well?"

"Don't be moody, Jack. That was just to pass the time while you weren't here. He's not like you. I don't see him any more, anyway." She looked up into his face, twining her arm round his neck; her intentions were obvious. "Jack . . .?"

He bent and kissed her, half-reluctantly. He could smell cigarette smoke on her breath, but her lips were soft, parting under his. Her straw hat slipped back and fell to the ground, and he rested his face in her smooth scented hair; his arms crept round her and tightened, drawing her slim body close to his. "Oh, Harriet . . ." he murmured. Her fingers were in his hair, caressing the back of his neck with a practised touch, sending delicious sensations tingling through his body. It was a relief to let his physical responses take over, and to put aside any doubts he may have had as to her motives.

Suddenly she pulled away, taking him by the hand and leading him a few yards further on, to an open gate into the orchard. Behind the thick hedge, she drew close to him and looked into his face, her eyes soft and inviting. His senses quickened. He bent to kiss her again; she put a finger to his lips, and began to pull off his jacket and to undo the buttons of his shirt, slipping her hand inside against his skin. His blood beat up with insistent urgency. He pulled her to the ground beside him, exploring the fastenings of her garments, and kissed her fiercely while the shadows faded in the growing dusk.

Hospital Visit

"I'm glad you've found time to meet me before you go back," Alice told Jack. "Edward will be so pleased to see you."

"You look as if you could do with a break, yourself," he said, noticing how tired she looked. "You must be working much too hard." He couldn't help thinking of the contrast with Harriet's glowing outdoor healthiness. Alice had met him at Liverpool Street Station, and they had exchanged belated birthday presents, not having seen each other since their birthday in August. They were twenty now, though Jack thought Alice looked older. She was wearing a dark-blue skirt and jacket and a white high-necked blouse, and had dressed her hair in a way that made her look more sophisticated than he remembered. Her pale face was thin and serious, but fatigue lent her a sort of grave beauty.

"Oh, I'm all right," Alice said. "I'm hoping to go out to France myself, soon. I've applied for a transfer to one of the base hospitals. You must have had a good rest, anyway. You look really fit and well."

He agreed, not telling her the real reason for his renewed vitality. The interlude with Harriet had given him a much-needed boost, putting aside the doubts which had worried him since the swimming-party with Stephen; even the prospect of returning to the front could not dim his optimism, and he was looking forward to seeing his friends again.

This mood was somewhat subdued when he entered the surgical ward in the Wandsworth Hospital, and saw the rows of men with their bandaged wounds and amputated limbs. He felt almost ashamed to be so obviously fit and healthy in their midst. This aspect of war was unfamiliar to him – he was accustomed to seeing dead men, and casualties being carried away on stretchers, but had not till now been brought face-to-face with the longer-term effects of injury. It was only luck, he thought, that he wasn't lying there with a pinned sleeve where his arm should be, or with half his face missing.

"What will these poor blighters do after the war?" he wondered.

It was very different from the ward Jimmy had been in, with the men teasing each other, smoking and laughing. There was a gramophone playing, but through the music Jack could hear the continuous groaning of a man who lay with his entire chest and abdomen wrapped in bandages. He wondered how Alice could stand it, working in a ward like this one. For his part, he'd rather be in the front line. Surely Edward couldn't be in such a dire state as some of these men? Alice had said he was recovering well, and was expecting to be sent out to a convalescent hospital very soon.

They found him sitting in an armchair reading, dressed in blue convalescent uniform, with his head lightly bandaged. He stood up to kiss Alice and shake hands warmly with Jack. It was the first time they had met since joining up, more than two years ago, and Jack looked at Edward with interest, realizing that they would soon be brothers-in-law. It was an odd thought; Jack couldn't imagine his mother having the Sidgwicks round for tea, or himself being invited to a dinner-party with the doctor and his family. For Alice, with her intelligence and self-education, the social adjustment wouldn't be so difficult; she already seemed to have left the kitchen and scullery of Greenstocks far behind. It would have been far stranger if she were going to marry Philip Morland – "perish the thought," Jack thought. Edward, for all his public-school background and perfect manners, was a good sort, and well-suited to Alice. He asked Jack a lot of questions about his experiences, and told them some funny anecdotes, which Jack countered with some of his own. It turned out that they had been to some of the same towns and villages in France, and they gave each other tips about the best pastry shop in Béthune and where supplies of chocolate could be found in Albert. Jack knew perfectly well that officers had access to all sorts of places barred to the other ranks, but he appreciated Edward's tact in treating him as an equal.

"Did Alice tell you she's applied to go out to France?" Edward asked Jack, who nodded. "I wish we could persuade her not to go."

"But I'm hoping to go to the same hospital as Lorna," Alice said, "and that would make up for a lot."

"Yes. But you know what it was like for Lorna, at first — living in a tent, all through the winter, sloshing about in mud —"

"It sounds as bad as the trenches," Jack said.

"But I really do want to go," Alice said firmly. "It's where nurses are most urgently needed now, and Lorna says the conditions have improved recently. Please don't worry, Edward."

Realizing that it was almost time to leave, Jack decided to withdraw tactfully to allow Edward and Alice a few moments alone together.

"Good luck then, if you get out to the front again," he told Edward.

"Thank you — and you too," Edward said. "It was kind of you to find time to come in. I know how quickly time goes when you're on leave. Well, good-bye, till we meet again."

How long would that be, Jack wondered? He thought of all that had happened since the last time the three of them had met; they were different people now, changed by their experiences. He glanced back superstitiously. Edward was holding Alice's hand, and gazing at her in such a way that Jack felt he was intruding into a moment of intimacy simply by looking at them; Alice's eyes were soft with tenderness, her face beautiful in the dim light of the ward. Jack turned away, feeling both touched and excluded by what he had seen, knowing that what he had shared with Harriet had been nothing like this. He wondered briefly whether Edward and Alice had ever been lovers in the physical sense; he supposed not, Edward was too much of a gentleman to risk compromising Alice in that way, especially under the present circumstances, when any love affair could be briskly and brutally terminated.

One thing Jack was sure of – he could not imagine Alice smoking, or drinking in a public house.

Through the Wire

Jack rejoined his company, finding his friends out of the line and billeted in a school-house in Albert, but resentful and full of complaints.

"Parades in the day and working parties all night – when are we expected to sleep?"

"Two hours compulsory sleep in the afternoon, only you're kept awake by other companies parading outside – Sergeant-Majors screaming fit to wake the dead –"

"As bad as being in the front line, it is."

"You're right there, Victoria," Charlie said.

"*Victoria?*" Jack repeated. The small dark-haired man thus addressed was new to the platoon, evidently having arrived during Jack's absence.

"His surname's Cross, so of course we call him Victoria," Stephen explained. "I don't think anyone knows what his real name is."

"It's Archibald," the new man said, grinning. "I reckon I prefer Victoria."

Jack soon found out that Philip Morland had added to his unpopularity by forbidding the men to play Crown and Anchor, the popular gambling game with which they passed their spare time.

"Told me to send anyone found playing it to the orderly room," Charlie said bitterly. "Course we all know it's official-ly banned anyway, but I wouldn't mind betting he's the only officer who won't turn a blind eye."

"And we're not to call Charlie by his first name, now he's Lance-Jack," Stephen said. "Mr Morland's instructions. He won't tolerate such familiarity," he added in a reasonable imitation of Philip's clipped accent.

"It's all right for him," Victoria said. "He's got his home comforts nicely laid on."

"What do you mean?" Jack asked.

"Billeted with a young French widow – him and Mr Rowley. Husband a Corporal in the French army, killed in '14. She's a nice bit of officer's rations if ever I saw one. He's got a cushy one there all right."

According to rumours passed on by Philip Morland's batman, Charlie said, Philip was occasionally having his meals prepared by the attractive widow instead of dining in the B Company Officers' mess, and was receiving other favours besides.

"Lucky blighter," another man joined in. "Wouldn't mind being in his shoes. You want to apply for a commission, Charlie – get your share."

"You forget I'm a married man," Charlie said with dignity.

Jack found himself a spare bed and began putting out his few belongings, thinking about this latest gossip. He found it hard to reconcile the idea of amorous philanderings with Philip's rigidly formal manner in his dealings with the men.

"You know what I found out on leave," he told Stephen as they cleaned their boots ready for parade. "When His Highness first came out, I sent my sister a letter telling her all about him – she already knew him from home, and knows I can't stand him. Anyway, I can't remember what I put now, except I know it wasn't very polite. Well, she told me that the letter had been half crossed-out by the censor, not that bit, but all the place-names and whatnot. It only struck me then that it could have been him doing the censoring. It never crossed my mind at the time."

Stephen gave a hoot of laughter. "Knowing your luck, it would be. You can't seem to do anything right where he's concerned. But surely he would have said something about it, or crossed out all that as well. It was most likely some other officer."

"Well, I suppose it won't do him any harm to know what we think of him," Jack said. "Except it won't make life any easier for me."

"I shouldn't worry about it," Stephen said. "Just be careful what you write in future. My folks got a letter from me that had been so mucked about with, all it said was *'Dear Ma and Sarah, hope you are well, love Stephen.'*"

During the next few weeks, as the days shortened into winter, the men resigned themselves to a routine of slogging up to the line and back with duckboards or frames or ammunition, enlivened from time to time by the bursts of shelling which too often made these trips hazardous. The trenches were in a bad state, having been lived in and constantly bombarded since July 1st, and the job of repairing them and pumping out the muddy water seemed endless. The lush, pleasant landscape of early June already seemed a lifetime away, Jack thought, growing accustomed to his present surroundings of expanses of mud, denuded stumps of trees, shattered dugouts and piles of rubble, and the remains of civilization behind the line – shelled cottages with their inside walls exposed and contents spilling out, gardens reduced to craters, a narrow stretch of railway line smashed and disused, a church standing defiantly among the ruins. It seemed impossible that spring and summer could ever return to this desolate country.

In December, after a short spell away from the line, B Company returned to the front to relieve men who looked more haggard and exhausted than any Jack had seen before. "Good luck, mate – you'll need it," one of them remarked cynically, passing him in the communication trench. A sleety rain was already falling, and continued to do so for the next day and a half. It was impossible to stay dry in the front line or to find anywhere to sleep untroubled by dripping water or crawling rats, or out of hearing of the whizzbangs which hurtled overhead with nerve-shattering regularity.

"Well," Stephen said with an attempt at cheerfulness, "at

least, if it gets any colder, it'll turn to snow. That'll be better than this wet."

"Oh, shut up, Cartwright," Victoria said amiably. "Remember last winter? Like playing at bloody Eskimos."

The men were huddled dismally in a dugout shrouded in groundsheet-capes, waiting for their mess-tin to boil for some tea. A tread sounded in the doorway, and Stephen, who was facing the opening, stood up and saluted. The others followed suit as Philip Morland came in, followed by Sergeant Jones.

He looked round at the group in the dugout. "I want some volunteers for a trench raid tomorrow night. Instructions from Battalion Headquarters. Would anyone like to volunteer? If not I'll have to pick five men." His gaze passed over Will Fletcher and Victoria and rested for a moment on Jack, as if offering a challenge.

"I'll go, sir," Jack said promptly. He wasn't going to have Philip Morland thinking he was windy.

"And me, sir," Stephen said.

"Good man, Cartwright. Anyone else?"

The others were looking down at the ground, not wanting to bring themselves to his attention.

"Very well, I'll see if anyone else is willing, and if not I'll be back."

Jack turned on Stephen as soon as Philip had gone. "What the bloody hell did you say you'd go for?"

Stephen looked startled. "Same reason as you, I suppose. Mind you, they could have waited for a spell of better weather. I suppose the staff up at Battalion HQ are sitting in their nice cosy dugout with a map and a pencil and paper and glasses of whisky, thinking it's time for a bit of entertainment."

"I'm surprised His Royal Highness hasn't managed to get himself out of it," Jack said. "He ought to stick to what he's best at." He couldn't resist giving the others the benefit of his updated impersonation, strutting and standing to attention in woodenly exaggerated mimicry. He looked the men up and down and stiffened his face in an expression of severe disapproval. "You, Private Fletcher," he barked, "your hair's at *least* a tenth of an inch too long – get it seen to at once. Private Cartwright, your sewing thread is two shades lighter than the regulation khaki – you're a disgrace to the regiment. Lance Corporal Jenkins, have you been permitting these men to enjoy themselves? Don't let me hear of such an outrageous thing again. Men of the 3rd Epping Foresters are not here to enjoy themselves. Any man showing signs of enjoying himself will be given two days' field punishment."

He was so absorbed in his performance that it took him a few seconds to realize that the delighted laughter of the other men was dying away, and that Stephen was looking at the entrance, his eyes wide and face horrified. Dropping his pose abruptly, Jack glanced round. Philip Morland was standing in the curtained doorway, staring at him with the expression of cold disdain Jack had caught so perfectly.

"God Almighty, I've done it again," Jack thought, his high spirits fading abruptly. "Why am I such a bloody idiot?" There was a long pause, during which all the men in the dugout seemed frozen into immobility.

Then a shell salvo whined overhead, breaking the silence. Philip said quietly, "Cartwright, Smallwood, report to Captain Snell, now, with Sergeant Jones. There's to be a briefing on the raid."

Following Philip out through the low doorway, Stephen turned and caught Jack's eye, letting out his breath and shaking his head slowly in disbelief. Jack grimaced back and mimed cutting his throat with the edge of one hand. He let the sacking curtain fall behind him, already hearing the renewed, stifled laughter of Will and the others.

At two a.m. next night, Jack was waiting in the support trench trying to calm the now-familiar cramp of fear in his stomach. He wished he had time to dash around to the latrine again, but it was too late for that now; he'd have to wait till he got back ... *if* he got back ... The men had had a swig of whisky each, and he could still taste the fiery warmth in his mouth, but it was doing little to steady his nerves. The twenty-minute bombardment was beginning, concentrating on the stretch of German trench where, if all went according to plan, Jack and the other twenty men would shortly be arriving ... "*If* the wire's been cut this time," he thought. "God, why did I *offer* to do this?" It was far too late to change his mind, even if such dithering would have been tolerated for one moment; the trench was packed with men – half from A Company, half from B – carrying rifles, bags of Mills bombs and Very lights. The howitzers and 18-pounders behind were ready to renew the bombardment on the opposite trenches as soon as the raiding party sent up a signal to indicate that they were retiring. Sergeant Jones was giving his group some last-minute reminders: "Remember, no one is to turn back, C.O.'s instructions." An icy sleet was falling, soaking Jack's woollen gloves and the balaclava he wore under his helmet. It would be like porridge in No-Man's-Land, he thought, shifting his weight nervously from one foot to the other, feeling the suction of wet mud under his boots. Philip Morland, who was commanding the whole party, stood with one foot on the ladder, looking at the luminous dial of his watch.

It was time to go. Philip led the way up the ladder and through a gap in the wire. The two groups split up, each led by its own Sergeant, making for separate gaps. Jack was through, Stephen slightly in front of him. No-Man's-Land was a gluey morass, pitted with water-filled shell craters and littered with the débris of war – old boxes, loose strands of wire, bits of shells, bits of bodies too, most likely, Jack thought, trying not to think what might be under his feet. A machine-gun rattled to the left; the crump of the heavy guns boomed – just the normal sounds of night-time at the front, nothing to indicate that the Germans opposite had seen them ... They squelched on, finding themselves at the German wire at last, locating a gap – it was cut then, for once, Jack thought, relieved that he wasn't going to die hung on the wire like the men he had seen on July 1st, but now there was nothing to stop him from reaching the trench ahead. The men filtered through and spread out again, Philip Morland slightly ahead of Jack, creeping forward to the brink of the trench – closer than Jack had ever been to the enemy; he would certainly see Germans now, he thought, and their instructions were to kill some . . .

A shape moved in the gloom ten yards to Jack's right, a grey human shape, with a rifle aimed at Philip. There was no time to think twice – Jack's own rifle was in position, and he took aim and fired, seeing the head snap back as the body crashed against the side of the trench. God, he had killed a man . . . his first definite kill . . . but there was no time to stop and philosophise . . .

"Smallwood, Morgan, stay here and give cover," Philip said. "Now!" he yelled to the rest.

Rifles cracked around them, another grey figure fell, men were tumbling and jumping into the trench, and the separate explosions of Mills bombs were merging into one continuous rumbling, pierced by screams and yells . . . What was happening? Why weren't German reinforcements coming? Jack could hardly believe that the raid was going according to plan. The sergeant from A Company was emerging from a cellar, waving a roll of papers. "All dead in there, Mr Morland," he shouted to Philip. But bombs were being hurled back now from further along the trenches, bursting; Jack saw one of their own men go down . . . another movement, higher up . . .

"Germans behind the traverse," he shouted.

He sensed Philip's hesitation.

"We've done what we was told, sir," the Sergeant shouted. "Sound the whistle . . . get the men together . . ."

Philip did so. Men were emerging from the dugouts, spilling into the crowded trench, scrambling over the parapet;

Jack kept his rifle trained on the edge of the traverse. Philip fired his Very pistol straight up, sending the red light flaring. The last man was up now, staggering to his feet, running awkwardly; they were on their way home, leaving at least two dead in the trench, but they had done what they came to do ... the men were strung out, struggling through the mud; Jack saw Stephen among them. Their own artillery was opening up again on the trench they had just left, the shells screaming overhead. A machine-gun behind them chattered, and Jack saw Philip Morland stagger and fall, heard him cry out . . . God Almighty, what to do now . . .?

The rest of the men, further to his right and led by Sergeant Jones, had run on, out of sight now in the gloom. He couldn't leave Philip. Curse it . . . a star-shell was exploding overhead, casting an eerie, greenish light. Jack flung himself to the ground, waiting until the last flickers had died away. He crawled back to Philip, and found him huddled in a shell-hole, groaning, and clutching his thigh from which blood oozed in a dark patch. Jack crouched beside him.

"Mr Morland! Are you hurt bad, sir?" He was only too aware of the precariousness of their situation – it would only take one of their own shells to drop short, and they'd be done for . . . "*Mr Morland!*" he shouted again. "We must move on! It's too dangerous here . . ."

Philip looked up at him. "I can't . . ."

"You must! I'll support you . . . can you get up?"

"I can't," Philip repeated. "You go on. I'll wait here until the bombardment's over."

Shells were already bursting close by. Hot air fanned Jack's face, and a shower of earth and mud sprayed over both of them. God, they must get a move on – "You must come with me!" Jack yelled. "You'll be blasted to bits here –" He felt almost beside himself with frustration – it was fear preventing Philip from moving, not his injured leg, he felt sure, though that looked bad enough – they'd both die here at this rate, blown to pieces by one of their own shells. He started to pull Philip by the arm, and Philip gave him a look of such blind panic that Jack was suddenly reminded of the time when he'd lost his nerve facing the hedge on Galliard. Well, they'd got a big hedge to face here all right, both of them . . . History was repeating itself with a vengeance . . .

"Come on!" he shouted.

If they didn't get clear by the time the barrage finished, the German snipers would certainly pick them off. But Philip was giving in now, getting up awkwardly, trying to walk. He couldn't put his injured leg to the ground, and Jack ended up half-carrying him, slinging Philip's arm round his neck and taking as much of his weight as he could. They staggered on, the shells dropping safely behind them now, thank God . . . Once Jack lost his footing in the sticky mud and fell, Philip collapsing with him, and they had to extricate themselves from the slime and start forward again, Jack all the time expecting machine-gun bullets to slam into them from behind. But they were almost at their own wire by now, and – thank God – Stephen and another man were coming out to help them, carrying Philip the last few yards, and lowering him safely over the parapet.

Jack felt his legs collapse beneath him as he fell into the trench. "Well done, Smallwood, you did brilliantly," he heard a voice saying. It was Captain Snell, come to see the raiding party back in.

"Thank God you're all right," Stephen said, helping Jack to his feet.

Stretcher-bearers were hastily applying a field-dressing to Philip's wound, putting him on a stretcher and laying a blanket over him. He had obviously lost a lot of blood; his face was white in the dim light, racked with pain, as he mumbled a brief report on the raid to Captain Snell, who bent over him to listen. It was still raining, and the blanket would soon be soaked; Philip would have a long uncomfortable journey through the waterlogged communication trenches. Jack looked at him and managed an exhausted grin, and Philip reached out and grasped his hand.

"You saved my life, Jack," he said. "I won't forget that."

"That's all right, sir," Jack said.

The stretcher party carried Philip away, and Captain Snell ushered Jack and Stephen into the nearest dugout for hot tea laced with rum. "God, I saved him twice tonight," he thought, remembering the German sentry. "And I killed a man." He felt curiously unimpressed by the thought, feeling as little emotion as he used to when snaring rabbits. Four of their own men had been left dead in the German trenches, Captain Snell told them.

When he had had his tea, Jack squelched back to his own dugout with Stephen. He felt utterly drained, too exhausted to talk. He collapsed on his pile of sacks, plastered with mud as he was, and slept.

A Letter from Harriet

Jack was awoken shortly after dawn by the cheerful whistling of a Sergeant who was distributing the Company's mail. Stand-to must have finished by now, he thought, looking at the grey light filtering through the sacking curtain. Charlie and Will had already gone; he and Stephen must have been allowed to sleep on because of their part in the raid. He stretched stiffly, remembering the events of the night, and looked across at the sleeping Stephen. who was in a state of indescribable filthiness, even his eyebrows caked with dried mud. Jack realized that he must be similarly dishevelled himself. He stood up and looked down at his clothing, which was encrusted with dirt and stained with Philip Morland's blood.

"Smallwood in there?" the Sergeant's voice called out. "Letter for 'im."

Jack reached out and took the envelope, addressed to him in pencil. The handwriting was unfamiliar, not Alice's, Emily's or his mother's, the only people who wrote to him regularly. Thinking it might be from Jimmy, whose convalescence looked like lasting nicely into the New Year, Jack ripped open the envelope.

"Dear Jack," he read, *"I said I would writ to you this time, and so here it is, but a bit of a surprise I expect. I am not much good at writting letters but thougt I ougt to tell you that I think I am expecting. If I am the baby will be due in June. Doctor Sijwick said it is allmost sertan. I do not know what to do wether to get rid of it or not. I have not tolled my parents but I will have to soon. I thougt I ougt to tell you seeing it is yours. Are you comeing home again, or if not will you rite me a letter. Yours sinserly, Harriet."*

"God Almighty," Jack said aloud, and "God Almighty," again.

"What's the matter? What's happening?" Stephen yawned, stirring.

"I've just found out that I'm going to be a father," Jack said.

"A what? A *father*?" Stephen was suddenly fully awake. "Are you joking? How could that have happened?"

"Well, how the hell do you think it happened?" Jack said, amused in spite of his shock. "How does it usually happen?"

"No, I mean . . . you didn't say anything about . . ."

"It was when I was home on leave," Jack said. "You know Harriet, the girl I told you about, who I used to see before the war. Well, she and I . . . you know."

"What – just once, or more than once?"

"Well, a few times." Jack felt himself blushing beneath his dirt. "What difference does that make?"

"None, I suppose. Only it seems unlucky, if she's expecting. Or lucky, depending on how you look at it."

"I don't see what's lucky about it." Jack was still trying to assimilate the new information. His leave in September seemed years away, the village and its inhabitants remote; the hours he had spent with Harriet had retreated into the distant past, a fading idyll. He didn't know what he felt.

"Well, I think I might be pleased, if it was me. What will you do?"

Jack stretched out his legs and looked at his puttees, which were indistinguishable from the mud which plastered them. "I don't know. What can I do?"

"You could marry her," Stephen said seriously.

"But –" Jack fell silent, considering the idea. Would Harriet marry him, if he asked her to? On the other hand, what alternatives were there? She could "get rid of" the baby, as she had mentioned in her letter – Jack had heard that an elderly woman in the village had helped several local girls out of similar predicaments. But he felt rather shocked by the casualness of Harriet's suggestion, feeling an instinctive revulsion at the idea of terminating a life before it was begun. He found himself taking an unexpected pride in the thought that Harriet was carrying his child. Only a matter of hours ago he had killed a man; now he found that he had played his part in creating a new life. It was as if the two lives cancelled each other out. He thought about the dead German, remembering the body slumped against the side of the trench. He was glad he hadn't had the chance to look more closely; it was easier to contemplate having killed an anonymous Hun, rather than think of him as an individual, with a wife and family of his own, perhaps . . . But life was cheap; the company's best sniper had picked off six Germans in one day, and four of the men who had been waiting in the trenches with Jack a few hours ago were now dead. It was a matter of luck that he wasn't one of them, lying there rotting, or hastily buried in the mud. If he had been killed there, Harriet's letter would never have reached him, and he would have died without knowing he had fathered a child.

"Perhaps I could," he said, thinking of Stephen's suggestion. The novelty of the idea was appealing. In a few months' time – if he survived – he could have his own family, a wife and child . . . He couldn't begin to think of the difficulties the situation would create – where they would live, how much longer the war would last, whether he could support a family, whether Harriet would even want to consider being married to him. He turned the idea over and over in his mind.

"You ought to think about it seriously, before you decide anything," Stephen said. "But you've got to think of Harriet, haven't you – what's best for her. You've left her in a bit of fix, after all."

"Well . . ." Jack began. Stephen, completely inexperienced with girls as far as Jack knew, instinctively saw Harriet as a wronged maiden, whereas Jack suspected she was well able to take care of herself. "I know she doesn't love me," he said abruptly. It struck him that, for all the joy of his physical union with Harriet, there was little else besides; in comparison, the unspoken current of affection between himself and Stephen ran far deeper. They shared everything: the hardships, the boredom, the anxiety, the risks . . . Jack couldn't imagine that he would ever establish such a bond with anyone male or female – in civilian life, if he ever returned to it.

Stephen said, with naive simplicity, "She will, if you marry her."

"Are you two still chewing the fat in there?" Charlie squelched in, bringing them some tea. "Strewth, you're both in a state. You'd better try to get some hot water and clean yourselves up. What was it like, last night? Heard young Morland got a cushy one. McLachlan's taking over, new bloke, only just got his second pip. I hear you covered yourself with glory, old son," he added, looking at Jack.

"Covered myself with filth, more like," Jack said, yawning.

"Don't be so modest. He went back for Mr Morland, when the rest of us didn't know what had happened," Stephen told Charlie. "Captain Snell said he'd done brilliantly."

"Well, you and Morland are such good mates, of course," Charlie remarked drily. "How did he do, until he got hit?"

"He did all right," Jack said.

Part Four: 1917

Wintry Sea

Alice looked over the gunwale at the heaving swell of waves below. The sea was a dull wintry grey, like the sky; a cold wind tugged at her cape, whipped loose strands of hair against her face and made her eyes water. It was difficult not to think of U-Boats, not to imagine what might happen if a torpedo slammed into the side of the ship beneath her. The ship carried only civilians, and should have been safe under the terms of the Hague Convention, but Alice had already heard of civilian and hospital ships which had been torpedoed; in reality, no-one was safe. Looking at the distant blur which was the coast of France, Alice thought of all those she knew who had crossed this stretch of sea: Jack, Edward, Lorna, Philip, Tom; and those others who would not return – Ted, and Dick, and Rosie Taplin's fiancé, and several others from the village by now, including poor Harry Larkins who had survived the fighting on the Somme only to die weeks later from gangrene infection . . . What would 1917 bring, she wondered? It was only mid-January, but already people were predicting that the war would last out the year, and into the next. She turned her back on the rawness of the wind and retired below, where she took two letters from her valise and re-read them.

The first, from Jack, had arrived shortly before she had left the hospital in south London.

"*Dear Alice,*" he had written, "*I hope this reaches you before you go to France, and I hope all goes well for you when you get there. You will be very suprised to hear that I am getting married to Harriet, probably before you and Edward, as soon as I get a few days leave, I am not due for any yet, but I* might be able to get it for a special reason. You probably think it is all a bit sudden. Well it is, and there is a good reason for that, there is a baby on the way. I expect you're shocked and think we should have been more careful, well we should but there it is, and plenty more in the same boat in this war I'm sure. I have written to Ma and I expect she will be pleased when she gets used to the idea, she will have another grand-child and you will be an aunt again. Anyway Harriet will have to stay living with her folks until I get back for good, then we will have to think what to do, I don't know what, it seems hard to think of life without the war. The baby will be due in June, just think of me a father! It seemed odd at first but now I like the idea. Please wish me luck, and I hope I will see you again before long, we are out of the line for a bit, after having a hard time. Mr Morland was badly wounded in the leg in a trench raid and will be a long time recovering I think. I hope Edward is well and doesn't get to the front too quick, give him my best regards, and I hope you will try not to work too hard, you did look tired when I saw you in London. Till I see you again, and I'll be a married man by then and perhaps even a Dad, Your brother Jack."

Alice carefully put the letter back in its envelope. She had recovered from the initial shock the news had given her, but had grave misgivings about the proposed marriage. In her eyes, no-one could be good enough for Jack, and Harriet cer-tainly fell a long way short of the ideal. Having worked with her for so long, Alice was well aware of her flightiness, and her lack of appreciation of Jack's qualities. "But I really shouldn't judge her," she thought. "She might have changed since then; everyone has." Perhaps, with the responsibilities of mother-hood, Harriet might settle down and make a good wife for Jack. Well, everything was decided now; all Alice could do was to wish them both luck. It was a pity, though, for Jack to limit his opportunities while he was still so young; she wondered what he would do when – *when* – the war was over, unable to imagine him returning to village life. He certainly wouldn't want to go back to Greenstocks, she thought, but with a wife and a child to support he would have to accept whatever work he could find.

The second letter was from Edward, who had rejoined his battalion in Arras. *"It is a very imposing city,"* he wrote; *"I am sending you a photograph of the Grande Place, as it was in peacetime. Much to my surprise, I have been promoted, and am in command of my company – so I am now Captain Sidgwick! You will be very interested to hear of news I heard from the Morlands, when my parents and I went to dinner at Greenstocks shortly before my return. The Morlands had been to visit Philip in hospital in London (as you may already know, he was badly injured whilst leading a raiding party – his leg was broken and he suffered severe loss of blood). I don't know whether Jack will have told you about his own part in the raid: apparently he went back into shellfire to help Philip, and carried him to safety almost unaided. The Morlands are full of praise for Jack, as apparently Philip would quite possibly have died from loss of blood even if he had survived the shelling. It seems that Jack is likely to receive a Distinguished Conduct Medal, on Philip's recommendation, and I am sure it is richly deserved. You must be very proud of him."*

How typical of Jack, Alice thought, not to have mentioned his achievement! It was a strange turn of events, for Philip Morland to be singing Jack's praises, instead of criticizing him; though now, ironically, their paths would not cross again for some time, with Philip in hospital. She thought of the DCM with a glow of pride – Jack seemed to be springing all sorts of surprises. She was relieved, too, that the tone of Edward's letter suggested a recovery from the depression which had assailed him recently. He had not wanted her to go to Étaples, but this, she knew, was only part of the reason for his low spirits.

She had last seen him on Christmas Eve. Since leaving convalescent hospital, he had been sent on a training course, and had been on his way home to spend Christmas with his family before rejoining his battalion. Alice was unable to take any leave over the festive period, but had been allowed to have the afternoon off, and she and Edward had walked in St James' Park and along the Embankment. The small restaurant in which they had tea afterwards was crowded with officers about to return to France. Alice soon noticed that their presence seemed to upset Edward, and that his manner was becoming increasingly strained and withdrawn. His hand was trembling as he lifted his teacup; he noticed it at the same moment as Alice, and put the cup down quickly.

"Let's pay our bill and go," Alice said softly, reaching across the table and taking his hand.

Outside in the street he took a deep breath of the cold evening air. "I feel so guilty, knowing what the men are suffering," he told her. "I'd almost rather be out there – even though I know what to expect . . . it isn't the danger that I dread so much as the knowledge that I shall have to lead my men into impossible situations, to pretend that I believe in what I'm doing . . . having to persuade them, threaten them, even . . . and I've lost so many, Alice, so many good men . . . boys, really, most of them . . ."

She took his arm and pressed herself close against his side as they walked, knowing that this small comfort was all she could possibly offer him. He had seemed so composed, so in control of himself on her visits to the hospital that she had underestimated the effect of the constant strain and responsibility. He never spoke much to her of the dangerous situations he had been in, but he had, after all, been through the fighting at Loos and on the Somme, had seen countless men killed and brutally wounded, had lost almost all his fellow officers on July 1st. It was hard to believe that he was still only twenty-two.

"Oh, I'm sorry to be such a miserable wretch, Alice," he

said, stopping suddenly and clasping both her hands. "We're together, and it's Christmas, and I love you, and next time we meet will be for our wedding."

Alice thought of this conversation now as she refolded the letter and put it back into her valise, with Jack's. The wedding was planned for April, although they both knew how difficult it was to make definite arrangements; Edward's leave could be cancelled without notice, and Alice didn't know yet what pressures would be waiting her at Étaples. And Edward was in Arras, halfway between the Somme and the mining area around Loos . . . April seemed a very long way off. The only cheering prospect in the immediate future was that she would, with any luck, be seeing Lorna in Étaples. They had written to each other regularly, but had not met for many months, and Alice felt that even the occasional meeting would help to relieve her burden of anxiety.

Hours later she was unpacking her few belongings in a small hut which was to be her accommodation at No. 24 General Hospital, Étaples. In the train from Boulogne, she had watched the passing scenery with interest, knowing that both Edward and Jack had travelled this stretch of line on their journey to the base camp; merely being in France made her feel closer to them. The hospitals and the camps were at the edge of the town, adjoining open country. The tents, warehouses and long, low buildings covered a huge area, with the coast stretching away on the other side of the railway line, the sea a distant glimmer beyond grass-tufted dunes and acres of pale sand. The sea-breeze blew strongly inland, laced with salt and the scent of pine trees. It was refreshing, Alice thought, after the grime and darkness of blacked-out London; she hoped she could look forward to spending her time off exploring the coast and estuary, instead of the too-familiar city streets and parks. She had only been to the seaside on three or four occasions, and those visits had been to popular Essex resorts, crowded with tourists. This deserted, wind-swept coast appealed to her desire for peace and solitude, both of which had been denied to her for many months.

"I'm putting you in a surgical ward," the Matron told her. "Sister Thompson will be glad of someone experienced – she's been desperately short-staffed."

Sister Thompson, a small-built woman not much older than Alice, was delighted to be sent a new member of staff, particularly as another nurse had just gone down with flu.

"I'm afraid you'll be thrown straight in at the deep end," she told Alice, giving her a brisk tour of the ward. "There are so few of us here that we all do whatever needs to be done, from bedpans to helping in the theatre. The surgeons there are working all hours of the day and night."

Alice received the briefest of greetings from the other staff on the ward before plunging into the familiar routines. She found that the ward was less formal than the one she had left in London – everyone was far too busy to bother with formality – but the work was far more gruelling. She thought she had toughened herself to the horrible variousness with which human flesh could be mutilated, but now found herself coping unaided with wounds even worse than she had seen before. The adjoining operating theatre provided a constant supply of patients coming round from anaesthetics, with newly-amputated limbs to be dressed.

"At least a quarter of the men here are dying," Sister Thompson told her. "I'm afraid that all we can do is make their last few hours as comfortable as we can." Alice frequently came back from her lunch break to find screens round the bed of a patient who had died during the short time she had been out of the ward.

It was often difficult to remember that she had trained herself to accept death and suffering without emotion. If she stopped to think about the succession of wounded and dying men she had seen since she had begun nursing at Broadlands Hall, she found herself in the grip of a futile, pointless anger at the politicians and generals behind the war, who could apparently do nothing to stop the endless human wastage, and could think of no other strategy than to pit human flesh against machine-guns and explosives.

It took her a few days to locate Lorna, who was working in another ward and had just started a spell of night-duty. Eventually she was directed to a mess-room, where Lorna was having supper with a group of nurses and orderlies.

"*Alice!*" Lorna was on her feet at once, clasping Alice in a bear-hug. "I was wondering if I'd ever see you! How long have you been here? Which ward are you in?"

She still had the vivacious manner Alice remembered so clearly, but her movements seemed driven by a sort of desperate energy, as if she were afraid of succumbing to exhaustion if she relaxed for a moment. Her blue, dark-lashed eyes were exactly like Edward's, Alice thought, and held the same expression of dimmed sadness that she had seen in his.

"When did you see Edward last – how is he?" Lorna asked when Alice had told her about her ward.

"I saw him on Christmas Eve, although I've heard from him since, as I expect you have. Well, he looked . . ." She hesitated, then decided that Lorna would want the truth. "He was showing signs of strain. I think the effects of fighting he'd been in took a long time to emerge – it seemed he was coping so well, when he came home at first. But he did sound better in his last few letters – I think it was almost a relief, to be back with his battalion. And he's been promoted to company commander," she remembered to add.

"Yes, I know – you'll soon be Captain and Mrs Sidgwick! Doesn't it sound grand? And he wrote to me about Jack's DCM – you must be very proud."

"I am, of course. And did you know about Jack and Harriet?"

Having found out each other's location and hours of duty, they met whenever they could in the following weeks, and

Alice often thought that without Lorna's company she would have found it hard to keep going. The stream of dying and wounded men, the stench of gangrenous wounds, the delirious cries and groans, and the sense that she could never work hard enough to cope with it all, would have been impossible to bear if it had not been for the walks with Lorna along the coast and to Paris Plage. It had been a hard, bitterly cold winter, but with the dawning of spring the windswept sandhills and dunes and pine-woods provided an invigorating contrast to the atmosphere of the hospital. Apart from the distant rumble of the heavy guns, it was almost possible to imagine the war out of existence.

"Did you hear about Frau Zellern being sent back to Germany?" Lorna said on one of these walks. "It was compulsory repatriation – if she'd been a man, she'd have been sent to a prison camp."

"But she hasn't got any relations, has she, in Germany?" Alice asked.

"No – it must be awful for her, alone, and with the food shortages to be faced. Dorothy and the others were furious, but there was nothing they could do. I suppose they'll try to get her back again, after the war . . . we all talk about *after the war*, don't we, as if everything's going to be just as it was?"

"What will you do, yourself?" Alice asked. "Go back to London?"

"I'm going to work as a pacifist," Lorna answered promptly. "Yes, I shall live in London, and earn my living by teaching, and meanwhile write articles and pamphlets, if I possibly can. We must never forget – and future generations must never forget – this appalling, tragic waste of life. There must never be another war."

"No." Alice squinted in the bright light, looking up at a trio of Sopwith Pups which were flying in low over the glittering sea. "If women had any say in the running of the war, it might be different."

"We will have earned our place in whatever remains of society, at any rate," Lorna said confidently. "The Government must surely give women the vote – there'll be an outrage if they don't. And of course women will still have opportunities to work, when the war ends. There will be so few men . . . And women who would have devoted themselves to being wives and mothers will find that there just aren't the men to marry.

Lorna had been seeing an older man, Alice knew, an officer in the Royal Army Medical Corps who was separated from his wife. They were both silent for a moment, looking out at the calm sea and thinking of the men they loved. Then Lorna said, "There's a cottage along here, in that clump of trees, that serves delicious coffee. Shall we go in, out of the wind?"

The Hotel in the Pines

Another spring, Alice thought, looking at the spears of growth thrusting through soil in the carefully-hoed strip of garden outside the mess-hut. It was April; the days were beginning to lengthen, and the air to contain hints of warmth to come, after the bitter winter. In less than a month's time she was to marry Edward. Jack and Harriet had been married at the end of February, in the village church at home; Alice had been unable to get leave, but had sent a present, a small painting of the beach at Hardelot. Jack had been able to take only four days' leave, and was already back with his battalion. Alice found it hard to think of him as a married man, and suspected that he would, too, having had such a short time to acclimatize.

Her mother had written to tell her about the wedding, and to say that the banns had been read for Edward and herself. "*It was a shock for some people in the village, I dare say,*" her mother wrote, "*but Mrs Sidgwick has been very nice to me, and says she is looking forward to having you for a daughter-in-law, and she is sure you will make Edward happy. Harriet looked very nice, I will send you a photograph as soon as I can, she is keeping well and still living with her parents, it is strange to think of our Jack as soon being a father but he looked very happy and proud, he seems to have grown up a lot since he went away but then it has been more than two years. Mr Philip is out of hospital now but on crutches, his leg has mended badly and they say he will have a limp, so he is out of the war. Emily's Tom has been very lucky too, he was sent out in the winter as you know, got wounded in the hand* on his first time over the top, bad enough to get him sent home for good as he can't handle a rifle again, but not very good for farming as it is permanent damage."

At least one of the family had definitely been spared, then, Alice thought as she read on. Her mother went on to describe the current difficulties in getting coal, the urgings to cut down on food, and rumours that rationing would soon be brought in.

Jack wrote to her from the front, "I am very very sorry but having had a few days leave to get married I do not think I shall be able to get home for your and Edward's wedding, there are blokes here who have been waiting months for their leave, it's a great pity but I will get home if there is any chance at all, even for one day. I am in the line again but it is very quiet here, the next main action seems to be planned for further up."

Further up . . . the phrase sent Alice scurrying to look at a map of the Western Front. Jack could mean right up in Belgium, in the Ypres Salient, which had seen such bitter fighting since the outbreak of war; on the other hand, Arras was further up than Jack's battalion, which was still in the Somme sector . . . it would be too cruel for Edward to find himself involved in yet another major offensive.

Alice was thinking of this now as she returned to the ward after lunch. A tall officer in uniform was standing with his back to her at the ward entrance, looking in. He turned at the sound of her footsteps, and she swayed and almost fell over with the shock, leaning against the wall to steady herself.

"Edward!"

"Alice – thank goodness I've found you! I never thought I would, in this maze of huts." He held her in his arms to steady her, much to the interest of a pair of convalescent patients emerging from the ward on crutches.

She was almost crying with shock and relief. "But what are you doing here? How did you get here?"

"I managed to get a lift up from Arras in an RAMC van. Is there any chance of you getting the afternoon off?"

"I'll try . . . Can you wait here for a minute?"

She could hardly bear to leave him, certain that he would turn out to be a figment of her imagination if she took her eyes off him for even a few moments. She dashed into the ward; found Pauline, the other VAD who was just going off duty, and gabbled out an explanation. Pauline agreed to swap afternoons off, and Alice fetched her coat and hurried back to tell Edward.

"How long have you got?" she asked him.

"Just today."

"Where shall we go? Have you had anything to eat?"

"No, not since last night."

She thought for a moment. "There's a restaurant along the coast a short way – shall we walk there?"

"Yes – anywhere, if it's not too crowded."

"The only thing is – I know it sounds ridiculous, but nurses aren't allowed to be seen with officers, of any rank. If you start to walk up that way, I'll catch up with you in a few minutes – I'll be up before Matron otherwise. What about Lorna? Do you want to try to find her?"

"Later perhaps, but I must see you alone first."

There was something wrong, she was sure, something he was keeping back from her. She had to let him out of her sight again while she waited, seething with frustration at the stupid rules, until she thought he would be clear of the hospitals and camps. She caught up with him on the coastal road, where a stiff, salt-laden breeze was blowing inland. He turned to face her, holding both her hands.

"I'm terribly sorry, Alice," he began. "We shall have to postpone the wedding – all leave's been cancelled, after tomorrow. I only heard yesterday – I just had to see you . . ."

"All leave cancelled –" she stopped walking. "You mean –"

Another offensive, yes. To move the line forward from

Arras and to capture Vimy Ridge."

"Oh, *Edward*." She heard the flat despair in her voice. "I mean, I don't mind about the wedding particularly, but another big push . . ." She knew only too well what that meant. "Will you definitely be in it?"

"Yes."

"Oh, God, it's so unfair –" she burst out, knowing as she spoke that it was a stupid thing to say – when was fairness ever a consideration?

"Nothing's fair in this war, and I've been lucky so far."

He kissed her, and the salt wind made her eyes run with tears, and whipped loose strands of her hair against his face. "Don't cry, darling," he murmured, pressing his cheek against hers and stroking her hair. But he did not tell her not to worry; they both knew how futile such advice would be. She choked back her sobs – she had to, for his sake. It must be far worse for him, knowing what he would be facing, and leading his men into, in a few days' time. Meanwhile, she told herself, they were together, and they must make the most of what little time they had.

It was a crisp, bright day. The blue sky was streaked with cloud, and the clear air brought out the vivid colours of the coast; the sand gleamed white, and the sea was a distant silver sword throwing light back at the sun. The small hotel on the coastal path had a dining-room which looked over the dunes; it was empty, apart from two young nurses unknown to Alice, who left shortly after she and Edward were shown to a table. Edward ordered an omelette, salad and fruit, and Alice drank coffee, watching him eat, and wishing she could preserve this moment for ever, with him safe and whole in front of her.

"When will you have to start back?" she asked him when he had finished eating and they had ordered more coffee.

"Tomorrow morning, early."

Their eyes met, and she knew that the same thought was in both their minds; a notice outside the hotel had said that there were rooms free. He hesitated, clasping her hand across the table, his eyes questioning her. She said softly, "Go and speak to the receptionist."

"You mean . . . you'll stay with me?"

"Yes. Go on."

He went out, and she heard him talking to the receptionist in French, and giving their names as "Capitaine et Madame Sidgwick." A few minutes later the hotel manager showed them to a room upstairs, and left them. Alice wondered whether he had guessed that they weren't really married, but she didn't care. It made no sense, with the threat of separation ever-present, to worry about convention, and the formality of being married could make no difference to her feelings for Edward, or his for her.

The room was clean and bright, sparsely furnished, with a white-counterpaned bed, a chest-of-drawers, a fringed rug, and windows overlooking the sea. They stood for a while, looking out at the shifting pattern of the cloud shadows across the sand, and the pine trees tossing in the wind. Alice could feel her heart pounding as she stood beside Edward, his arm tightening around her waist. For all her professional familiarity with men's bodies, she felt suddenly shy of his; looking at his taut profile, she realized that he felt the same apprehension. Then he turned to her, stroking her cheek with gentle fingers. "Alice, are you quite sure?"

"Yes," she murmured. "I love you – what more can we ask for?"

"I can't help thinking that it's wrong of me to ask you to – to stay with me."

"You didn't ask me. I wanted to stay. Do you think I could go back to the hospital, and send you off down the road to Arras, knowing that we could have been together?"

His arms were round her, his face in her hair. "Thank God I came – I didn't plan it like this, Alice, I just had to see you."

"I know you didn't plan it. But I'm glad."

He reached up to draw the curtains, dimming the light in the room. He pulled her against him and they kissed for a long time; then he drew away and said simply, "Come," and led her towards the bed.

Hours later she woke to see a pale grey light filtering through the curtains. Edward's arms were clasped around her; his eyes opened as she stirred, and he smiled at her without speaking. He was beautiful, she thought, even more than she had remembered, all the evenings she had gazed at his photograph before going to sleep. The photograph couldn't show the blue of his eyes, very intense now in the dim light, or the smoothness of his pale skin. His thick hair was almost black against the pillow, the faint scar from his wound running across his temple. She reached out to him, stroking the curve of his eyebrow, and he turned his head to kiss her hand, and said, "I love you, Madame Sidgwick."

"And I love you, Monsieur le Capitaine," she said lightly.

"Will you get into trouble at the hospital?"

"I shouldn't think so. I'll be back in time to go on duty, and only Pauline will know – the VAD who shares my hut. She won't say anything. I should think I'd be sent home in disgrace for sure, if Matron found out I'm a wicked fallen woman."

"Do you feel wicked?"

"No. I feel lovely."

"You are lovely."

They gazed at each other in silence for a few moments. It was nearly dawn, Alice thought, and before long they would have to get out of the warm bed and go their separate ways. How much of their precious time had they wasted with sleeping? She couldn't remember; she knew that they had dozed and wakened, and talked, and made love again . . . Tears smarted behind her eyes, and Edward's face reflected the same sadness.

"You don't have to go yet, do you?" His fingers were twining in her long hair, tickling her neck.

"What time is it?"

"Nearly five."

"Not yet . . . do you?"

"I should, but . . ." He held her close to him, brushing his lips against her shoulder and neck. "If ever a man had good reason for desertion . . . it'd almost be worth facing the firing squad, for this."

Arras

Lorna was sitting on her bed lacing up her shoes. "Edward was here?" she repeated in surprise.

"Yes, he came quite unexpectedly. I'm awfully sorry he didn't see you. He meant to come back, but . . . well . . ." Alice faltered and stopped, feeling rather guilty that Edward had left without seeing his sister.

"Oh, what a shame I was in the theatre all afternoon and evening, with no chance of getting away. I'd have loved to see him."

"I know – I *am* sorry. Lorna, he came to bring bad news. All leave has been cancelled because of a new offensive."

Lorna looked up sharply. "Oh, Alice! I suspected that something was about to happen, but he'll definitely be involved in it, then?'

Alice nodded mutely, and Lorna sighed and stood up, throwing her coat over her shoulders. They both knew what the coming days would bring in terms of casualties, and now the agony of doubt would be an additional burden.

"I hope you managed to get some time off while he was here, at least," Lorna said, closing the hut door behind her as they left.

"Yes. We walked along to the little hotel in the pine woods and had a meal, and . . ." She hesitated, but then decided that Lorna wouldn't be shocked. "We stayed there the night."

"Really?" Lorna gave her a sidelong glance. "You must be dreadfully worried, Alice, as I am, of course. I'm sure he'll write as soon as he can. Perhaps for once it'll be an attack that really does go according to plan, now that they're using tanks.

I hope Matron doesn't find out about your illicit outing," she said, lightening her tone. "Do you know, there's a VAD in my ward whose father is a Colonel, and she's not even allowed to go out alone with him when he's at the Base? It's absolute madness, isn't it? Why they can't treat us as responsible adults, I really don't know. God knows, we work hard enough to earn whatever pleasures we get during our times off."

By next day, the crump of the guns rumbled on the wind, heralding the attack, and Alice's knowledge that Jack wasn't involved in the latest push was balanced by her awareness that Edward certainly was. The wards were cleared; all the patients who were well enough to be moved had been sent to Boulogne and on to England. At least the convoys would be arriving sooner than they had in London, Alice thought. She found herself hoping again that Edward would receive some minor wound within the first few hours of the fighting, and arrive in the first convoy.

The weather had turned suddenly chilly, bringing flurries of snow. "Snow in April," Alice thought, shivering with the cold as she came out of the ward. It was like the winter over again, shuddering at night beneath inadequate blankets, and having only icy water to wash in. She thought of the men in the front line, who had already suffered intensely in the bitter winter weather. In battle, Edward had told her, men who had managed to advance and hold their position were often cut off from their battalion for several days, with nothing to eat but the iron rations they carried in their packs. Under those circumstances, he said, there was no choice but to take extra rations from the dead lying around. "Oh, Edward . . . where are you now?" she wondered. Her anxiety became a relentless physical ache, a hopeless longing for him. Surely some instinct would warn her if he were in a crisis – although, she remembered, twins were often said to have psychic powers of communication, yet neither she nor Jack had ever experienced anything of the sort, for all their closeness.

The casualties started to arrive – desperately wounded men with haggard faces, some suffering from exposure after having lain out in the freezing conditions. In spite of the carnage, Alice found it almost a relief to be in action; the long hours and endless hurrying to and fro at least saved her from the worst excesses of brooding. She discovered that two men in her care were from Edward's battalion; one of them was delirious, but she pestered the other for whatever information he could give her, though he wasn't able to tell her much, having been wounded within minutes of going over the top. The convoys kept arriving, and still there was no note from Edward – but no bad news either, Alice told herself, clinging desperately to this small comfort.

"Go off-duty now, Alice," Sister Thompson told her late one evening, looking round the door of the sink-room. "You haven't had a break for hours. I'm just going off myself, now that Sister Webster's here."

"I'm all right. I'll just finish this first."

A sinkful of dressing-trays waited to be cleaned and disinfected, Alice plunged them into the stinging hot water, glad to be out of the rush and hurry of the ward for a few moments. The few moments of isolation were both a relief and a danger, for she knew that only the constant demands of work kept her from giving way to her emotions. Now, she felt that her strained nerves were ready to snap. "I can't stand it . . . I can't stand it," she thought desperately. "There *must* be a letter soon . . . there *must* . . ."

She tidied the sink-room and went back to her hut, grateful for the few hours of respite offered by sleep. Sleep helped to pass the hours, and tomorrow, surely, news would come.

She slept as if drugged, and was woken by a knocking on the door of the hut. Pauline had not yet returned from night-duty, and her bed was still neatly made. Alice climbed reluctantly out of bed, pulled on her dressing-gown and opened the door.

"Alice . . ." It was Lorna, and the expression on her face was enough to tell Alice why she had come.

"Is it . . . is it Edward?" she whispered. She could hardly force out the words.

Lorna nodded. She handed Alice a telegram, and covered her face with both hands.

Alice read, "DEEPLY SORRY TO TELL YOU EDWARD DIED OF WOUNDS, APRIL 12TH. TELEGRAM RECEIVED TODAY. NO FURTHER INFORMATION, WILL WRITE." It was from Dr Sidgwick.

Lorna was still standing in the doorway, choked sobs shaking her body. Alice led her inside and sat her down on the bed, embracing her while she wept. She felt numb, too numb for tears herself, only conscious that she had been waiting for this.

Old Ford Road

In spite of Lorna's urgings to accompany her back to Little-hays, Alice insisted on staying at the hospital.

"It won't do you any good – you're working yourself to exhaustion," Lorna said, troubled.

"I want to be exhausted. It's the only way I can keep going."

"Please, Alice – won't you come with me? You can see your mother again, and Emily. Surely it would be easier for us to go together."

"No. Thank you for thinking of it, but I can't go back to the village, I just can't," Alice said. "Not yet."

She had gone about her work mechanically since the telegram had arrived, hardly aware of what she was doing. She gave up as much of her free time as she could, wanting to tire herself so completely that she would pass into the oblivion of sleep as soon as she stopped.

"You're looking so pale and thin, I'm sure you shouldn't be working," Lorna said anxiously. "Your ward sister has noticed it, too. Alice, you remember what you told me about Edward's visit – you don't think there's any chance you might be pregnant, do you?"

"No. I already know I'm not. I wish I were – if only it could have been as easy as it was for Harriet – there would have been something left of Edward, to love –"

"I know. Oh, I do so wish it could have turned out that way, too. You poor darling . . . Can I really not persuade you to come with me, for my sake, if not for yours?"

"I will go back, some time," Alice said. "I ought to go and see my mother, she'll be so upset . . . and I'll visit your parents, but please, not yet. I couldn't bear it. There are so many memories of him, everywhere . . . and I can't face people's sympathy either, not yet."

Eventually Lorna left to catch the train to Boulogne, promising to write, and Alice went back to her ward. Later that day, she was told to report to Matrons's office, and found herself receiving unwanted sympathy.

"I was terribly sorry to hear of the sad news about your fiancé," Matron said kindly. "You must be dreadfully upset, especially as you had planned to marry quite soon, I understand. Sister Thompson is very worried about you, you know – she tells me that you won't take time off, and that you're working yourself much too hard."

"I'm not working any harder than everyone else, Matron. And it's what I want, really it is."

"You must allow yourself to come to terms with your grief, my dear," Matron said. "You shouldn't try to shut it away, which is what you're doing now. Wouldn't it be sensible to take a week's leave?"

"No – please, Matron." Alice was almost in tears of desperation. "I'd really be much better off staying here."

She *was* suppressing her grief, she knew – Matron was right. She had looked at Edward's photograph one last time, and then put it away with all his letters in the bottom of her trunk. He was gone, and she could not bear to look at his face, or his familiar handwriting. He had died of wounds, had not even been granted the mercy of an instant death whilst in action; Alice knew too well what agonies of protracted suffering could be concealed by the official phrasing. She wondered if she would ever know how he had died, whether some kind fellow officer would have time to write with details, and whether perhaps it might be better not to know.

Spring was returning, after the late cold spell. Daffodils were blooming in the little stretches of garden around the wards, and the mild weather enticed off-duty nurses and officers out to the estuary and coast, and to the more urban delights of Paris Plage and Le Touquet. Alice stayed in the ward as much as she could, and spent her off-duty time in the mess-room or in her hut, not wanting to walk out along the path she had walked with Edward, or to see the little hotel where they had spent their first – and now only – night together.

She received letters of condolence from some of the most unexpected people, besides the family: one came from Philip Morland, and another from Jack's friend Stephen, who had never so much as met Edward or herself. Alice was surprised by such thoughtfulness, having supposed that death must be commonplace by now, hardly warranting more than passing comment. She sent replies to everyone who wrote, and corresponded regularly with Lorna, who had been detained at home for more than the expected week by a severe attack of flu. The numbers of severe casualties in her ward gave her ample opportunity to immerse herself in work, and she tried to stifle illogical feelings of resentment towards the men in her care, for having survived the fighting when Edward had not.

In early June, Lorna, who had recovered sufficiently to think about returning to France, persuaded Alice to take a few days' leave and to meet her in London. *"You don't have to come home to the village, if you'd still prefer not to,"* she wrote. *"I shall be staying in London to visit Dorothy and Mathilda in the East End, and I thought you might find it interesting to come. We might even see Sylvia Pankhurst; Dorothy and Mathilda are working with her at Old Ford Road."*

Alice re-read this letter several times, feeling tempted away from the hospital for the first time. It would be comforting to see Lorna again; she was her closest friend, now, the only person whose company she wanted. At last she wrote back, *"Thank you for inviting me – yes, I would like to come. I'm not sure how long I will stay – perhaps just a day or two. Then, if you're coming back here, we could travel together."*

The Channel crossing was very different from her first one – the sea calm and blue under a serene sky, passengers sunning themselves on deck. The threat of the U-Boats remained, for the Germans had now declared unconditional submarine war, but Alice gave little thought this time to the prospect of a sudden watery death. She stood on deck watching the coast of France recede, half-wishing she hadn't agreed to Lorna's suggestion. She had too much time to think, away from the ward routine.

Early in the evening she arrived at Charing Cross to be met by Lorna, who took her to the small guesthouse in the Strand where she had booked rooms.

"While you unpack, I'm going to go downstairs to see if we can get some dinner," Lorna said as soon as they arrived. "And I shall leave you alone to read these." She took two letters out of her bag and handed them to Alice. "The first one is from a Captain in Edward's battalion, and the second is from Edward to you, written just before he died. It was forwarded with his belongings. I didn't want to risk posting it on to you.

Alice sat down abruptly on the bed, and Lorna left her. She looked at Edward's handwriting on the envelope, and put it down quickly, deciding to read the other letter first. It was from Captain James Addenham, of the 5th Epping Foresters.

"Dear Doctor and Mrs Sidgwick," it read, *"You must by now have received the terrible news of your son's death. I am writing to offer you my sincerest sympathy and that of my colleagues, and to tell you something of the circumstances.*

Edward was commanding his company on the morning of April 11th, in a snowstorm. His men were held in reserve but were suddenly called on to reinforce A Company, which had been beaten back. Finding that A Company's commanding officer had been severely wounded, Edward gathered up the stragglers and led the renewed assault. He had made considerable progress towards his objective when he was hit by shell fragments and mortally wounded. I saw him when he was brought in to our front-line trench shortly afterwards, and I did not think there was any chance of his survival. I last saw him being carried down to the Aid Post. He had already been given morphia and I do not think he was conscious enough to suffer. He died next day at the Casualty Clearing Station, and was buried in a small British cemetery close by.

We are all deeply saddened by his death, especially as it happened so close to his wedding. He was a first-class company commander and was liked and respected by everyone, officers and men. I had only known him since he took over his company in January, but I had formed a great liking for him. He will be greatly missed."

Alice's hand was trembling as she picked up the second envelope and opened it slowly. She took out a short letter, written on one side of the page only.

"My darling Alice," she read, "I got back to Arras late last night. The journey was a very slow and tedious one, because of all the troops and traffic bound for the front. I can't tell you how dreadful I felt to leave you that morning, after such a short time together; but I am glad that I saw you, even if it should turn out to have been our last meeting. If the worst should occur I do hope you will never have cause to regret anything that has happened between us. I often worry that I have caused you unnecessary anxiety, through asking you to marry me while the war is still in progress – but I cannot honestly regret it. You have meant so much to me, through all these bitter months, and I truly do not know how I would have faced it without you. I pray that I will come through somehow, and that I will be back in England to marry you before the summer is over; that you really will be 'Madame Sidgwick' very soon, and that we will be husband and wife in fact, as we already are in everything but name. I love you.

Edward."

Alice's eyes were blurred before she had finished reading, and Lorna returned shortly to find her huddled on the bed with tears streaming down her face.

"I'm sorry, Lorna," she sobbed. "He's gone, and he was so lovely . . ."

"Yes, I know he was," Lorna said, sitting down beside her. "And don't apologize, you foolish girl. I'm glad you're letting yourself cry at last."

"Be prepared to see the worst of the bomb damage," Lorna said as she and Alice finished breakfast next morning. "We'll be walking through some of the streets that were hit. The mess will take weeks to clear up, I should think."

"Bomb damage?"

"Yes – oh, I suppose you haven't seen the newspapers. There was an air raid three days ago – the worst one of the war so far. It was Gotha aeroplanes, masses of them, making for Liverpool Street Station, apparently."

"How terrible! Were many people killed?"

Lorna nodded, and Alice finished her coffee in silence, realizing that her preoccupation with her own concerns had prevented her from taking much notice of current events.

When she and Lorna walked round to Old Ford Road, she was dismayed by the aftermath of the raid; people were making half-hearted attempts to tidy up the débris of broken glass and masonry and smashed tradesman's barrows, and a tarpaulin shrouded a dead horse. In one of the streets, women and elderly men were wandering about looking as shell-shocked as patients Alice had seen on her ward, while children stared at the shattered shop-fronts, wide-eyed and silent. London was a dangerous place, she realized. She was shocked, too, by the visible signs of poverty around her: women waited in long lines outside food shops, clutching empty straw baskets, and thin, sickly-looking children clung to their mothers' aprons or searched in the gutters.

"These poor people!" she said to Lorna. "How do they survive?"

"It's a struggle, literally a life-and-death struggle," Lorna replied. "Some of the families have suffered dreadfully – at the beginning of the war, there wasn't even a separation allowance for soldiers' wives. Some of them were left to bring up families of seven or eight children on nothing. Sylvia Pankhurst has done wonders – getting milk for children, and starting up cost-price restaurants.

"Surely the Government should have done something, from the start?" Alice exclaimed. "It's a disgrace, to leave the wives and children of the fighting men to starve!"

"Yes. And this hardship isn't going to disappear when the war ends," Lorna said.

There was another war to be fought here, Alice thought, looking around her: a war against poverty and deprivation.

Arriving at 400 Old Ford Road, they went through a large hall set out as a canteen with rows of trestle tables and benches, and found Dorothy and Mathilda busily engaged in food preparations in the large adjoining kitchen. They could stop working only briefly to exchange greetings and news.

"I'm afraid we must carry on. We'll have nearly two hundred people to feed at midday," Dorothy explained.

"We'll help," Lorna offered. "What can we do?"

"Are you sure?" Mathilda said gratefully. "Well, I'll get some aprons, and you could get the gas stoves going and boil water in these big saucepans, and Alice, perhaps you wouldn't mind chopping these onions for the pot . . ."

Alice felt glad to throw herself into the rush of activity, chopping vegetables, sorting cutlery, cutting bread. Customers were queuing before midday, and she was sent to collect their tickets as they came in. They were mainly women with children, and elderly people, but there were one or two men of military age on crutches or with arms in slings.

"Those who can afford it pay tuppence for their meal, a penny for children," Mathilda explained, "and those who can't pay get their tickets free. But when they come in to eat, no-one knows who's paid for their tickets and who hasn't."

It was rewarding work, Alice decided. The atmosphere was cheerful, all the helpers working flat out cooking and washing up and serving food, and when every seat in the canteen was taken there was a hubbub of conversation livelier than she had heard in months. She was amazed to see how resilient people could be, confronting whatever fate dished out to them with a sort of stoical determination.

"Now we clear up and start preparing for the evening meal," Dorothy said when all the customers had gone, and Lorna had gone with Mathilda to collect more supplies of vegetables. "But I must find time to take you and Lorna round to the Mothers' Arms."

"The Mothers' Arms? What is it?" Alice asked.

"It used to be a public house, the Gunmakers' Arms. Now Sylvia's converted it into a nursery and school, mainly for war orphans. Would you like to get some tea going for us, while I clear the tables?"

"I was so sorry to hear about Frau Zellern being sent back to Germany," Alice said, when they were sitting at the scrubbed table with mugs of tea. "It must have been awful for her, going back on her own."

"Yes. But we'll do everything we can to get her back. Of course, we wouldn't have come back to London if she'd still been with us – things would have been worse for her here than they were in Essex, with all the hatred of Germans."

"It's so stupid, isn't it? The fighting men don't hate the German soldiers – they seem to have more hatred for their own generals, from what . . . from what Edward says . . . said . . ."

"I'm so sorry, my dear," Dorothy said gently, and Alice, feeling her eyes stinging with tears, stood up quickly to refill the teapot.

Later, Dorothy took Lorna and Alice round to the Roman Road and left them in the converted bar-room of the pub, now a lecture-room and clinic. They looked around with interest at the light, modern decor: white-painted walls hung with pictures from children's books, bright chintz curtains at the windows, long wall-cupboards full of toys.

"It's lovely!" Alice said, remembering the dreary, colourless surroundings of the school she had attended in the village.

"Sylvia Pankhurst is a marvellous designer," Lorna said. "You should have seen some of the things she did for the WSPU, in the old days."

Upstairs, they found that the children were having their rest hour, babies in cots or baskets, the older children on mattresses on the floor, under the supervision of a young nurse. Alice and Lorna tiptoed around the room looking at the sleeping faces. Alice spent a long time gazing at one tiny, dark-haired baby, with a stab of regret that Edward hadn't left her a child. It would have left her in a difficult situation, she knew – how could she have kept herself? And it still wouldn't have been easy to be an unmarried mother, even though the war must have started to change the old prejudices. "But anything would have been worth it," she thought. She would never have a child now, she supposed, unable to imagine herself ever wanting any other lover or husband, now that Edward was gone.

"Do you teach the children, as well, the older ones?" Lorna was whispering to the nurse.

"No. There are specially trained teachers, who use the new Montessori method. It's a modern style of teaching, where the children learn through activity. And there's no strict discipline of the old-fashioned kind – the children learn to co-operate with each other."

"It's been such an interesting visit," Alice told Lorna as they made their way back to the Strand later. "It was a revelation to see something so *positive*, so forward-looking, after all we've seen of suffering."

She felt almost ashamed to be taking a flicker of interest in anything other than her own grief.

"I thought you'd be impressed," Lorna said. "By the way," she added. "did I tell you that when I called to see your mother, she said that Jack's coming home on leave in a few days' time?"

"Jack? Really?"

"His baby's due any day now, his and Harriet's."

"Is it? Goodness – I'd completely forgotten – how could I have?" She walked in silence for a few moments, then said, "You know, I think I might go back to the village after all."

Wiring

"Some thick clouds coming over now," Stephen said. "You'll be able to go out soon."

"What time are you relieved?"

"Two o'clock."

"I should be back in by then. First one in gets some tea going, all right?" Jack fumbled in his pockets for a cigarette, to quell the sickness in his stomach. It was only a wiring party, not a trench raid or an attack, but the prospect was enough to make his hands shake. Young Will had got a shell splinter in his eye, last week, on a routine patrol; he'd be out of it all right now, but it was a high price to pay, the loss of one eye . . . at least he'd have one good one left, Jack supposed, more than some blokes had finished up with.

He took a few drags of his cigarette, and then risked a look over the parapet. The moon was still casting a faint cold light, but not enough for a sniper to pick him out. Nothing much was going on tonight, just the occasional Very light in the distance, and the faint rumble of guns. Behind him, boots tramped on the duckboards and muffled voices cursed: carrying parties, bringing up rations and ammunition, and, if they were lucky, mail. He heard Jimmy's voice: "Not too bad here, lads, only two feet deep –"

Jack ducked below the parapet as a light soared and flared closer to. He must have spent many hours on sentry duty as Stephen was now, or at morning and evening stand-to, looking out across No-Man's-Land. In some dawns it had struck him as having a terrible savage beauty, when the sky and the torn earth were tinted with the same warmth, the glow from the east threw the shattered stumps of trees and the coils of wire and the nameless huddled shapes into silhouette, and the waterlogged shell-holes reflected light back at the cloud-streaked sky. But its more dreadful aspects could never be forgotten for long, when you were sharply aware that the area was a slaughterhouse, and the shell-holes reeked of cordite and decaying bodies, and the wire was a death-trap. There were rumours now of a renewed offensive in the Ypres Salient. "Knowing our luck, we'll be sent up there next," Jack thought.

For now, there was only tonight to get through, and then they'd be out of the line and he'd be going home. It would be good to be clean again, to have a proper wash and to get his uniform deloused. It would be a mixed sort of homecoming, though; the baby would be due any day now, but the whole family must be saddened by the news of Edward's death. Poor Alice; she hadn't deserved that – not that anyone deserved anything they got in this godforsaken war; poor Edward, too, he was a good bloke and a good officer too, from what Jack heard. He couldn't see Alice ever getting over it. What would she do now, after the war? Stay on as a nurse, perhaps . . .

McLachlan was making his way along the trench, collecting the members of the wiring party together. There was more cloud cover now, blotting out the moon.

"Here we go then. See you later," Jack said to Stephen, dropping his cigarette end into the mud.

"Good luck, Jack."

The wirers made their way out to the gap, carrying stakes and hammers and coils of wire. It was too quiet tonight, Jack thought, ominously quiet; he would have preferred teeming rain or a brisk wind, to drown any accidental noises. It was difficult to unravel the wire, and if anyone were butter-fingered enough to let go of an end it sprang back with a clink, which to Jack's ears seemed to reverberate along the entire front. The gap was not a big one, and they were able to fix the wire with staples and twists, but all the time the uncanny silence was screaming in his ears, straining his nerves to breaking-point. You always thought your nerves would snap, he thought, that you'd go berserk and run out screaming, like he'd seen some blokes do; but you always managed to keep going just that little bit longer, keeping your sights trained on the next meal, the next bit of kip, the next mail-bag, the next time out of the line. Spend much time thinking any farther ahead than that, and you'd go insane for sure . . . Thank God – the last strand was fixed now, and McLachlan was inspecting it, and they could go back in and brew up the tea.

But McLachlan was whispering, "I want to check further along on our front. Smallwood, come with me. Everyone else, you can go back in."

Stifling a curse, Jack followed. McLachlan wasn't a bad bloke, very thorough where it counted, not too hot on the more trifling points of detail. They crept along in the darkness. Jack hoped the sentries knew they were out; there had been cases of men shot by their own company, who mistook them for German raiders. It would be a bloody silly way to go, Jack thought.

They heard the scream of a shell salvo coming over, out of the blue. It was close, but not close enough for them to bother throwing themselves to the ground; they had a fine, practised judgement in these matters. Most of the shells flew harmlessly overhead, but one exploded further back the way they had come; Jack heard the muffled burst as if it had fallen in the trench, followed by yells and moans, and clods of earth splattering the ground. "God, someone's copped that lot," Jack thought, his heart pounding. Was it the section of trench they had just left, or further along?

McLachlan stood still, waiting to see if it was the beginning of a hate or just a random outburst. "I don't think Jerry's seen us," he whispered. "Just giving himself something to do. We'll make our way back – the wire's intact."

They crept back alongside the trench. Jack could still hear

the moaning ahead, and sounds of digging, and the tramp of feet: stretcher-bearers on their way up, he supposed. They passed the stretch of wire they had just repaired, and by now it was only too evident that the shell had burst in the part of the trench where Jack had stood smoking and talking to Stephen. The sandbags were torn, scattering their contents . . . part of the parapet had collapsed . . . Victoria was there as sentry, where Stephen had just been standing . . . was it Stephen who had been moaning so terribly, or was it gone two o'clock – would he have been relieved, and be making tea in the dugout?

Jack scrambled into the trench over the debris, after McLachlan.

"Who was hurt?" McLachlan asked Victoria.

"Private Cartwright, sir, badly wounded, and Private Willis hit in the hand."

"Stretcher party here?"

"Yes, sir. Just gone down the communication trench."

McLachlan started to organize repairs to the damaged parapet, but Jack, without waiting for instructions, set off down the communication trench, his only thought to find out what had happened to Stephen. Oh, Jesus Christ . . . *badly wounded* . . . that could mean anything . . . he hurried on along the sinking duckboards, blundering against the trench walls, pushing past two men who were coming the other way. "'Ere, steady mate, what's the 'urry?" one of them complained.

The stretcher-bearers were ahead of Jack now, making their way slowly. He stumbled up behind them, anxiously eyeing their burden.

"How is he?"

"Bad, mate. Friend of yours?"

"Yes . . ." Jack bent down to the body on the stretcher, his breath coming in harsh bursts. Stephen looked up at him without recognition, his eyes unfocused. Jack saw at once that he was wounded to death – his face already looked grey, even in the dim light, and under the blanket the front of his tunic was mangled and torn, dark with blood, from the chest down.

"Oh, God . . . *Stephen* . . ." Jack lifted Stephen's hand and clasped it. There was a faint answering pressure and Stephen turned his head slightly, but then his eyelids closed and his fingers slowly went limp in Jack's grasp.

"Sorry, mate. He's a goner," one of the stretcher-bearers said. "Couldn't do nothing for him."

"Is he dead?" Jack asked flatly.

"'Fraid so. Awful shame, isn't it – only a young chap, by the look of him."

Jack gave Stephen's pale face a last look, then turned without a word and began to walk slowly back. He hardly knew what he was doing, wouldn't have bothered if a shell had burst right in front of him, sending him after Stephen. Figures appeared in front of him, Jimmy, and McLachlan. Jack was weeping without restraint, not caring.

"Is it Cartwright? Dead?" McLachlan asked.

Jack nodded, unable to speak.

McLachlan gave a disgusted gesture. "Oh, God. One of our best, and we were just due to be relieved. I'm sorry, Smallwood. You were good friends, I know."

"Come on, mate. Come and have a sit down, and some tea and rum," Jimmy said kindly, putting an arm round Jack's shoulders. Jack allowed himself to be led away to the dugout, and Jimmy got some water brewing, and some other men who had been on the carrying party came in and heard what had happened. There was nothing more to be said; it was all too familiar. Jack sat dumb with misery, looking at the makeshift bed where Stephen had slept, and at his few belongings.

The tea must have been heavily laced, for he fell into a heavy sleep after drinking it, waking automatically in time for stand-to. He remembered what had happened: Stephen was dead. He turned his face to the wall, not wanting to remember. His eyes ached with tears, and the physical pain of

223

his sorrow thudded deep in his chest. What was the point of it all, what was the point in going on? How could you believe in anything, in a world where such things were allowed to happen? Stephen shouldn't have died; quiet, gentle Stephen, who should never have been in a war at all, should have been at home in London looking after his brewery horses . . . killed by a stray shell, not even in an attack . . .

"Come on, mate." Jimmy was nudging him with his foot. "Stand-to in five minutes."

"All right. I'm coming."

"There was a letter for you in the mail last night. Here." Jimmy handed it over.

Jack took it suspiciously. What was it this time? Not more bad news – but what more bad news could there be? It was his mother's handwriting. He opened the letter slowly.

"*Harriet had her baby last night, a lovely boy,*" he read. "*Mother and baby are both doing well. I hope you will be home on leave next week as planned. Many congratulations.*"

God Almighty, he thought, it was just like last time, life and death ironically mixed, one life abruptly stamped out, another beginning. He was a father, a *father* . . . he could hardly take it in, after the shock of Stephen's death.

"It's good news," he said to Jimmy. "You'd better congratulate me. I've got a baby son."

Greenstocks

The village seemed almost unaffected by the war, Alice thought. Apart from the fact that there were no young men about, its streets and cottages and church were exactly as they had always been. The weather was warm, and the gardens and hedgerows were colourful with early summer growth; it was like the hot summer of 1914, when she and Edward had first started to become fond of each other. She had put off her return because of the painful memories she knew would be stirred by the familiar surroundings, but now found comforting rather than disturbing. Edward was everywhere – in the churchyard, by the bridge, in the lanes – but she was glad now that she could picture him so clearly, and hear his voice speaking to her. It would be worse, she thought, if even these comforts were lost.

She turned her back on the village, walking through the hayfields. The grasses were tall, almost ready for mowing; the silvery flower-heads, interspersed with big ox-eye daisies, swayed with each breath of light wind. She was on her way to Greenstocks, having been invited there to tea by Mrs Morland. It was the second afternoon since she had returned, to stay with Emily and her mother; they had all wept for Edward, and she had visited the Sidgwicks, and she had wept some more, and for the time being her tears were spent.

She had been to see Harriet at her parents' cottage, finding her flushed and healthy. The baby boy was tiny, with unfocused eyes of milky blue, and a few strands of light hair, and plump curled fingers with miniature nails. Alice thought he was beautiful, and couldn't wait for Jack to come home and see him.

"He'll love him," she said. "What are you going to call him?"

"I don't know yet. We'll decide when Jack's home."

Harriet looked as if motherhood suited her, to Alice's relief; she had been afraid that the enforced marriage would turn out badly. But Harriet was lucky, Alice thought wistfully. She would have a good husband in Jack, and now a lovely baby, and she looked well content, showing no sign of regret.

"I'll probably go back and work as a Land Girl, when the baby's old enough to stay at home with Mum," she told Alice. "We'll be needing the money."

There were Land Girls working on several of the farms now. Food production was vitally important in these times of shortages. There was no time to keep up the old standards of maintenance; Alice saw now that the Greenstocks gardens were overgrown, with weeds poking through the gravel, the lupins sagging across the path and the peonies bowed down with the weight of the heavy blooms. It felt strange to be walking up to the front door of the house instead of going round by the kitchen entrance, and stranger still when a young girl in a white cap and filled apron opened the door and showed her into the drawing-room. Alice had an uncanny feeling that the war years had slipped away, and that she ought to be in the kitchen straightening her cap and preparing to bring the tea things in.

Mrs Morland and Madeleine were waiting in the drawing-room, and Philip followed Alice in, walking heavily and leaning on a stick.

Mrs Morland greeted Alice effusively. "My dear! How are you? Do sit down."

Philip shook Alice's hand, and Madeleine kissed her. Madeleine was as pretty and fresh and well-dressed as ever, and Alice wondered whether the war had really touched her at all. She was engaged to marry Geoffrey Montjoy, Emily had said; he had been declared unfit for active service, and had stayed at home working in a bank in Chelmsford.

"We were terribly sorry to hear about poor Edward," Mrs

Morland said. "Such a dreadful waste, and so close to your wedding . . ."

This was the worst bit. Alice was determined not to cry again; she answered their questions, and was glad when the maid brought the tea in and Mrs Morland handed it round – "Not much cake, I'm afraid, it's so hard to get sugar" – and the dangerous moment was safely negotiated.

"How is Harriet?" Madeleine asked. "We heard that she had her baby, a son."

Alice told them about her visit. "Jack's expected home tomorrow, if nothing happens to cancel his leave . . . you know what it's like." But did they, she wondered, apart from Philip?

"I'd like to see Jack, if he can spare the time," Philip said. "Would you tell him?"

"Yes, all right," Alice said, puzzled. She glanced at Philip. He had not said much, so far; he had a somewhat remote, withdrawn air. War must have changed him, she thought. She had somehow imagined him to be immune. He had grown a moustache, and his face was thinner than in the old days, with hollowed cheeks. He looked less arrogant, less sure of himself than he had been, Alice thought, interested by his connection with Jack.

"Philip has a suggestion to make," Mrs Morland said mysteriously.

"Really?"

"Yes," Philip said. "I don't know what Jack's plans are, for himself and Harriet and the baby. I imagine they'll be wanting somewhere to live – they can't stay with Harriet's parents for ever. I was wondering whether he and I could help each other out. I know we haven't always seen eye to eye, but – well, I wouldn't be here now if it hadn't been for Jack, as you know. He risked his own life to save me, and I shall always remember that. All our differences seem a very long time ago now. I'd like to put them behind me, and I hope Jack will."

"I'm sure he will," Alice said. "It all seems so – so irrelevant, now, what happened before – Jack was just a boy then. I'm sure he has no bad feelings."

"I hope you're right, Alice." Philip looked at her gravely for a few moments, and she felt, oddly, that he was seeing her for the first time as a person; as if he had never really noticed her before, all the years she had worked in his house as a servant. He continued, "Well – after the war, I mean – I'm thinking of getting this place going as a stud farm, breeding and training horses. I shall need a good head groom, someone who can handle the youngstock and stallions, and do a bit of breaking. Sedley's too old for that sort of game, and he's thinking of retiring shortly in any case. There'd be a cottage, of course – I was wondering whether Jack would be interested?"

"I should think he'd love it," Alice said, thinking of Jack's old enthusiasm for the horses he had ridden and looked after. "I'll tell him what you say – of course, the war could go on for some time . . ." They were all talking as if it were going to end tomorrow, she thought. But Philip's plan would certainly solve a lot of problems for Jack, giving him security, and work he would enjoy.

"Yes, please do tell him," Philip said. "I'd like to discuss it with him in more detail."

"If we can help Jack out, we'll be only too delighted," Mrs Morland said. "We know how much we all owe him. Now, tell us a bit about your own work in France. We're full of admiration for what you've been doing."

Alice told them a little, and then Madeleine asked her about her own plans for the future. She hesitated. "Well, I shall go back to France until the war's over, and then . . ." Again, she had the sense that they were taking a lot for granted, assuming that the war would end soon, and that the Allies would win it – how might life be changed, if things turned out differently? No-one knew; it was foolish to make plans, but she had often enough found herself doing it . . . "Afterwards, I really don't know."

She was filled with a sudden conviction that she couldn't come back to live in the village. What did the village have for her now? What would she do? Return to domestic service? It wouldn't suit her, she knew, looking across the room at the grate she had cleaned out on countless occasions, the mantelpiece she had dusted and the brasses she had polished. Life here would go on in much the same way, she supposed, the new maid taking over where she had left off, but she couldn't see herself having a place in it. The war had changed her, she knew, as surely as it had changed Philip and Jack, taking away her future as well as distancing her from her past, leaving her stranded. It would be all right for as long as the war lasted, but what then? What could life possibly offer to compensate for her loss?

She listened absently to Mrs Morland and Madeleine's conversation about the food shortages, glancing up once to find Philip's eyes fixed on her in concern. She looked away, discomfited, and said, "I must be going – thank you so much for inviting me."

"I'll walk up the drive with you," Philip said quickly, rising awkwardly to his feet.

"Do come again, my dear – it's been lovely to see you again," Mrs Morland said, pressing Alice's hand. "And don't forget the message to Jack."

Alice supposed that Philip wanted to talk of his plans in more detail. They walked slowly up the drive, Alice slowing her pace to Philip's clumsy step-and-lurch, and resisting the professional urge to take his arm and help him. Philip said nothing at first, absorbed in the effort of walking, but where the driveway met the open fields he stopped and turned to face her.

"You will let me know, Alice, if there's anything I can do to help – anything at all?" he said.

"Yes, thank you. I'll tell Jack what you said."

Philip frowned slightly. "I don't mean just what I said

about Jack. I mean, if there's anything I can do for *you*, please tell me. I mean it." He held out his hand.

"It's very kind of you. Thank you, and goodbye," Alice said, somewhat confused. She shook his hand quickly and hurried off up the drive; for some reason, the exchange had brought back searing memories of Edward, and she struggled not to give way, to steer her thoughts back in a safer direction. Philip's behaviour was as surprising as it was uncharacteristic, she thought. What could he have meant? Why should she expect him to help her? She turned at the lane entrance to look back.

He was walking slowly towards the house, leaning heavily on his stick, as if the short walk had been too much for him. Behind him, dwarfing him, the house rose, solid and four-square, backed by its huddle of trees, typifying all that was permanent and unchanging, comfortable and conventional. Alice turned again and walked on, so that the house was hidden by the trees bordering the lane. There could be no more looking back; Greenstocks was in the past now, irrelevant. She thought of the entirely different surroundings she had seen so recently in the East End, the undernourished children, the shabby streets, the determination of people to survive against all odds. There was so much to be done there, she thought, with a sudden intuition that her future would lead her to London, away from the village. Lorna would be living in the city, for her pacifist work. Perhaps they could rent a flat together, and she could write to Dorothy and Mathilda and ask if there was any work for her in the canteen or with the orphaned children. There was positive good to be done there, she thought. Nothing would compensate her for Edward, but it would give her a beginning – a new aim in life, a sense of doing something worthwhile – something she had never expected to feel again.

It began to seem such a marvellous idea that she felt like writing to Lorna at once, instead of waiting until she got back to France.

Jack returned home later that day. Alice thought it would be tactful to leave him to spend the evening with his new family, but next afternoon she answered a knock at the door of Emily's cottage to find him standing there with Harriet and the baby.

"Oh, Jack!" She felt overcome by emotion at the sight of him. They had last met in September, and so much had happened since then, to both of them . . . and these last few days, she had been desperately afraid that something would prevent him from returning.

He embraced her, and she pressed her cheek against the rough fabric of his jacket. "Alice . . . I couldn't believe it when Harriet told me you were at home, too. God knows, you could do with a few days away from – from all that."

He looked and sounded worn out, and she gazed at him anxiously as they went indoors. He had looked so fit and well last time she had seen him that the contrast was disturbing. "Oh, if only he didn't have to go back," she thought. He had done enough, surely . . .

Mrs Smallwood was lifting her new grandson out of the carrying basket, looking at him delightedly. "Isn't he a lovely little thing? Isn't he just the image of Jack?"

"Yes, I suppose he is," Alice agreed, privately thinking that it was much too soon to tell.

"We're calling him Stephen," Harriet told her. "Jack wanted to. Stephen Smallwood."

"It's a nice name." Mrs Smallwood handed the baby to Jack, who put him carefully into his basket and tucked the blankets around him with gentle hands. Alice felt rather touched at the sight of her brother in this unfamiliar role, and could see that he was adapting to it quickly.

Later, she and Jack walked up to Hill Spinney together. It was her last evening; tomorrow, she would travel back to

London and on to France, and Jack would follow a day later. They stopped in the same gateway where she and Edward had stood nearly three years ago, and looked down across the valley. The sun was setting hazily, and the air was still warm, laden with the scent of honeysuckle from the hedges, where a few late bees droned. Everything was growing luxuriantly; the cattle grazed in the lush meadows, and the hedgerow was splashed with dog-roses. The towers and chimneys of London were blue smudges far in the distance. Farther away still, a faint tremor vibrated the air: the heavy guns, in France and Belgium.

Jack seemed preoccupied, staring down into the valley, his mouth set in a hard line. Something was on his mind; whether it was the thought of going back, or something more specific, Alice couldn't tell.

"Did you name the baby after your friend Stephen, in the platoon?" she asked. "He wrote me a nice letter – when Edward died – even though he doesn't know me. He must be such a kind person."

Jack said nothing for a moment, continuing to stare into the distance. Then he answered, "Was. He was killed, the night before I came out of the line."

"Oh, Jack!" Alice exclaimed. "How terrible. I'm so sorry – you were close, weren't you?"

"I loved him, really," Jack said awkwardly. "You do, under those circumstances. I hoped you'd meet him, one day. He was hit by a stray shell, no warning at all. I was wiped out when he died . . ." He blinked furiously several times, drew a khaki handkerchief out of his sleeve and blew his nose. "But I don't have to tell you about that, do I? You know, worse than I do."

"Yes . . ." Her own tears were threatening now, for Jack as well as for herself and Edward.

"I'm sorry, Alice." Jack slipped his arm through hers, squeezing her fingers against his side. "I've been so wrapped up in my own thoughts, I haven't even asked you how –

you're coping."

"I'm coping, somehow. There's no alternative, is there?"

"You deserved each other, you and Edward," Jack said quietly.

They stood in silence for a few moments, absorbed in their individual thoughts. Alice thought of Edward standing in this same spot, and how solid and real he had seemed then, just as Jack was now. "Dear Jack. He must come through . . . he must, whatever happens," she thought, and clung more tightly to his arm, as if somehow that would keep him safe.

"We've gone through a lot, haven't we, both of us?" she said aloud, trying to sort her thoughts into some sort of order. "But in spite of everything, I'm still glad to have loved Edward, even though he's gone – how could I regret it? And it must be the same for you . . . you wouldn't have wanted anything else, not to have known Stephen . . ."

"No," Jack said. "I wouldn't have chosen that."

"And we both have a future to think of, in spite of all we've lost," Alice continued resolutely, "You with Harriet and little Stephen, and I –"

She remembered that she hadn't yet told Jack about Philip's suggestion, or about her own plans. They turned away from the gateway and walked on slowly uphill, arm-in-arm as she talked. They passed into the cool shadows of the trees, and behind them the distant crump of heavy guns trembled on the still air.

About the author

LINDA NEWBERY taught English in a comprehensive school until she decided to commit herself full time to her writing. Her novels for teenagers include The Shouting Wind trilogy, which focus on teenage dilemmas, the rapidly changing world they live in and particularly the opportunities that have presented themselves to women over the last decades.

Linda also writes stories and poems for younger children and enjoys researching her novels in great detail, even once parachuting from a Cessna aircraft in order to describe the experience convincingly.

She lives in Northamptonshire with her husband and three cats.

VOYAGE
by Adèle Geras
ISBN 1-903015-00-6 £4.99

The story of four young Russian Jews, Mina and Daniel, Rachel and Yasha and the journey that takes them from Tsarist Russia to New York in 1904. The four begin the voyage as strangers, linked only by sadness and uncertainty. Sometimes they even wonder if America really exists. One thing is certain, they can not turn back. The conditions on board the ship are harsh but love and friendship still flourish. Noe of them knows what awaits them in America but they are carried forward, like all immigrants, by the belief that a better life is awaiting them.

A moving and inspiring story of courage and love by the much acclaimed author of *Troy*.

A QUESTION OF COURAGE
by Marjorie Darke
ISBN 1-903015-21-9 £5.99

Set in the period of women's battle to win the vote, young Emily Palmer, a seamstress in a Birmingham sweatshop, becomes passionately involved in the early heady days of the movement. In pursuit of what she believes Emily leaves behind her home, her family, her job and her town. But as time goes on, while she never questions the justice of the cause, she begins to worry about the violence employed by the suffragettes. After a spell in prison, Emily finds the courage to speak out, not only against her enemies but also against her friends.

A wonderful portrayal of a strong young woman finding her own voice, in a time of turbulent social change, a really compulsive read.

PLAYING BEATIE BOW
by Ruth Park
ISBN 1-903015-11-1 £5.99

Abigail is lonely and confused and longs to escape from her problems. Her wish comes frighteningly true when her world alters almost beyond recognition and she finds herself trapped in another time! Through hardships and dangers she finds true friendship and even love and her adventures force her to confront what her real values are.

But there are people she must help before she can return home, including a strange, wild child called Beatie Bow . . .

This story is set in Sydney now and in the last century, where Ruth Park one of Australia's most beloved writers lives.

THE DEVIL'S ARITHMETIC
by Jane Yolen
ISBN 1-903015-10-3 £5.99

Hannah is to discover for herself the frightening reality of the tales her Grandpa tells of his times in the concentration camps. Suddenly she is sucked from the safety of her family in New York as they gather for Passover and finds herself living in Poland in 1942. Through strange and mysterious twists of time and fate, Hannah discovers that through her bravery and her caring, she too can contribute to the past and make the future a better place.

Jane Yolen is one of America's most popular and prolific writers.

Barn Owl Books

THE PUBLISHING HOUSE DEVOTED ENTIRELY TO
THE REPRINTING OF CHILDREN'S BOOKS

RECENT TITLES

Arabel's Raven – Joan Aiken
Mortimer the raven finds the Joneses and causes chaos in Rumbury Town

Mortimer's Bread Bin – Joan Aiken
Mortimer wants to sleep in the bread bin but Mrs Jones thinks not

The Spiral Stair – Joan Aiken
Giraffe thieves are about! Arabel and her raven have to act fast

The Secret Summer of Daniel Lyons – Roy Apps
Tom pretends to be Daniel Lyons and part of the exciting new world of film in 1909

Your Guess is as Good as Mine – Bernard Ashley
Nicky gets into a stranger's car by mistake

The Gathering – Isobelle Carmody
Four young people and a ghost battle with a strange evil force

A Question of Courage - Marjorie Darke
Emily joins the Suffragette movement and finds love as well as a cause to believe in

Voyage – Adèle Geras
Story of four young Russians sailing to the U.S. in 1904

Private – Keep Out! – Gwen Grant
Diary of the youngest of six in the 1940s

Leila's Magical Monster Party – Ann Jungman
Leila invites all the baddies to her party and they come!

Vlad the Drac – Ann Jungman
The adventures of a diminutive vegetarian vampire who lives with a
family in London

The Silver Crown – Robert O'Brien
A rare birthday present leads to an extraordinary quest

Playing Beatie Bow – Ruth Park
Exciting Australian time travel story in which Abigail learns about love

The Mustang Machine – Chris Powling
A magic bike sorts out the bullies

The Phantom Carwash – Chris Powling
When Lenny asks for a carwash for Christmas, he doesn't expect to get one,
never mind a magic one.

The Intergalactic Kitchen – Frank Rodgers
The Bird family plus their kitchen go into outer space

You're Thinking about Doughnuts – Michael Rosen
Frank is left alone in a scary museum at night

Strange Exchange – Pat Thomson
The exchange is supposed to be with a French boy but an alien turns up instead

Jimmy Jelly – Jacqueline Wilson
A T.V. personality is confronted by his greatest fan

The Boy Who Sprouted Antlers – John Yeoman
When Billy says he can sprout antlers he doesn't really expect it to happen

The Devil's Arithmetic – Jane Yolen
Hannah from New York time travels to Auschwitz in 1942 and acquires wisdom